THE
DOLLMAKER
OF
KRAKÓW

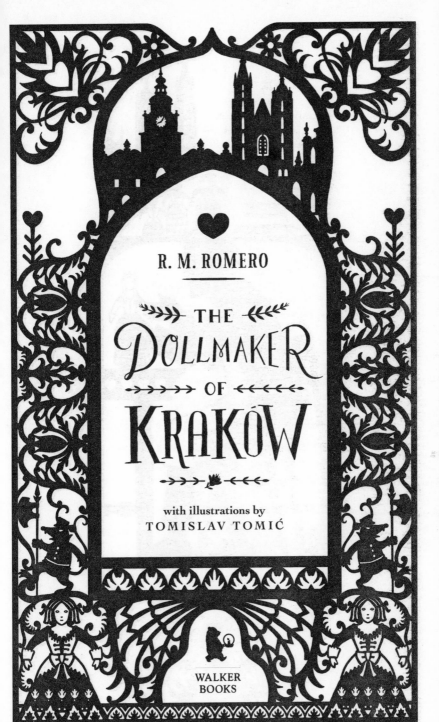

R. M. ROMERO

THE DOLLMAKER

OF

KRAKÓW

with illustrations by
TOMISLAV TOMIĆ

WALKER
BOOKS

First published in Great Britain 2017 by Walker Books Ltd
87 Vauxhall Walk, London SE11 5HJ

2 4 6 8 10 9 7 5 3 1

Text © 2017 Rachael Romero
Jacket illustration © 2017 Lisa Perrin
Interior illustrations © 2017 Tomislav Tomić

The right of Rachael Romero, and Lisa Perrin and Tomislav Tomić to be identified as author and illustrators respectively of this work has been asserted by them in accordance with the Copyright, Designs and Patents Act 1988

This book has been typeset in Sabon and Cochin

Printed and bound in Great Britain by Clays Ltd, St Ives plc

British Library Cataloguing in Publication Data:
a catalogue record for this book is
available from the British Library

ISBN 978-1-4063-7563-3

www.walker.co.uk

For the children
who were lost in
the Holocaust.

And for River,
who sent me flowers
from over the sea.

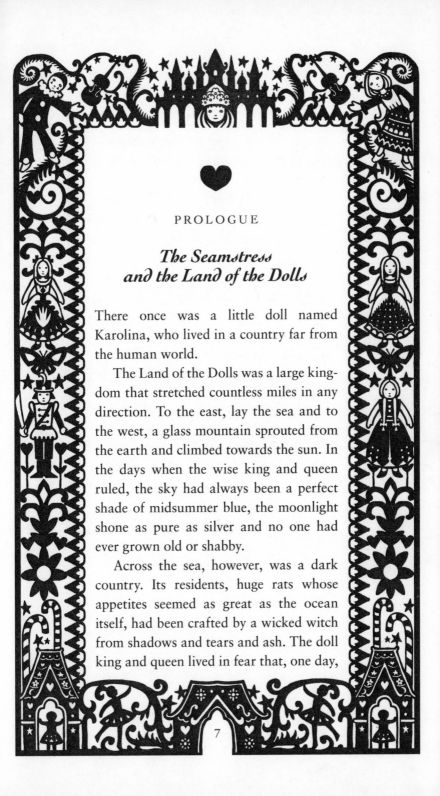

The Seamstress and the Land of the Dolls

There once was a little doll named Karolina, who lived in a country far from the human world.

The Land of the Dolls was a large kingdom that stretched countless miles in any direction. To the east, lay the sea and to the west, a glass mountain sprouted from the earth and climbed towards the sun. In the days when the wise king and queen ruled, the sky had always been a perfect shade of midsummer blue, the moonlight shone as pure as silver and no one had ever grown old or shabby.

Across the sea, however, was a dark country. Its residents, huge rats whose appetites seemed as great as the ocean itself, had been crafted by a wicked witch from shadows and tears and ash. The doll king and queen lived in fear that, one day,

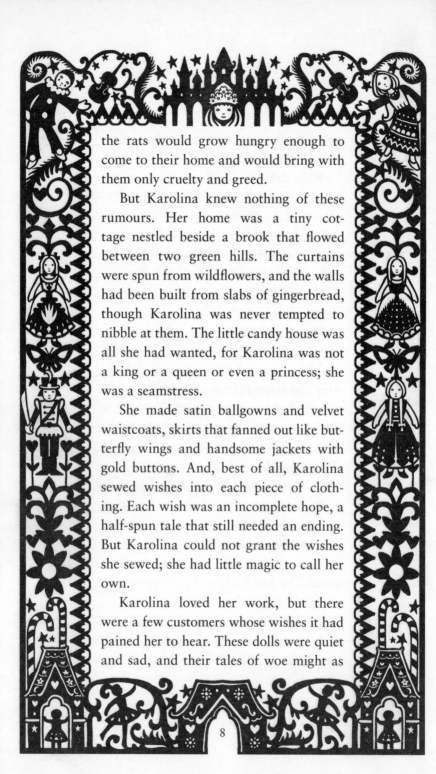

the rats would grow hungry enough to come to their home and would bring with them only cruelty and greed.

But Karolina knew nothing of these rumours. Her home was a tiny cottage nestled beside a brook that flowed between two green hills. The curtains were spun from wildflowers, and the walls had been built from slabs of gingerbread, though Karolina was never tempted to nibble at them. The little candy house was all she had wanted, for Karolina was not a king or a queen or even a princess; she was a seamstress.

She made satin ballgowns and velvet waistcoats, skirts that fanned out like butterfly wings and handsome jackets with gold buttons. And, best of all, Karolina sewed wishes into each piece of clothing. Each wish was an incomplete hope, a half-spun tale that still needed an ending. But Karolina could not grant the wishes she sewed; she had little magic to call her own.

Karolina loved her work, but there were a few customers whose wishes it had pained her to hear. These dolls were quiet and sad, and their tales of woe might as

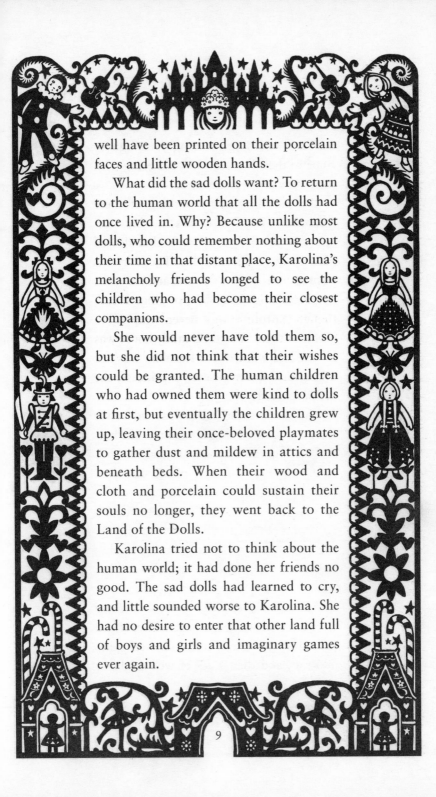

well have been printed on their porcelain faces and little wooden hands.

What did the sad dolls want? To return to the human world that all the dolls had once lived in. Why? Because unlike most dolls, who could remember nothing about their time in that distant place, Karolina's melancholy friends longed to see the children who had become their closest companions.

She would never have told them so, but she did not think that their wishes could be granted. The human children who had owned them were kind to dolls at first, but eventually the children grew up, leaving their once-beloved playmates to gather dust and mildew in attics and beneath beds. When their wood and cloth and porcelain could sustain their souls no longer, they went back to the Land of the Dolls.

Karolina tried not to think about the human world; it had done her friends no good. The sad dolls had learned to cry, and little sounded worse to Karolina. She had no desire to enter that other land full of boys and girls and imaginary games ever again.

One day, the rats did indeed come to the shoreline of Karolina's country. They overthrew the king and queen with their iron bayonets and sharp teeth, and unleashed their own brand of terror. Karolina was forced to flee away from the invaders and their pyres, into the deep, dark woods. Her dress was in tatters and her cheek was cracked.

It was in the woods that she met a toy soldier named Fritz, and together, with the help of a kind wind, Dogoda, she found she was destined to return to the human world after all.

CHAPTER 1

The Dollmaker

Karolina awoke in her new world with a glass heart.

It was a heart that felt as if both roses and their thorns grew within it, for it held all the happiness and sorrow she had ever experienced in the Land of the Dolls. When she moved, it rattled against the glossy wood of her chest panel.

Trembling, Karolina raised a hand to her face. It took only a single touch for her to realize that the crack that had raced up her cheek in the Land of the Dolls was gone. Lowering her arm, she saw her fingers were smudged with blush-pink paint that smelled fresh. The kind wind had told her that someone in this human world had called out to her. So that person – whoever it was – must have been

 11

the one who had fixed her face and placed the glass heart inside her.

Karolina glanced around and saw that she had been set on top of a high table amid wood shavings and coils of ribbon. While she was not made of glass or porcelain as some of her friends had been, she did not want to fall from her perch, so she stayed very still to avoid losing her balance. To her right was a huge shape like a mountain, though it was not as high as the ones in her country. A long, rough cloth had been draped over it. Karolina could not imagine what might be hidden underneath it.

Across from the table, a large window looked out into the darkness, which was broken only by the faint yellow glow of street lamps. They were not made of peppermint sticks, as the ones in the Land of the Dolls had been, but instead rose like dark, sturdy trees from the cobblestones. The world outside did not look inviting, but the room around her reminded Karolina of her cottage: warm and friendly. However, this shop – for it was a shop – was not full of ballgowns and jackets and scarves, as her cottage had been.

It was full of toys.

There was row upon row of rocking horses whose flanks had been painted with daisy chains and autumn leaves. There were stuffed-toy animals of many different shapes and sizes on the shelves, their tiny thread-mouths smiling.

And, best of all, there were dolls everywhere. None of them had scratched faces or limbs scorched by fire. They all seemed at peace, ready to love and be loved.

They were *safe*.

These other toys weren't like Karolina, though. None

of them had greeted her or even moved. They weren't alive and had no hearts of their own, and Karolina knew as well as any doll that only a creature with a heart could be truly alive.

Nevertheless, Karolina envied the silent toys a little; her glass heart had filled up with grey dread. She was alone. Where was the person the kind wind had said would be waiting for her?

The clatter of approaching footsteps made Karolina go rigid. A door at the back of the shop opened, and a man appeared. He had a red beard, as if the Morning Star had briefly touched it with her fingertips, and wore a pair of white pyjamas. He rubbed at his green eyes as he limped towards her. Now that he was closer, Karolina saw that the stranger was neither a little boy nor an old man, but somewhere in between. Karolina imagined that if he picked her up, she would stand only a little taller than his hand, which was speckled with the same pink paint that now coated Karolina's fingers.

He must be the person the wind had told her about, the one who had repaired her face and given her a new heart!

The man – the Dollmaker – sat down on the stool beside Karolina, wringing his hands. She could see that his face was streaked with tears that looked fresh. They had turned the pale skin of his cheeks as red and angry as battle cries.

"The Great War was more than twenty years ago," the Dollmaker said to himself. "It's 1939. I'm home in Kraków. I'm *home*. The nightmares aren't real."

It hadn't occurred to Karolina that there was such a thing as war in the human world too.

If the Dollmaker had been another toy, the right words to comfort him might have come to her, but she could not

think of anything to say. Being able to show pain with tears so openly seemed to her like a terrible magic trick, one that humans performed almost without knowing it.

His hands trembling, the Dollmaker removed the cloth from the mountain – revealing that it was no mountain at all. It was a grand doll's house that stood three storeys high and was the perfect size for Karolina. Her head would not scrape its ceilings, nor would she have to strain to reach the kitchen table or open the wardrobe she saw in the high attic bedroom. The window boxes overflowed with cloth roses, and a sleek black cat sat on the railing of the upstairs balcony. Karolina particularly liked this; the cat would gobble up any rats who strayed near.

The Dollmaker set to work putting the finishing touches to the roof's edges using a slim knife. His hand moved so quickly that Karolina doubted he could have stopped even if he had wanted to. He carved a wavy, delicate design that was so smooth it reminded her of cake icing.

As he worked, the Dollmaker's tears stopped, and Karolina thought she understood why. Creating something had always made *her* feel better. It was only when her hands were still that fear threatened to overtake her heart.

Karolina breathed in deeply. This world, this place … it smelled familiar, like dust and cinnamon and fields of yellow flowers. Had she been here before? There was no precise way to describe the strange feeling that was washing over her, cutting her as deeply as the Dollmaker's knife would have. But the more Karolina tried to grasp at that feeling, the more she felt that she was trying to catch a dream between her small hands.

Maybe the Dollmaker would be able to answer her questions.

Karolina took a step towards the doll's house, trying to think what to say. But in her haste, she tripped over the hem of her long red skirts and gasped loudly. Her arms wheeled at her sides as she struggled to regain her footing. She managed to right herself before she tumbled over.

This was *not* how she'd wanted to introduce herself, but it was too late to do anything else now.

"Hello," Karolina said, and waved. "I'm Karolina."

The Dollmaker dropped the knife, and his face turned whiter than smoke. "Oh no. It's finally happened," he said. "I've finally lost my mind."

Karolina knew that the Dollmaker *hadn't* gone mad. "There's nothing wrong with you," she said.

The Dollmaker sprang up from his stool, backing away. "But ... but you can't be real. Dolls can't talk. I must be tired – I'm seeing things."

"You do look tired, but I promise, I'm just as real as you are," said Karolina. In truth, it was almost as if the Dollmaker were the strange one, the sole human in the world of the toys, and she simply a natural extension of the shop.

"But I made you," the Dollmaker said. "And I can't make something that comes to life."

"Gardeners do it all the time with flowers," said Karolina. "And you didn't really *make* me. My soul already existed – you just called out to me, and the wind brought me to you. I thought you already knew that."

"I don't remember calling to anyone. I was just trying to recreate a doll my mother had made and..." The Dollmaker shook his head rapidly. "Oh, why am I talking to a toy? This is all too much." He slumped against the side of the table, the movement causing the hem of his

pyjama bottoms to hike up several inches. Karolina saw that his leg was made from the same pale wood *she* had been carved from.

"I didn't think humans could be made out of wood," said Karolina, cocking her head to the side so that she could study the Dollmaker's leg from a different angle. He seemed so flustered that she thought he might not respond. But after a long moment filled only with the weighty ticking of a nearby clock, he did.

"Only my leg is made of wood," the Dollmaker said. "The rest of me is made of something a bit softer."

"Can I see it?" Karolina said.

The Dollmaker averted his gaze. "It isn't very ... pretty," he said. "Most people don't like to look at it for very long."

"Why?" asked Karolina.

"People don't like seeing broken things," the Dollmaker said.

"You're not broken," said Karolina, planting her hands on her hips. "I'm made of *all* wood, and you don't think I'm broken, do you?"

"No one has ever put it like that before," said the Dollmaker. He rolled his pyjamas up to reveal a wooden leg strapped to what remained of his original limb, which was encased in a leather slip.

Apparently, things weren't as different in this world as Karolina had originally feared. "I like your leg," she said.

"You're one of the few who do," said the Dollmaker. Then he asked, "You're actually a living doll? You're ... you're not someone who was turned *into* a doll, are you?" His hair had fallen over his temples, partially obscuring his eyes, and now he pushed it back impatiently.

"I think I would remember being human," Karolina said. "But I only remember being a doll."

"Amazing," the Dollmaker said softly. He sat back down on his stool and leaned forwards, as if he intended to snatch up every one of Karolina's words with his callused hands.

Seeing that he was growing more comfortable with her, Karolina tried a question. "You said your mother made a doll like me. What did you mean by that?"

"My mother loved making things. Many years ago, she made a doll that looked just like you and told me that, one day, I should give it to my own child. But when my mother died after the war, that doll was lost. So I decided to remake her." The Dollmaker's voice gave way to a pause that somehow seemed louder than any word he had spoken yet. Then he said, "And I made you."

Had Karolina known the Dollmaker's mother? Maybe that was why everything here felt so familiar. "Is that why you make toys? Because your mother did?"

"In a way. It only started when I couldn't sleep in the field hospital after I lost my leg." The Dollmaker patted his knee. "It gave me something to do when everyone else was asleep. It still does. My dreams can be ... unsettling. Wars are hard to forget."

"I have dreams like that too," said Karolina. "Sometimes, I close my eyes and I see every awful thing that happened in the Land of the Dolls."

"The Land of the Dolls?"

"It's where I used to live before you called to me and I came here," Karolina explained. "Just like you live in..." She tapped her chin, considering. Had the Dollmaker mentioned exactly where this was?

"Kraków," the Dollmaker told her. "This is the city of Kraków in the Republic of Poland."

"Kraków." The city's name felt fresh and crisp on Karolina's tongue, like an apple slice. "What's it like? Is it a good place?"

"I believe so. I love it very much." The Dollmaker motioned towards the window. "I made a model of the city, if you'd like to see it."

Karolina bounced from one boot-clad foot to the other. "Yes, please," she said.

The Dollmaker went to pick her up, then stopped, his hands hovering above her. "May I move you?" he asked. "I don't want to be rude by carrying you if you don't want me to."

"I don't mind being carried. Your legs are so much longer than mine. It would take me for ever to walk across the room," said Karolina. She raised her arms, and the Dollmaker lifted her off the table.

As he walked over to the window, Karolina caught a glimpse of her reflection in the glass pane and a little more of her anxiety left her. The Dollmaker had captured her likeness perfectly; she had the same golden hair and large cornflower-blue eyes as she'd possessed in the Land of the Dolls.

"You did a very good job of making me," Karolina told the Dollmaker. "Thank you."

"You're welcome," the Dollmaker said. He seemed eager to change the subject, however, and pointed downwards. "Now, look at Little Kraków."

CHAPTER 2

Hidden Magic

The model of the Dollmaker's city had been placed in the shop window. A building with two golden towers and a huge statue of a stern-faced man stood in its centre. Pigeons and people gathered around it in equal numbers, while small figures made their way to the stocky houses and shops surrounding the square. The Dollmaker himself was part of Little Kraków, standing in front of his shop with a doll in one hand and a cane in the other.

It was the two figures in the corner – a young knight with a golden sword and the dragon slinking towards him – that took Karolina's breath away, however. "That knight – where does he live?" she asked.

"That's Prince Krakus and his home was the Wawel

Castle," the Dollmaker said. He tapped a small building whose facade had been painted to resemble red bricks. A blue river curled around it like a cat.

"I want to meet him," said Karolina. "How long would it take me to get there? It doesn't look *too* far away."

"The real Kraków is a bit ... bigger than the parts of it I put in the model. I'm afraid that it would take you a very long time to walk to Wawel Castle," said the Dollmaker. "And I hate to disappoint you, but the prince and the dragon are part of Kraków's history – not its present. I only put them in the model because I liked their story so much."

The news broke over Karolina like a gust of winter wind, chilly and unwelcome. "If the knight doesn't protect the people in this city, who does?"

"Well," said the Dollmaker, "right now, we have an army and a navy who can help us. But I'm afraid for my country. There are storm clouds gathering around us."

Thinking of the soldiers in their brilliant silver uniforms who had served the queen, Karolina said, "But armies can't always protect their people." Then she added, "I thought this world would be safe."

"It's ... not always safe," said the Dollmaker.

Karolina pointed out into the darkened square. "I don't see anything dangerous out there," she said. "Are you sure that the prince and the dragon are gone? Their magic seems grand and powerful. Maybe they could help end the war in the Land of the Dolls."

"I wouldn't have thought there could be a war in a world full of toys," the Dollmaker said.

"There is a *real* war happening now, with battles and wounds and everything," said Karolina.

"Who started it?"

"Rats." Karolina shivered. Her enemies may have been worlds away, but that had not lessened her fear of them. "Awful rats who came from across the sea."

"Rats?" said the Dollmaker. "As in the little creatures who live in alleyways?"

"Little?" Karolina blurted out.

"I assume they *weren't* little, then?"

"No," Karolina said. "They were huge and mean. But I'm not there any more, just like you're not at war any more. The kind wind saved Fritz and me, even if I don't know where Fritz is and—"

"I'm so sorry. I didn't mean to upset you," said the Dollmaker.

"You're forgiven," Karolina said. She pressed her hand against the pad of his thumb, then, on impulse, wrapped her small arms around it. It wasn't a proper hug, but it would have to do.

When she released him, the Dollmaker said, "I have a book that has the story about the prince and the dragon upstairs. I can go and get it, if you'd like to read it."

"That would be helpful," Karolina said. She had not yet given up hope that the prince and the dragon had gone into hiding, the way she and many of the other dolls had in the forest. If she could find them, they might be able to save her people.

The Dollmaker returned Karolina to the table and said, "I'll be right back." But before he left, he added, "Please don't leave while I'm upstairs. Please."

Karolina gestured to the front door. "I can't," she said. "That door's too big for me to open on my own."

"I don't mean leave the shop." The Dollmaker suddenly

looked much younger than he was, like a fear-stricken boy instead of a man. "What if ... what if you go back to being an ordinary doll?"

Karolina had not thought of that. What if the kind wind returned and swept her up just as she was getting to know the Dollmaker?

Understanding Karolina's silence, the Dollmaker said, "I'm so sorry. I didn't want to worry you." He flinched, and it made Karolina wonder how much of his life had been made up of apologies – even when he had done nothing wrong.

"You don't need to be sorry," said Karolina. "I don't know everything about how magic works, but dolls don't leave this world until their bodies fall apart. And my body is brand new." She wiggled her tiny fingers, which were just as nimble as they had been in the Land of the Dolls. "I think I'll be staying for a while."

The Dollmaker's smile was one of tired relief. He opened the door at the back of the shop and vanished up the stairs, leaving Karolina alone with the silent toys.

The Dollmaker returned five minutes later with the book tucked under his arm. The cover was connected to the binding by only a few fragile threads, and the image printed on it – that of a girl in a dark forest Karolina felt she knew all too well – was worn and faded.

The Dollmaker placed the book on the table. "This was my favourite when I was a boy – and my mother's before me," he said as he began to turn the pages. They were delicate and yellow, as if they had taken in all the sunny

afternoons the Dollmaker must have spent reading the stories. "Ah! Here we are – 'Prince Krakus and the Dragon'."

Karolina skimmed through the story, her disappointment building with each word she read. "Prince Krakus *killed* the dragon?" she exclaimed. "What a waste of a perfectly good dragon. He should have made it his friend instead – that's what the king in the Land of the Dolls would have done."

"Now that I think about it, that probably would have been a better idea," said the Dollmaker. Karolina gripped several of the pages in one hand and, with a grunt, flipped them over. An illustration of a group of knights greeted her, their swords gleaming as they raced towards the gates of a castle. "Look at all these knights. If they *could* come to the Land of the Dolls, they could help us beat the rats. Especially if they were as big as you."

The Dollmaker traced a finger down the winged helmet of one knight. "They do look fierce," he said. "If only they could come to life and help you." He closed his eyes, and beneath his finger, the drawing on the page stirred. Karolina blinked, thinking she must have imagined it. But the image quivered again. The knights on the page were *moving*. Karolina heard their capes flapping in the wind and the crashing sound their horses' hooves made as they struck the ground. The noise grew louder and louder, as if the knights were approaching them from a great distance.

The Dollmaker must have heard these noises as well. His eyes snapped open, and he looked down at the page, his jaw dropping. "What...?"

Happiness snagged in Karolina's throat, leaving her almost breathless. "You're bringing them to life," she managed to say. "You really can do magic!"

At once, the picture ceased moving and the sounds of the knights stopped. But that sense of magic remained; Karolina could feel it warming the air around them.

"I didn't do that!" the Dollmaker exclaimed. "I couldn't have. I've never done anything like it before."

"You called me here and gave me a heart, and now you made the book come to life too," said Karolina. "You might even have enough magic to save the Land of the Dolls. Maybe that's why the kind wind brought me here! And in return, maybe I can do something for you."

"You really don't need to," the Dollmaker said in a rush. "I still don't believe I'm the magician you think I am. But, either way, I don't expect that."

"But it wouldn't be fair if I didn't help you too." Karolina looked around the shop, trying to figure out how she could assist the Dollmaker. It was not until she heard the rustle of her own skirts that she knew what she *could* help with. "I'll sew clothes for the toys," Karolina declared. "Then you can sell them. I was a seamstress back home, and I'm very good at it."

"I imagine you are," said the Dollmaker. "But other than the rats, I know nothing about your home."

"Where should I start?" said Karolina.

The Dollmaker waved his hand. In that moment, he *looked* like a magician, one who could command the stars – even if he did not see it himself. "At the beginning," he said.

In the Land of the Dolls, Karolina told him, the river beside her cottage would rouse her each morning with a song, and the trees were weighed down with candy apples. The

sunlight itself tasted as sweet as buttercream. It was a place where love lasted for ever, and no one was ever discarded.

"The way you describe the Land of the Dolls makes it sound perfect," the Dollmaker said.

"Oh, it wasn't – even before it was invaded." She flipped a plait over one tiny shoulder, and it slapped against the Dollmaker's elbow. "The stuffed rabbits were always nibbling on your clothes, and you start to get sick of candy apples after a while."

"I still think I'd like to be a toy there." The Dollmaker's laughter broke off into a yawn, and Karolina turned to look at the grandfather clock. Both its hands pointed to twelve, begging them to retire for the night.

"Can we go out into Kraków tomorrow?" Karolina said. "There could be more magic hidden somewhere."

The Dollmaker did not seem very keen on that idea. He shifted uncomfortably and said, "I think people would react strongly if they saw you talking. It might be best if we stayed inside for a bit, until you know more about this world. I could use the time to work on my magic and finish my project." He pointed to the magnificent doll's house.

"I understand," Karolina said. "But you will show me Kraków one day, won't you?"

"The next time I have to make a delivery," said the Dollmaker, "I will take you with me."

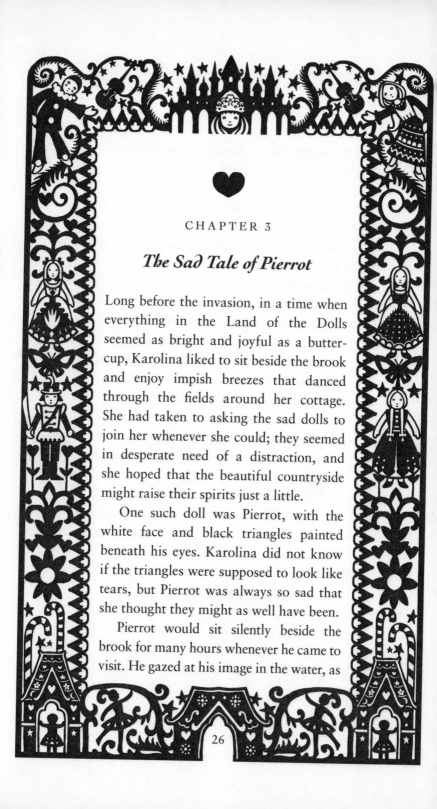

CHAPTER 3

The Sad Tale of Pierrot

Long before the invasion, in a time when everything in the Land of the Dolls seemed as bright and joyful as a buttercup, Karolina liked to sit beside the brook and enjoy impish breezes that danced through the fields around her cottage. She had taken to asking the sad dolls to join her whenever she could; they seemed in desperate need of a distraction, and she hoped that the beautiful countryside might raise their spirits just a little.

One such doll was Pierrot, with the white face and black triangles painted beneath his eyes. Karolina did not know if the triangles were supposed to look like tears, but Pierrot was always so sad that she thought they might as well have been.

Pierrot would sit silently beside the brook for many hours whenever he came to visit. He gazed at his image in the water, as

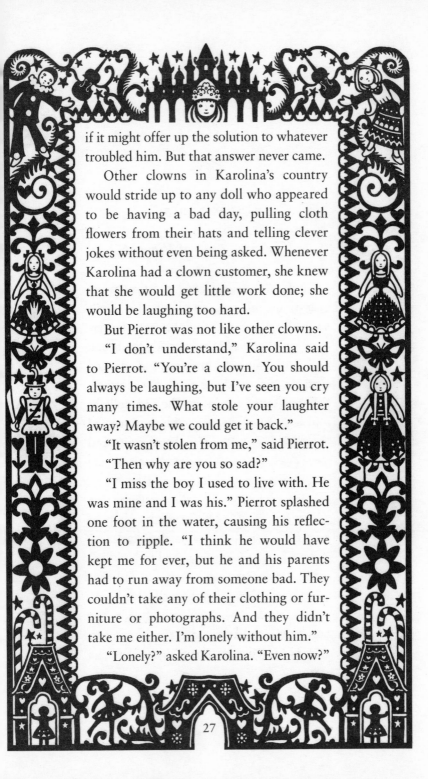

if it might offer up the solution to whatever troubled him. But that answer never came.

Other clowns in Karolina's country would stride up to any doll who appeared to be having a bad day, pulling cloth flowers from their hats and telling clever jokes without even being asked. Whenever Karolina had a clown customer, she knew that she would get little work done; she would be laughing too hard.

But Pierrot was not like other clowns.

"I don't understand," Karolina said to Pierrot. "You're a clown. You should always be laughing, but I've seen you cry many times. What stole your laughter away? Maybe we could get it back."

"It wasn't stolen from me," said Pierrot.

"Then why are you so sad?"

"I miss the boy I used to live with. He was mine and I was his." Pierrot splashed one foot in the water, causing his reflection to ripple. "I think he would have kept me for ever, but he and his parents had to run away from someone bad. They couldn't take any of their clothing or furniture or photographs. And they didn't take me either. I'm lonely without him."

"Lonely?" asked Karolina. "Even now?"

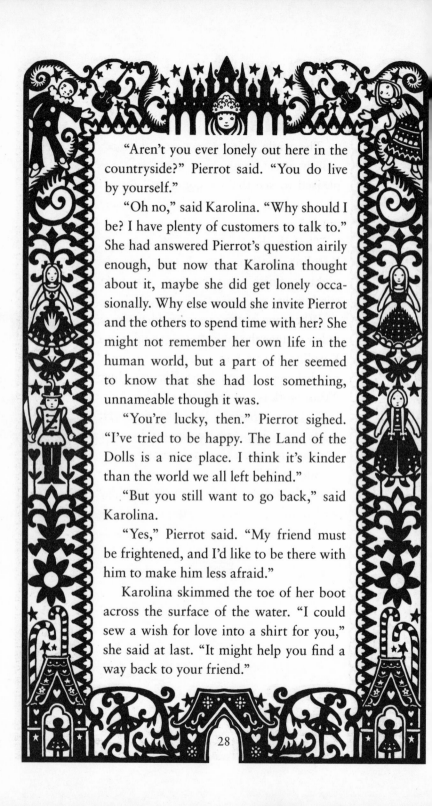

"Aren't you ever lonely out here in the countryside?" Pierrot said. "You do live by yourself."

"Oh no," said Karolina. "Why should I be? I have plenty of customers to talk to." She had answered Pierrot's question airily enough, but now that Karolina thought about it, maybe she did get lonely occasionally. Why else would she invite Pierrot and the others to spend time with her? She might not remember her own life in the human world, but a part of her seemed to know that she had lost something, unnameable though it was.

"You're lucky, then." Pierrot sighed. "I've tried to be happy. The Land of the Dolls is a nice place. I think it's kinder than the world we all left behind."

"But you still want to go back," said Karolina.

"Yes," Pierrot said. "My friend must be frightened, and I'd like to be there with him to make him less afraid."

Karolina skimmed the toe of her boot across the surface of the water. "I could sew a wish for love into a shirt for you," she said at last. "It might help you find a way back to your friend."

The smile that crept across Pierrot's mouth was fragile, but Karolina was pleased to see that he could still muster up a smile at all. "I would like that very much."

Though the clown's shirt was simple, Karolina worked steadily through the night to finish it, wanting to get every stitch right.

When one of the queen's soldiers came to her cottage the following morning to ask Karolina to sew him a uniform, he could not help but comment on Pierrot's shirt. "Your work is stunning," he told her.

"It's for a friend," Karolina said. "He made a very important wish, and I want it to come true more than anything."

She could not move mountains or draw the moon down from the sky, but wishes...?

Wishes she could help with.

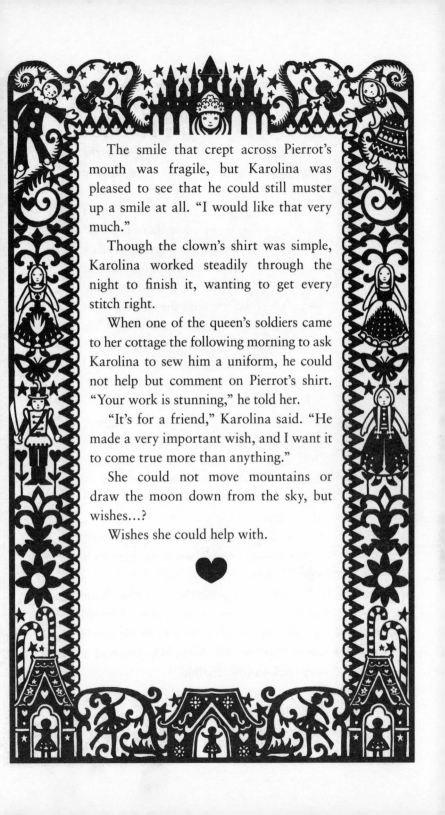

CHAPTER 4

The City of Kraków

In the morning, after the sun rose, the main square of Kraków filled up with people.

Some had easels and notebooks tucked under their arms. Others were carrying baskets of bread or tools to construct more splendid buildings. They were all different and colourful in their own ways, though Karolina did not see any of them performing magic like the Dollmaker.

The Dollmaker came downstairs to the shop when the grandfather clock in the corner struck nine o'clock. He had donned a pair of silver spectacles and proper clothing in place of his pyjamas, and his limp was lessened by the use of a cane.

"Good morning," Karolina said.

"Oh ... good morning," the Dollmaker said. He adjusted his glasses, tilting them one way, then the other. But Karolina did not melt back into one of his dreams.

"Did you sleep well?" Karolina said.

"I did," the Dollmaker replied. "I slept better last night than I have in a long time." He unlocked the door to the shop and turned the sign propped in the window from CLOSED to OPEN. As he did, Karolina caught a glimpse of the lettering on the door: CYRYL BRZEZICK, TOYMAKER.

Cyryl Brzezick.

What a curious name the Dollmaker had!

"I do hate to say it, but I think it would be best if you didn't try to speak to any customers who come in today," the Dollmaker said as he plodded over to one of the shelves to straighten a cuddly elephant that had fallen onto its neighbour, a giraffe. He gave each an affectionate pat.

Karolina had thought he might ask for her silence. If a toymaker had difficulty with the idea that one of his toys might strike up a conversation with him, other people in this world might struggle with it even more.

"I understand," Karolina said, her shoulders drooping a little. "But can I stay with you and watch? I'll be quiet and I promise not to move."

"Yes," said the Dollmaker. "I could use the company."

The lively chaos in Kraków increased as the day went on, and many people came inside or peered into the shop window. The round-faced children took a special interest in it, and their mouths dropped open in awe when they saw the rows of dolls, and Little Kraków.

Two such children and their mother entered the shop shortly after it opened, their arrival signalled by the jaunty sound of the bell above the door. Karolina watched as the little boy and girl chose two toys and bounced up to the Dollmaker's work table with their mother in tow. The girl held a soft doll with red hair made of yarn; the boy clutched a teddy bear wearing a bow tie. The toys already looked loved by their new owners.

"We'd like to buy these, please," their mother said. "Oh, yes. Of course." The Dollmaker got off his stool awkwardly, his wooden leg showing briefly from below his trousers. The woman stared at him for a moment longer than Karolina thought was necessary. The Dollmaker rang up the purchases on a bulky metal machine that clicked and whistled when he pressed its buttons, as if it too were secretly alive. He did not look at the woman as he accepted the money she gave him. "Thank you for stopping in," he said softly. "*Miłego dnia*. Have a nice day."

The woman nodded, eager to be on her way. The two children sped giggling towards the door with their new friends.

The Dollmaker watched them go, his smile growing more and more tattered around the edges.

"It wasn't nice of that woman to stare at you," said Karolina once they were alone again.

The Dollmaker took off his glasses and began to clean them aggressively using the corner of his shirt. "It doesn't bother me," he said.

Karolina sat down with a grunt. "You're not a good liar," she informed him.

"No," the Dollmaker said wearily. "I'm not."

As the days passed, Karolina realized that the only person who visited the Dollmaker without their children was the flesh-and-blood counterpart of one of the figures in Little Kraków, a baker named Mr Dombrowski. He brought a pastry for the Dollmaker, and many complaints about his ungrateful wife or the poets and artists gathered in the café next to the shop. But his favourite topic to gripe about seemed to be the country of Poland.

"I thought we were going to be a great nation when we became independent," Dombrowski said. He hovered near the Dollmaker's work table at the back of the shop. All Karolina could see was the baker, whose body was as round as the roll the Dollmaker had eaten for breakfast.

"We are a great nation," the Dollmaker said, smiling at the baker. "And Kraków is a great city. After all, how many other cities can say they were founded by a prince who fought a dragon?"

"*Bah!* Dragons don't exist. You've been spending too much time around your toys and your fairy stories," said Dombrowski. Spittle flew from his mouth in a shower, and a droplet landed on Karolina's cheek. She wanted to wipe it away with the hem of her red skirts, but she didn't want to break her promise to the Dollmaker by moving.

What had happened to Dombrowski to make him lose his faith in dragons? Had he *ever* believed in them? Karolina hoped so. An entire lifetime spent without believing in anything marvellous would be gloomy and dull.

"Germany – now, there's a great nation," Dombrowski went on. "Haven't you been reading the newspaper? The German army marched right into Czechoslovakia and took the country. No one argued with them. Imagine being able to do that!" He pounded his big fist on the table for

emphasis, and Karolina toppled over onto her side.

"Adolf Hitler is a dangerous man," the Dollmaker said, righting Karolina with an apologetic grimace. "There's nothing good about what he's doing."

Dombrowski shrugged. "Didn't you say that your family name was originally Birkholz before you changed it? That has to be German. And you fought with Germany in the last war."

"My father was German, but he moved to Poland when he was a child. I was a member of the Polish Legions during the war," the Dollmaker said. "We were fighting on the same side as the Germans back then, but I felt proud to be Polish, and I still do."

"What is in Poland? Salt and pine trees and potatoes," the baker said. "You could sell this place and start a new life in Germany with all that money your father left you. I'm sure you'd be welcomed with open arms."

"I'd give the money back if it meant my parents were still alive," the Dollmaker said. Karolina hadn't known that he didn't have any family left. It was sad to think of him without parents, but she understood, as the Dollmaker himself surely must, that no amount of money could buy back a soul. Death was fair in that regard. "It's been nice to have the shop, though. I like to think it's a place where people can forget what they've lost."

"Hardly," the baker said, rolling his eyes. "Everyone in Kraków lost someone, and no amount of frippery is going to make them forget it. You won't ever give up your silly dreams, will you, Cyryl?"

Before the Dollmaker could respond, Dombrowski stalked out of the shop, muttering as he went.

Karolina thought that both men's lives would have been

far better if the baker had been able to appreciate the simple beauty the Dollmaker brought into the world. But she could see that Dombrowski was not a man who changed his mind. If he scoffed at the idea of dragons, he would never believe in the Land of the Dolls or its inhabitants.

The Dollmaker slouched on his stool. "Perhaps he's right," he said, as Karolina stretched her stiff limbs. "These days, poets write about the end of the world instead of true love, and artists paint what they saw through the smoke of the battlefield instead of painting fairies. I've been running this shop for almost twenty years, and what do I have to show for it? I don't even have a family of my own."

"You've never been married? Not ever?" asked Karolina, surprised. If someone as irritable as the baker had a wife, why hadn't the Dollmaker been able to find true love?

"No," the Dollmaker said. The look in his eyes was distant, as if he were quietly poring over the many futures that had been lost to him. "I'm afraid I'm not very good at talking to people."

But people loved the toys he made, thought Karolina, and that was a *little* like loving the Dollmaker himself. How could she make him believe that?

"You make the children who come here happy," Karolina said, laying a hand on the Dollmaker's wrist. "You helped them find new friends. And you wouldn't believe how many dolls wish to be loved – it was all my friend Pierrot ever wanted. Don't listen to that grouchy old baker. What you do matters – and your magic will do even more good in the future. I just know it."

"I can only hope," the Dollmaker said.

CHAPTER 5

Rats

The day the rats declared war on the Land of the Dolls, the sun was shining as brightly as ever. They trampled sugar daisies, fouled rivers and composed violent ballads. And wherever they went, they stole from the dolls.

As more rats appeared, no doll dared come to Karolina's shop. If they had paid a visit, it would have been with one wish in mind: for the rats to leave the Land of the Dolls for ever. And that wish was far bigger than anything Karolina could grant.

Since the rats arrived, Karolina had not left her cottage. She had only peeked through her flowery curtains at the rats marching on the road with their huge, rusty axes and tar-black eyes.

One morning, she heard a knock at her door. Karolina stiffened and grabbed her silver needle. It wasn't a true sword, but what else did she have to defend herself with?

"Who's there? What do you want?" called Karolina.

"Karolina, it's Marie!" a voice said. "Please, can I talk to you?"

Marie? What was Marie doing here now?

Karolina opened the door and saw one of the sad dolls standing on the step. Karolina remembered sewing each of the splendid gold butterflies onto Marie's skirt and the wish she had woven into them: that Marie would be reunited with a human girl in the far-off city of Paris.

"You shouldn't be outside!" said Karolina. "Do you know how many rats are around?"

"That's why I came here," said Marie. "It's not safe to stay in the Land of the Dolls any more. I'm going to try to find a way back to the human world."

"Our army will send the rats back over the sea soon," said Karolina. She glared at the road, hoping for once that there was a rat sulking nearby who might hear her prediction and tremble.

Marie looked down at her pink

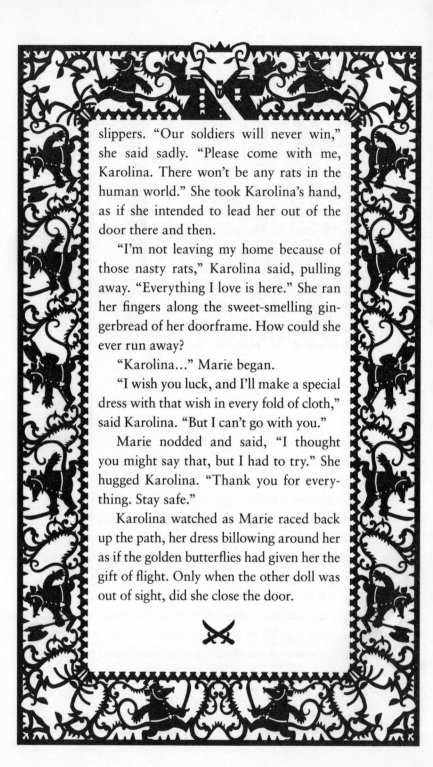

slippers. "Our soldiers will never win," she said sadly. "Please come with me, Karolina. There won't be any rats in the human world." She took Karolina's hand, as if she intended to lead her out of the door there and then.

"I'm not leaving my home because of those nasty rats," Karolina said, pulling away. "Everything I love is here." She ran her fingers along the sweet-smelling gingerbread of her doorframe. How could she ever run away?

"Karolina…" Marie began.

"I wish you luck, and I'll make a special dress with that wish in every fold of cloth," said Karolina. "But I can't go with you."

Marie nodded and said, "I thought you might say that, but I had to try." She hugged Karolina. "Thank you for everything. Stay safe."

Karolina watched as Marie raced back up the path, her dress billowing around her as if the golden butterflies had given her the gift of flight. Only when the other doll was out of sight, did she close the door.

CHAPTER 6

The Magic Shop

With Karolina's encouragement, the Dollmaker practised his magic.

He made the wooden figures move through their miniature Kraków, their actions mechanical and jerky. He placed his hands over the illustrations in his books of fairy tales, and the ink figures acted out their stories again and again for him and Karolina. He turned the dying sunflowers he purchased in the main square into silk.

But as wonderful as this magic was, Karolina knew it would not be enough to defeat the rats. The drawings of the cackling witches and golden knights could only tell the stories that were already on the page, and the wooden figures in Little Kraków could not speak their minds the way

Karolina did, let alone go to war. The Dollmaker's magic was small and soft and beautiful, just as Karolina's had been in the Land of the Dolls.

"I'm so sorry this isn't more helpful," the Dollmaker said to Karolina. They had been looking at one of his books, but now he closed it and nudged it to the side, too disheartened to watch the drawings any longer.

"It's not your fault," Karolina said. "I think magic has a mind of its own sometimes. Do you know how many times I tried to wish the rats away? And it *never* worked."

The Dollmaker drummed his fingers on his wooden leg, considering this. "Perhaps if I keep trying, I might be able to master it."

"Don't give up," said Karolina. "I have enough faith for both of us."

Apart from Karolina herself, the most extraordinary thing in the shop was the doll's house her new friend was building tirelessly. Every evening, the Dollmaker worked on it, and on a new doll who was to live there, a girl with dark corkscrew curls and sparkling, mismatched eyes. The left was spring green and the right was sea blue.

While the Dollmaker whittled with his knife, Karolina sewed new clothes for the other toys. Tonight, she was stitching a pink dress for a doll named Lucja. But Karolina could not focus on the roses she was embroidering on Lucja's collar. She was too interested in the doll with the mismatched eyes.

"She looks like she should be a princess," said Karolina. "She's almost as wonderful as *Lady with an Ermine*."

Lady with an Ermine was Karolina's favourite work of art. The Dollmaker owned a copy of it that had been painted by one of the artists who spent their days in the nearby café. The original painting by Leonardo da Vinci was in the Czartoryski Museum, a small building with a cheery green roof, on the other side of the main square. The woman in the painting seemed to hold a thousand secrets in her hint of a smile. Her white ermine circled her arm like a wisp of smoke, its own eyes gleaming mischievously.

"I'm not an artist like da Vinci," the Dollmaker said. But he was smiling; he always seemed happy when he talked about the doll's house and the doll inside it. Those two toys seemed to mean more to him than anything in the shop save Karolina. "I just hope Mr Trzmiel is pleased with my work."

"Mr Trzmiel?"

"Oh, Jozef Trzmiel is the man who asked me to make the doll's house. It's for his daughter's ninth birthday," said the Dollmaker. He reached into the drawer of the work table and pulled out a photograph from the stack of receipts and sketches for new toys. "See? The doll is supposed to look like Mr Trzmiel's daughter. Her name is Rena."

Karolina tilted her head in order to see the picture, which featured a beaming young girl in the middle of a field. It seemed as if the meadow itself had given her the wreath of cornflowers that she wore. "She seems lovely," said Karolina.

"Her father seemed kind as well," the Dollmaker said. "I have to deliver this doll's house to him next week. I hope I don't get too lost trying to find his home – I don't know Kazimierz very well. Why don't you come with me?"

"To Kazimierz?" Karolina asked. She knew all about

Planty Park and the train station and the beautiful river by the Wawel Castle from the Dollmaker's model of Kraków. But she had not heard of Kazimierz.

"It's the Jewish district of the city," said the Dollmaker.

"Jewish?" Karolina asked. "I heard that terrible Hitler on the radio yelling that the Jewish people aren't like the Germans and are hurting Germany. Then you changed the station." To be perfectly honest, Karolina hadn't given it much thought. The Dollmaker always changed the station whenever the leader of Germany spoke. She thought he must hate the way Hitler was always shouting.

The Dollmaker said, "I didn't realize you could understand German."

"*You* can speak it, and your mother learned German from your father, didn't she? That must be why I can understand it too," said Karolina.

"I hadn't considered that," said the Dollmaker. His paintbrush paused on the windowpane he had been touching up. "As for Hitler… He hates everyone who isn't like him. I'm ashamed of the type of place my father's country has become because of Hitler." He fell silent for a moment, lost in this black thought. Then he resumed, saying, "Jewish people like Mr Trzmiel practise a different religion than I do – they aren't Christian. They have a different relationship with God than I do."

Karolina said, "Oh. That's a foolish reason to hate someone."

"Yes," said the Dollmaker, "it is."

The Dollmaker did not appear to want to discuss the matter any further, and Karolina decided to turn to a more cheerful subject. She laid Lucja's dress out on the table so that the Dollmaker could examine it.

"What do you think?" she asked.

The Dollmaker peered over the rim of his glasses. "That's marvellous," he said. "Especially the little roses."

"Pink roses are for gentle people. Or for gentle dolls," Karolina said. "There's a language for flowers. Red for passion, white for purity, pink for hope and gentleness."

"Your red dress suits you, then," the Dollmaker said, chuckling.

CHAPTER 7

The Trzmiels

Rena Trzmiel's birthday dawned hot and sticky, and the Dollmaker's face gleamed with sweat as he and Karolina made their way down the hill towards the Kazimierz district.

Peeking out excitedly at the city, Karolina flopped along in the satchel the Dollmaker wore across his chest. A dozen items, including small tables, beds and stoves, had been placed in the bag with her.

This was the first time the Dollmaker had taken Karolina out of the shop, and she revelled in the sight of Kraków as it unfolded before her. Everything about the city was even more magnificent than it had been in the Dollmaker's model, from the main square – the Rynek

Główny – to the Wawel Castle, which loomed above the rest of Kraków like a king on his throne.

Kraków was nothing like the Land of the Dolls, where every doll knew all their neighbours. Karolina thought that she would have better luck naming every twinkling star on the night canvas than every resident of the Dollmaker's city.

But the Dollmaker did not give the crowds and the cloud-white buildings a second glance. He had lived in Kraków for most of his life, and so such things were as unremarkable to him as the glass mountain and sugar flowers had been to Karolina.

"I can't stand summer. It can't end soon enough," the Dollmaker grumbled above the doll's house in his arms. Its chimney struck his chin with every step he took so that a red welt had risen on his skin.

"You should take the tram," said Karolina.

"I'll be fine," said the Dollmaker. He lifted his thumb from the base of the house so that he could point towards the road. "It's all downhill from here."

Karolina sighed. The Dollmaker, she thought, really ought to look after himself better.

In Kazimierz, the houses crowded around one another like singers in a choir, and there were even more painters than in the main square. They sat with their easels on street corners and crouched over their watercolour dreamscapes. Every so often, a group of children would swarm around them, marvelling at the way their paintbrushes or sticks of charcoal flew across their canvases. The older residents of

Kazimierz – the women with their heads covered and the men with their long beards – merely shook their heads.

Jozef Trzmiel's flat was on the third floor of a sandstone building whose windows were as big as the eyes of giants. The Dollmaker frowned at the narrow, winding staircase inside, but he did not complain. Readjusting the doll's house so that it sat more squarely against his belly, he began to climb. The further up they went, the more sure Karolina felt that they must reach either a princess or a dragon at the top. Such characters were always found in the tallest of tall towers.

"Remember, you mustn't say a word while we're inside," the Dollmaker reminded her. "We don't want anyone to know that you're alive."

"I'll remember," Karolina said.

When they got to the third floor, the Dollmaker veered to the right.

"Flat Number Forty, isn't it?" he asked.

Karolina glanced down at the crumpled piece of paper that had fallen to the bottom of the bag. "That's what you wrote down."

After several failed attempts, the Dollmaker finally managed to knock on the door of Number Forty without dropping the doll's house. He tried leaning against the doorframe to support himself, only to pull back when his shoulder struck the small golden rectangle affixed to it. A six-pointed star decorated the top of it, and beneath it stood a lion that had risen up on its hind legs.

The door opened, and Karolina saw Jozef Trzmiel for the first time. The Dollmaker's customer was a tall, handsome man with dark curls. His features reminded Karolina of the statues she and the Dollmaker had passed, sharp

and well-defined. He wore a smile and a small circular hat that only covered the very top of his head.

It was one of the best smiles Karolina had ever seen, shining and genuine.

"*Dzień dobry*, Mr Brzezick. I'm glad you're here." Jozef opened the door even wider, and Karolina tipped her head to the side to better admire the large carpet, which depicted a red bird curled contentedly around an apple tree.

"*Dzień dobry.* Good day," the Dollmaker said. But his good leg had begun to buckle from the weight of the doll's house. Thankfully, Jozef noticed before his daughter's present went crashing to the ground.

"Here, let me help you. I'm so sorry you had to climb all of those stairs with it," Jozef said, grabbing the base of the house. "I thought we could set it on the table in the parlour."

Jozef steered the Dollmaker inside and down a hall lined with three oak-panelled doors. Several photographs in ornate frames hung on the floral-paper walls, most of Rena. The Dollmaker's new customer was in a few of the photos himself, usually beside a smiling woman with a round face. The warmth of that smile radiated outwards, as if she wanted to welcome Karolina and the Dollmaker into the house. But the woman herself was nowhere to be seen.

"This doll's house really is an extraordinary piece of art," said Jozef. "What a perfect present for Rena."

The Dollmaker blushed. Karolina thought he was not accustomed to having his work praised by other adults. "Thank you," he said as he and Jozef shuffled into the parlour.

Karolina had to squint against the sudden brightness of the afternoon sunlight spilling into the room. In its centre,

two velvet sofas faced each other, and a low table was squeezed between them. A pair of violin cases and a piano stood in the corner. The top of the latter was piled high with sheet music. The breeze coming from the river that flowed alongside Kazimierz had caused several of these papers to flutter down onto the carpet. It was exactly the sort of place that was perfect for dolls. If only Karolina's friends could be here!

"I'm sorry about all the clutter," said Jozef as he and the Dollmaker lowered the house onto the little table. "My wife used to joke that we needed to purchase a second flat for all my instruments."

"No, no. You have a lovely home," said the Dollmaker. He stooped over, opening the satchel to remove the delicate pieces of furniture inside. Karolina, feeling smaller than ever, held her breath. "Can you play all those instruments?" he asked.

"Yes," said Jozef. "But the violin is my speciality. I play for the symphony."

"How wonderful! I'm afraid I've never been to see a performance," the Dollmaker said. "But it would be very nice to attend a concert one day."

Karolina smiled sadly. It would be good for the Dollmaker to leave the shop and go to a concert. Though she knew such a performance could never compare to the concerts held in the Land of the Dolls.

Did the stars still play music back home? They'd gone quiet when the rats came, and it hurt Karolina to think about that endless silence.

"Does that doll in your bag go with the house?" Jozef asked, drawing Karolina back from her thoughts of home.

"No," the Dollmaker said quickly. He turned away

from Jozef and began arranging the tiny table and stove in the doll's house kitchen. "Karolina's more of an advertisement for the shop. If someone wants to see my work, I can show them this doll."

"That's a clever idea," said Jozef. He watched with admiration as the Dollmaker straightened the small wardrobe in the attic. "With something like that, you wouldn't need to take out an ad in the paper. Word of mouth can be better than—"

The front door swung open, and a voice floated down the hall, interrupting Jozef. "Papa? Papa, is that you?" The question was followed by the *clump, clump, clump* of small feet.

"Yes, it's me. I'm home early today," Jozef called. "Come and say hello."

The Dollmaker wobbled upright and positioned himself in front of the doll's house. Jozef gave him an approving nod. He clearly wanted his daughter's present to be a surprise.

A laughing boy and a girl appeared on the threshold a moment later. Karolina recognized her from the photographs. From her mismatched eyes to her brown curls, the resemblance between the girl and the doll in the white house was unmistakable. She *had* to be Rena Trzmiel.

Spotting the Dollmaker, Rena said, "*Halo!* Hello! Are you the new flautist for the symphony?"

Karolina tried not to giggle. The Dollmaker could barely keep up with the songs on the radio when he hummed along to them. She couldn't imagine him as a musician.

"No, sadly, we haven't found anyone to replace Mr Budny yet," said Jozef. "This is Mr Brzezick, Rena. He's going to be our guest today."

The boy whispered to Rena, "I should probably go if you have company. See you tomorrow at school. Have a happy birthday."

Rena caught his hand before he could start down the hallway. "Thank you. Goodbye, Dawid."

Her smile set the boy's cheeks ablaze, and he turned and raced out of the room. Rena hadn't seemed to notice that he had been blushing.

Jozef clapped his hands together and said, "Happy birthday, Rena!"

The Dollmaker shuffled to the side so that Rena could see her present.

"This is for me?" said Rena. Her eyes grew as wide as Karolina's in surprise.

"Of course it is," Jozef said. "Mr Brzezick made it for you so that all your dolls will have a place to live."

Rena's mouth fell open. Her teeth looked like little rows of pearls. "You made this?" she asked. "All by yourself?"

The Dollmaker seemed pleased. "Ah, yes. I did," he said awkwardly.

"It's beautiful."

Rena crept over to the doll's house, holding her breath as she approached. Was she afraid that the house would evaporate if she dared to touch it? But the doll's house remained its usual sturdy self as Rena skimmed her hand over the roof and down into the attic. "She looks just like me!" she said, gently touching the princess doll. "Oh, thank you, Papa! Thank you, Mr Brzezick!"

The Dollmaker glanced towards the door.

"You're very welcome. I … I should be going," he said. "I hope you enjoy the doll's house, Rena. Have a lovely birthday."

"Wait," said Jozef, stretching his arm out to bar the Dollmaker's path. "Would you like any tea before you go? You must be thirsty after carrying the house up all those stairs."

"I don't want to take up too much of your time," the Dollmaker said.

Karolina wished the Dollmaker wouldn't think of himself as an imposition. Why would Rena's father have invited him to stay if he didn't want him there? Jozef didn't seem like Mr Dombrowski, who moved through the world armed with a harsh word about everything.

"You wouldn't be," Jozef said, echoing Karolina's own opinion. "Please come and sit down while I make the tea. You've made such a special present for Rena – we'd like you to celebrate with us."

The Dollmaker removed his hat as he sat down on the sofa. Now, he ran his hands over the brim again and again, as if it were a little animal he hoped to soothe.

Jozef returned with a teapot in one hand and two cups balanced precariously in the palm of the other. The Dollmaker started to rise to assist him, but Jozef managed to make it to the sofa without dropping anything. "I'm more graceful than I look," he said. "I've had to learn since my wife passed away."

The Dollmaker's smile looked as if it had grown rusty from disuse. Inwardly, Karolina groaned. Here was someone who was being kind, and the Dollmaker was too nervous to be friendly in return.

It was Rena who saved the Dollmaker from his discomfort,

having spied Karolina peeking out from his satchel. "Your doll is so pretty," she said. "Did you make her to look like someone, the way you made mine to look like me?" She held the princess up against her cheek for comparison.

"I... No, no. She just ... looks like herself," the Dollmaker said. "Your doll was the first one I modelled on a real person."

"What's her name?" Rena said.

Oh, how Karolina wanted to tell the girl herself. The idea of being played with had *intrigued* her since the sad dolls had told her about it. In Rena's hands, Karolina could become someone else. A queen, a witch, a great general ... *anyone*.

Karolina allowed her head to fall against the Dollmaker's side, hoping that he would understand her silent wish.

"Her name is Karolina," the Dollmaker said. "It means 'song of happiness' in French."

"Really?" said Rena. She scooted across the carpet on her palms. "My name means 'song of joy' in Hebrew. Do you name all the dolls or just the ones you like best, Mr Brzezick?"

"All of them," said the Dollmaker. "It feels right."

"We artists should always name our work," said Jozef as he poured himself and the Dollmaker each a cup of tea. "I can't stand that some of the most beautiful pieces of music I play are untitled. They *deserve* titles."

"I agree," said the Dollmaker. He took Karolina out of the satchel, and as he held her out to Rena, Karolina had to refrain from kicking her legs in excitement. The Dollmaker had understood what she'd wanted! "Would you like to play with her?"

"May I? Please?" Rena shot a pleading glance at her

father. She seemed to want to meet Karolina properly as much as Karolina wanted to meet her.

"I don't see why not," Jozef said. "But remember, she doesn't belong to you. You have to be extremely gentle with her."

"I'll be very, very gentle," said Rena. Then she asked the question no one but the Dollmaker would have ever thought to ask. It was this question that made Karolina's heart sing like her name. "Would *you* like to play with me, Karolina?"

"Karolina admired your doll when I was making her," said the Dollmaker, "so I think that she would."

Rena took Karolina from the Dollmaker and thanked him. "I'm glad Papa let me play with you. I don't think Mama would have. She was stricter," Rena whispered to Karolina. She had lowered her face so close to Karolina's that her breath disturbed her feather eyelashes, making it appear as though she was blinking. "But I still miss her lots. I love my papa, but it's not easy without Mama here."

The princesses in the Dollmaker's books rarely had mothers themselves, although plenty of them had *step*-mothers. These were often wicked women who made the girls complete impossible tasks or sent them into woods teeming with monsters. With that in mind, it made sense to Karolina that the girl the princess doll had been modelled on had no mother.

But that did not make it any less sad.

Rena carefully placed the princess in her attic room. "I'm going to name my new doll Princess Wanda. She was a great lady who saved Kraków in a story," she said. "And what if you were a ghost haunting the princess? Not a scary ghost, but a protector ghost?"

Karolina, who had never been a ghost before, listened eagerly for Rena to tell her the rest of the story.

"My uncle is a terrible person who wants to take over my kingdom," Rena made Princess Wanda say, raising her voice to a squeak. "Will you keep me safe, Miss Ghost?"

"Of course," Rena made Karolina herself say, and Karolina was astounded to find that the girl had got the pitch of her own voice nearly right.

For the next hour, Karolina battled a wicked duke who was tormenting the princess. Together, in the story the little girl had crafted, she and the princess plotted a grand escape.

It was bliss. Was this what the sad dolls had remembered and longed for so fiercely? It felt so *right* to Karolina that she thought it must be. Why else would they have wished to come back to the human world?

Rena and Karolina might have continued playing had the Dollmaker not let out a hiss of surprise. Rena turned away from the house, taking Karolina with her as she did. The Dollmaker had managed to spill the better part of his tea in his lap.

"I'm so sorry," he said to Jozef. "I don't think I got any on your rug, but—"

"If you *did*, we could just move the sofa again," said Rena. "It used to be by the window until Papa spilled a cup of coffee over here." She knocked her fist against one of the legs, which was apparently covering the stain in question.

Even in his embarrassment, Karolina saw that the Dollmaker had to bite his lip to keep from laughing.

"Rena's right," said Jozef. "The stains are my fault. This rug belonged to an uncle – I think it's older than I am." He tapped his toe on the carpet rhythmically. It was as if he

54

were playing music even without the aid of his violin.

"I'll go and wash my hands," the Dollmaker said. "And I'll pay for the rug too."

Before Jozef could protest – and Karolina knew he was preparing to do just that – the Dollmaker retreated out of the parlour.

"Poor man," Jozef murmured to himself. "He seems so nervous."

Though her father had not been speaking to her directly, Rena added her own opinion. "Maybe. But I'm glad you invited him to stay for tea, Papa." She stroked Karolina's hair with so much care that it was as if she knew Karolina was real. It must be marvellous, Karolina thought, to belong to Rena Trzmiel.

"I'm glad too," said Jozef. He stood up and stretched, then walked over to inspect the doll's house more closely. The fresh paint gleamed like the white keys of his piano when the light struck them. "This reminds me of my father's work. Your zaydee was a carpenter. He was always disappointed I wasn't better at making things."

Rena used Karolina to point to the cabinet across the parlour. "You made that, though. Most people couldn't do that."

"And your zaydee and your mama were both quick to point out that it's lopsided," said Jozef. He shook his head. Then he held out his hand to his daughter and asked, "May I see Mr Brzezick's doll?"

Rena nodded and gave Karolina over to Jozef. "Her name is Karolina, Papa."

Jozef turned Karolina to the side and ran one of his hands down her gold plait. His fingers were stronger than Rena's, and he held Karolina the way she had seen the

 55

Dollmaker hold the painting of *Lady with an Ermine*, as if she were to be admired rather than loved. "Her hair looks so real. I wonder what it's made of. Horsehair, maybe? That's what the best violin bows are made from." He gave the plait a tug to test its material.

"Ouch!" Karolina said. It was the first word she'd ever spoken to a person who was not the Dollmaker – and right away, she wished she could take it back. The Dollmaker had never fully lost his belief in magic, and even he had been shocked by Karolina's ability to talk. What would another grown-up think of her?

Jozef looked at Rena. "Very funny," he said.

"I didn't do it," Rena protested.

"Then who did?" said Jozef. "Karolina's only a doll." He gave Karolina a prod with his index finger.

Karolina tried to ignore such rudeness – Jozef didn't *know* she was alive – but in that moment, she found she could not. "Please stop that," she said. "How would you like it if someone went around poking you without your permission?"

Jozef dropped Karolina with a gasp.

She hit the floor with a dull clunk, one that resounded through her wooden joints and left her hair slightly askew. But otherwise, she was undamaged.

"You should be grateful that I'm made from wood," Karolina said, even more annoyed now. She sat up to glare at the gaping man above her. "If I were porcelain, I'd be in a hundred pieces right now."

"I must be dreaming," Jozef said with a groan. He rubbed his eyes feverishly, as if he hoped he could wake himself.

Rena was staring at Karolina as well, but her expression

was not one of dismay or confusion. She looked enchanted.

"You're not dreaming," said Karolina. "Why would you dream about a magical doll? You grown-ups don't have much faith in magic."

"You can't possibly be talking," said Jozef. He peered at her through his fingers, the way Karolina did when she was listening to a particularly frightening part of a story.

"Well, I am," said Karolina. She was in no hurry to go through the exhausting conversation she'd already had with the Dollmaker. "You don't have to believe in me, but you ought to. Rena does, doesn't she?"

Rena nodded, refusing to glance away from Karolina, even for an instant.

Jozef started to reply, but at that moment the Dollmaker emerged from the bathroom, a damp towel in his hand. "Is everything all right? I thought I heard something fall..." He trailed off, seeing how pale Jozef had gone. The Dollmaker followed his gaze ... and the towel he was holding slipped from his hand.

"Your doll is alive," Jozef said.

"I *knew* it," Rena said. She squealed. "I just knew it!"

CHAPTER 8

Secrets Revealed

The Dollmaker strung together apology after apology. A streak of anger ran through his words, though it was not directed at the Trzmiels. It hadn't been Jozef or Rena who had shared his secret. That fault lay with Karolina and Karolina alone.

Jozef, dazed, had the sense to sit down. The Dollmaker poured him another cup of tea, which he accepted but had yet to drink.

The Trzmiels had been kind to the Dollmaker, and the last thing Karolina had wanted to do was ruin his afternoon with them. But now, it appeared that she might have done just that. The thought made her feel as if a heavy stone instead of her precious glass heart hung in her chest.

"We didn't mean to startle you," the Dollmaker said to Jozef. "I imagine it's ... a little difficult to understand."

"Please don't be angry. It's my fault," Karolina said. "I didn't mean to say anything – and I didn't *want* to frighten you either."

"When did you come to life?" Jozef asked. He rolled his teacup between his hands, perhaps to keep his fingers from doing a nervous dance on the arm of the sofa or the surface of the table. He had certainly been startled when Karolina had announced herself, but he was no coward; he had not run away from what he could not explain.

"A few months ago," said the Dollmaker.

"It was sixty-seven days ago," Karolina said promptly. "I can't believe you could forget a date like that. It's so important!" She flicked one of the buttons on the Dollmaker's waistcoat.

"Karolina's been alive all that time and you haven't told anyone? Not even the children who visit your toyshop?" Rena cried. "Why not?"

"It just seemed wise to keep it a secret. Especially nowadays," said the Dollmaker. "People react ... strangely to things that are different."

Jozef's hands stopped wandering around the teacup. Something about what the Dollmaker had said seemed to resonate with him.

"My grandfather once told me about a rabbi in Prague who brought a huge clay statue to life to protect him and his neighbours," said Jozef. "Is that what happened? Did you bring Karolina to life to help you in some way?"

The Dollmaker shrugged helplessly. "I don't know, Mr Trzmiel. I thought I was only making another doll. But she started chattering away at me one night," he said.

"According to Karolina, I called her here, but I don't know how or even why."

"I do not *chatter*," Karolina said, wagging a finger at him. She felt bolder in the company of so many people who saw her for who and what she was. "Chattering is for birds or monkeys. And you didn't give me wings or fur, so I can't be either of those."

Rena giggled, and even Jozef cracked a small smile at Karolina's indignation. It hadn't been her intention to amuse them, but at least Jozef was less wary now.

"Your grandfather's story is very interesting, Mr Trzmiel," the Dollmaker continued. "To me, Karolina has always felt like a magical creature that E.T.A. Hoffmann would have written about."

"Or Leśmian in the Sinbad adventure stories. But I've never been anywhere near the ocean or fought a sea monster like Sinbad," Karolina said, recalling one of the books the Dollmaker had shown her.

"I remember those stories. I loved them as a boy," Jozef said fondly. "But Mr Brzezick ... I don't mean to pry, but you really don't know where this magic comes from?"

"Unfortunately not," said the Dollmaker. "All I know is that Karolina needed a home, and I was just happy to have a friend." He ducked his head to take a sip of his tea. His loneliness lay across his face like an unhealed wound.

Yet the Dollmaker had never wanted anyone's pity. He had that in common with Karolina.

"There could be a purpose for your gift," Jozef said thoughtfully. "Even if it might not be clear to you what it is yet."

"Are any of the other toys alive?" Rena asked. The

question burst from her like a cork popping from the mouth of a bottle; she was almost vibrating with excitement.

"I'm the only one who is alive – it's because the Dollmaker made me a heart of my own," said Karolina. "I know there are other toys who can walk and talk somewhere in your world." She clicked her heels together with a giggle. Having the freedom to move about while Rena and Jozef were in the room made her feel giddy and light.

"I wish *my* dolls were like you," said Rena. "It would be so much fun. You're exactly the way I imagined you being, Karolina."

"The Dollmaker gave me the right shape for who I am," said Karolina. "The way a person looks doesn't say anything about what sort of person they are, but the way a doll looks says everything."

"Being a doll sounds simple. Or, at least, simpler than being a human," said Jozef. He took a sip of his tea and then went on. "I *am* truly sorry for dropping you, Karolina. I was surprised, that's all. I never thought I'd be meeting you today."

"We won't keep you any longer, Mr Trzmiel," the Dollmaker said. "Again, I'm sorry for" – he waved his hand – "all this."

"This has been the best birthday. May I come to your shop to see you and Karolina again?" Rena asked. "I won't be any trouble, and I promise I won't tell anyone she's alive. Papa won't either."

"I don't think anyone would believe me if I did," Jozef said.

"I..." the Dollmaker began. But Karolina was not about to let his shyness stop them from having visitors.

"You can come whenever you want to," Karolina

said, extending the invitation on behalf of herself and the Dollmaker. "And I hope you do."

"I was only supposed to deliver the doll's house and leave," the Dollmaker said as he and Karolina entered the shop again after their long and eventful afternoon. He put his hat on top of the grandfather clock as he passed it. Now the clock looked like a *real* grandfather.

"If they were really frightened of us, they would have thrown us out of their flat," Karolina replied. "I think we'll see Mr Trzmiel and Rena again soon."

The Dollmaker set Karolina on top of the work table. "I take it you liked playing with Rena, then?"

"I did," Karolina said. She tried not to sound too enthusiastic, but how could she conceal her happiness entirely? Dolls were like children; they could not hide their joy.

"I could still find you a home with a child. You could even go to live with Rena, now that she knows that you're … well, not like other dolls," said the Dollmaker. He pulled a dust rag from one of the drawers in the table and went over to the model of Little Kraków. With his back to her, Karolina had no idea what his expression was. Was it one of relief – or distress?

As much as Karolina had enjoyed her time with Rena, the girl's life was already full of friendship and love; she had Jozef and the boy she had been playing with, not to mention toys like Princess Wanda. Rena didn't *need* Karolina in quite the same way the Dollmaker did.

"I *want* to stay. The kind wind brought me to you, after all," said Karolina. "But if Rena or any of the other

children who come to the shop want to play with me, I wouldn't say no."

The Dollmaker turned back to look at her, and Karolina stretched out her arms as far as she could, as if to embrace the shop, as well as the Dollmaker himself. "As long as you aren't unhappy..." he said.

"I've never been unhappy here." Karolina hopped onto the Dollmaker's stool, then clambered down one of its spindly legs. "Even if sometimes you don't take care of yourself. Now, pick me up and I'll help you dust Little Kraków."

The Dollmaker complied, resting her in the crook of his arm. And for the first time, Karolina flew above Little Kraków and all its residents without the help of the kind wind.

CHAPTER 9

Gingerbread and Swords

The rats stole everything from the dolls.

They took opals and rubies and dreams kept in glass vials, silks and velvets, tables and lace curtains. They stole peppermint cobblestones and gnawed away at gingerbread walls.

The rats declared they needed it all, every last sugar biscuit, every ballgown, every violin whose strings still quivered with the laughter of the stars. They said they deserved it for having taken over the Land of the Dolls so quickly and with great skill.

When the invaders came to Karolina's cottage, they did not knock on the door. Instead, they burst through it, and Karolina cried out in surprise as they scuttled inside. The gown she was in the middle of stitching – one of deep blue silk – slipped to the ground. It formed a puddle on the floor.

The rats shoved and scratched at one

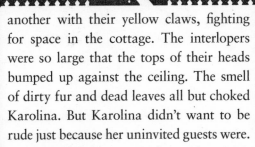

another with their yellow claws, fighting for space in the cottage. The interlopers were so large that the tops of their heads bumped up against the ceiling. The smell of dirty fur and dead leaves all but choked Karolina. But Karolina didn't want to be rude just because her uninvited guests were.

"May I help you?" she said, raising her chin as she had seen the queen do. The queen, Karolina thought, would have courage before the crooked teeth that surrounded her like prison walls.

"Get out," said the biggest rat. He held a hunk of sticky peppermint in his front claw, nibbling at it as he spoke. The sweets must have come from one of the lamp posts lining the road to Karolina's cottage.

When Karolina did not move, the rat drew his sword. "I'll ask one more time, and then I'll ask no more."

Sword or no sword, Karolina could not surrender her cottage when she'd worked so hard to make it her home. How dare he barge in and give her orders, as if he were a king himself. "This is my house," said Karolina, glaring. "You're the ones who need to leave."

The rat shoved the piece of peppermint into his mouth, spewing flakes as he chewed. "I'm warning you..."

"Please leave," Karolina repeated, and pointed to the door, hoping she looked fiercer than she felt.

"I did warn you," said the rat, his pink tongue plucking the stray crumbs from his whiskers. "Remember that later – I did warn you."

"What are you—?" But Karolina had no time to finish. The rat swung his sword and drove the blade so deeply into her cheek that the wood splintered. Karolina had banged her shins on tables and fallen over enough times in her life, but she'd never experienced anything as awful as this before. It felt as if a rope of flame had been laid across her face.

Karolina closed her eyes, fighting against the enormity of the pain. "You can't have my home!" she croaked at last. "You can't have my shop! You haven't given me anything for it in return."

"I give you your life," said the rat.

"That was mine already," Karolina protested.

"For now," the rat replied.

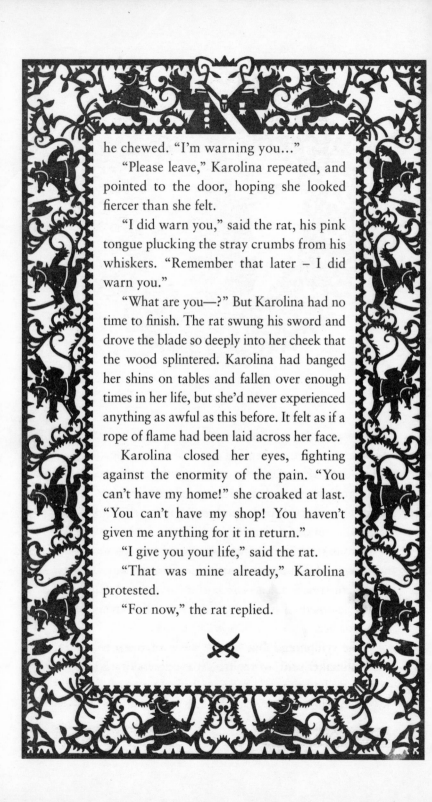

CHAPTER 10

Songs of Joy

A few days after the first meeting with the Trzmiels, the postman arrived with a letter for the Dollmaker. Inside were two tickets to the symphony: one for the Dollmaker and a smaller one decorated with bluebirds for Karolina.

Karolina could only assume it was Rena who had sent her ticket, and she turned it over and over in her hands. The seamstress was the one who usually made things for others; it was new and special for someone to make something for her.

"The symphony? But I don't have anything to wear," the Dollmaker said, worrying at the corners of his ticket.

"If we had time, I'd sew you a whole new outfit," said Karolina. She could already see the tunic and trousers she

67

would make for her friend. Karolina would sew her wish for the Dollmaker – that he would find the right words to do magic with – into the clothes.

Magicians needed the right words, and if her friend carried them with him, he might be inspired.

The Dollmaker sighed. "If only you could. I suppose I'll just have to buy something instead. I can't even remember the last time I dressed up!"

"Then we're going to the concert?" asked Karolina.

"The Trzmiels *did* invite us," the Dollmaker said carefully. "And I don't want to be rude."

The ivory-coloured building where the concert was to be held, the Juliusz Słowacki Theatre, was far grander than Karolina had imagined. With two round towers on either side of its entrance, and the six stone women atop staring proudly ahead, it looked like a palace.

The Dollmaker stepped into a lobby that seemed even busier than the main square. Everywhere Karolina looked, there were refined men in trim jackets and elegant women in their evening gowns that trailed behind them like midnight shadows of blue and black. The Dollmaker's new suit made him look like all the other concert-goers. But he did not join in their conversation and their laughter. Instead, he stood near one of the windows, drumming his fingers on the head of his cane.

"Maybe we shouldn't have come," the Dollmaker murmured. "I don't know anyone here. This isn't for people like me."

"You said yourself that it would be rude not to accept

the invitation," Karolina said. She was nestled inside the pocket of his jacket, but the lobby was so loud that she didn't think she had to be *entirely* silent – and the Dollmaker needed a bit of encouragement. "Don't worry. I know we'll have a good time."

The Dollmaker's attempts to avoid speaking to anyone did not last. A small hand tugged on his sleeve, and he turned. It was Rena! She wore a forest-green dress, and her hair was pinned back with a clip shaped like a butterfly.

"Mr Brzezick! Karolina! You came," she said. "Papa said you might be busy being magical so I shouldn't be disappointed if you couldn't come. But now I don't have to be."

"Hello, Rena," the Dollmaker said.

Karolina thought it would be up to her to carry the conversation for the time being. The children who came to the Dollmaker's shop were always entranced by the toys he made, but he was not used to them wanting to talk to *him*. No wonder he didn't know quite what to say.

Karolina held up her ticket. "I have my ticket," she said. "I like the bluebirds on it. Did you draw them?"

Rena nodded. "I did. They're my favourite birds." Inspired by this comment, the Dollmaker closed his eyes and let his fingertips brush Karolina's ticket. Karolina watched the birds begin to flit across the page, circling around its edges, as if they were trying to escape. When the Dollmaker removed his hand, they settled back into their original places.

Rena let her fingers stray to a corner of the ticket. Her touch was as tender as the Dollmaker's magic. "Can the birds come off the paper, Mr Brzezick?"

The Dollmaker's smile dimmed a little. "Unfortunately not. I haven't mastered that magic yet."

"He's working on it, though," said Karolina. She could be the voice of hope as well as reason, she thought.

Rena said, "Some things take lots of practice. If you ever need any pictures, I've got lots and lots in my room that you can borrow."

"That's a kind offer," said the Dollmaker. "I take it you like to draw?"

"More than anything," said Rena. "I like to watch the painters near our flat. Papa says I must be in all of their work because I'm around them so often."

"I'm sure they enjoy you being there," said the Dollmaker. Karolina felt proud of him; he met Rena's mismatched eyes as he spoke rather than staring at his shoes like he ordinarily did. It was nice to see him relaxing around someone for once.

"I hope so. I wouldn't want to get in their way." Rena pointed across the lobby and asked, "Do you want to say hello to Papa?"

"Yes," the Dollmaker said. "I'd like to thank him for the ticket."

Rena guided the Dollmaker across the lobby; she wove through the crowd like a ribbon. Soon they found Jozef, who looked more handsome than ever in his suit and black bow tie. His violin case was tucked beneath one arm, and the way he held himself reminded Karolina of her friend Fritz. The soldier had dedicated his life to his profession, and the same seemed to be true of Jozef.

Fritz would have loved to attend the concert, Karolina thought. How many times had they longed for the music that the stars had bestowed on them like kisses?

"Papa, look who I found," Rena said, bounding towards her father.

"Good evening, Mr Trzmiel," the Dollmaker said. "Thank you for inviting me."

"And me," Karolina said in a loud whisper.

"I'm glad you could join us," Jozef replied in the same hushed tone. His smile grew by the moment, like a flower opening in the sunlight. "I was ... well, I was beginning to think we had dreamed what happened. That would have been disappointing."

"Disappointing?" asked Karolina.

Jozef bent at the waist so that he could address Karolina more directly. "There's nothing as disappointing as realizing you only *dreamed* a good thing," he said.

"That *is* always sad," the Dollmaker said. Then he added, "I must give you something for my ticket, Mr Trzmiel."

Jozef held up his hand. "Please, call me Jozef. And don't worry about the ticket. It was no trouble at all. I love sharing music with friends."

"What will you be playing tonight?" asked the Dollmaker.

"Chopin's Concerto for Piano and Orchestra," said Jozef. "We play his work so often that I feel lucky I enjoy it so much. Otherwise, I'd be tired of it by now."

The Dollmaker laughed – and not just to fill the silence, as he sometimes did. "I feel the same way. My mother played the piano. She loved Chopin! But my father preferred Beethoven, and they argued about it more than once. His love of *Moonlight Sonata* was probably one of the only things from Germany my father held on to after he married my mother." The Dollmaker hummed a few bars of the song. It sounded like moonlight spilling over the eaves of a building.

But as beautiful as it was, Karolina was far more interested in what her friend had just told Rena and Jozef. The Dollmaker rarely mentioned his parents – or the hole their deaths had left in his world – even to Karolina.

"*Moonlight Sonata* is a good thing to hold on to. But I'd have to side with your mother," said Jozef. In the distance, a clock began to chime, and Rena's father sighed. "I should go and get ready. I hope you have a wonderful time."

"I'm sure we will," the Dollmaker said.

"I should go too," Rena said. "I'm sitting with my friend Bianka and her mother. Her father's in the orchestra, just like mine. He plays the cello."

"The cello?" asked Karolina.

"It's like a violin, only it's much, much bigger," Rena said. She stretched her arm up towards the crystal chandelier above them to indicate the size of the instrument.

"Goodbye," the Dollmaker said, waving to Rena and Jozef.

"Good luck!" Karolina called.

The Dollmaker's seat did not overlook the stage, so Karolina could not see Jozef as he played. But she heard his violin as clearly as if he had been standing right beside her. It was like he was casting a magic spell all his own, for his rich music was the sort that could wipe away tears and chase away entire flocks of nightmares. If only Karolina could bottle up the music like a potion! It wouldn't *save* her country, but it might bring joy to the dolls.

Karolina was about to tell the Dollmaker this when she looked up … and saw that his eyes were shimmering

with tears. But she knew instantly that these tears were not born from sorrow but from *happiness*. The absence of despair's weighty shadow made the Dollmaker look strong and joyful, the way Karolina thought he must have before the war had robbed him of so much.

The concert was the first of many meetings. Rena came to the shop as often as she could that summer, dragging her father behind her. Jozef was good-natured about her devotion to Karolina and the shop; Karolina never heard him complain about the visits.

He and the Dollmaker happily talked together for hours about art and music while Rena played with the other toys, Princess Wanda and Karolina. The two men discussed Chopin and Lutosławski, and the recently deceased Szymanowski.

"We're artists among our own kind," Jozef said one afternoon. He had brought his violin to play for them, and though Karolina enjoyed the records the Dollmaker had, nothing could compare with how vibrant live music was.

"I think that's very true. Maybe one day, we'll see your work in the Czartoryski Museum, right next to *Lady with an Ermine*," the Dollmaker said to Rena.

The little girl eagerly agreed. "I want to paint all my favourite places in Kraków," she said. "Like the Vistula river and the big trees in the House of the Living – that's where Mama's buried."

Karolina had never thought about cemeteries as houses – the Dollmaker had never mentioned the one his own parents were buried in – but she liked the idea that those

who had been lost could find respite from their pain. She thought it would be nice to some day have a place where the ashes of the dolls that the rats had burned could be at peace, beneath the boughs of the apple trees and the clear expanse of the sky.

That summer, all four chairs in the Dollmaker's room above the shop were occupied nearly every teatime. When the four were together, it seemed possible that Rena would indeed become a great artist when she grew up and that the happiness Karolina, the Dollmaker and the Trzmiels shared together would never end.

But such wishes felt almost disloyal to Karolina. She knew that in another world, far across the stars, her own people were suffering, and she vowed to do more to help them. Now that the Dollmaker had found friendship and peace in his own life, surely he and Karolina would be able to bring peace to her country too.

CHAPTER 11

The Witches

On the first day of September, the Dollmaker's radio announced that Hitler's army had invaded Poland. Britain and France, nations Karolina had only read about in books, declared war on Germany in response. And soon after, the Soviet Union attacked Poland as well, leaving the country divided in two.

None of the news was entirely unexpected, but Karolina knew that the Dollmaker had dreaded it for a long time.

For days, Karolina and the Dollmaker heard the German Luftwaffe planes shrieking above the rooftops of Kraków. The Dollmaker prayed. He worked his pink rosary beads between his fingers, as if they, like Karolina's stitches, might hold the power to grant wishes. When his prayers were not

 75

answered, the Dollmaker turned to pacing and listening to the radio that had replaced the half-finished dolls on his work table. The announcers gave terse accounts of troop movements and casualties. They grew less and less certain as the Germans came closer to the shining city.

The Dollmaker ran his hand down his wooden leg. Was he thinking of the battlefield and the awful years he had spent there? Karolina had to wonder. The lines on her friend's face looked deeper than ever, gutters that the ever-lengthening shadows pooled in.

"I don't even have my pistol to defend us with," he said. "I sold it after I came home from the last war – I didn't ever want to look at it again."

The radio's knob was large and stubborn, and it took Karolina several tries to turn it off. She couldn't stand to hear any more of the upsetting news. "Until the Germans come to Kraków, you can't do anything," she said.

"But they *will* come," said the Dollmaker.

Karolina couldn't argue with that, not even when the baker – who she always disagreed with on principle – expressed the same thought the following morning. "There's hardly any food coming into the city," Dombrowski said. "I'm down to my last few loaves, and I haven't got any flour to make more."

But despite his anxiety, the baker gave the Dollmaker a loaf of bread and would not take a single złoty for it. "If the Germans kill us all when they reach Kraków, what use will money be?" said Dombrowski.

The baker, like many people in the human world, seemed full of contradictions to Karolina. He was usually rude to the Dollmaker, but he *did* seem capable of kindness sometimes.

Dombrowski left before the Dollmaker could thank him for the bread, lumbering back to his shuttered bakery and his rowdy children. Karolina wished they had come outside to greet their father; she longed for the sight of *any* child. He and Karolina hadn't seen Rena since the Dollmaker had closed the shop at the start of the week.

Was Rena safe? Karolina remembered all too clearly what it had been like to be caught in the terrible gnashing teeth of history with nowhere to run.

By the second week of September, the members of the Polish government had fled to Paris. They told their countrymen on the radio that only outside of Poland could they hope to reassemble an army to take it back.

"The Polish government *will* come back, won't it? And make all the Germans leave?" asked Karolina. The words in the newspaper she was reading swam before her eyes. She didn't want to look at them, let alone believe them.

"I don't know," the Dollmaker said. He clutched his paper so tightly that the ink rubbed off onto the pads of his fingers, making him look more like a café poet than a shopkeeper.

Karolina waited for a moment, watching as the Dollmaker lowered his newspaper, then asked, "What do we do now?"

"We go on, I suppose," said the Dollmaker. He inched his hand across the table, and Karolina hugged as many of his fingers as she could manage to wrap her arms around. Inside her chest, her glass heart quivered. "Perhaps the Germans will mostly leave us alone. They've won, after all.

The Polish army is defeated. They have no reason to torment us any further."

"Maybe," Karolina said, touching her cheek. There didn't seem anything merciful about an army that invaded another country. She imagined the Germans would soon fill the government with their own men, just as the rats had.

It was not long before the shadow of the German army, the *Wehrmacht*, swept over Kraków. But the shining city was not heavily bombed the way other places in Poland had been. A city without an army to defend it was not a city enemy soldiers should bother destroying, as the mayor himself pointed out when he went to meet the Germans and begged them to enter Kraków peacefully. They had agreed, although the mayor mysteriously vanished soon after.

It had not been uncommon for lost things – house keys, flower petals and even single socks – to arrive in the Land of the Dolls from other worlds. But the mayor of Kraków was not likely to find himself on the shoreline of Karolina's home, however lost he was. A person was entirely different from a button or a half-finished poem that had wandered away from its owner.

Karolina and the Dollmaker watched the arrival of the invading soldiers in their green-and-black uniforms from the shop window. The grinning skulls and crossbones on their caps made it all the more difficult for Karolina to believe the promise the Germans had made to the mayor. If the invaders were not going to harm Kraków, why had they adopted this grim sign?

"The Germans allowed Poland to become independent

after the Great War, and now they want to take it back," the Dollmaker muttered as he and Karolina finally left the shop. He hadn't felt like going out, but he was down to the bread Dombrowski had given him and one cabbage. He couldn't spite the Germans by starving himself – and they always went to the market on Mondays.

As if to taunt the Dollmaker, a group of German *Wehrmacht* soldiers idled in front of the entrance to the Cloth Hall, passing a cigarette back and forth as they laughed over what was no doubt their good fortune. Not only had they survived many battles, they had won them.

Karolina, who was riding in the Dollmaker's basket, hugged his side. "They have no right to be here," she whispered. "They have their own country. They should go back."

"It never works that way," the Dollmaker said, keeping his own voice low. "That's usually why human beings go to war."

"I think the Land of the Dolls is better than any place in your world – even Kraków," Karolina said. "But that doesn't mean I'm going to invade your city."

"We're not very wise," the Dollmaker said. He lapsed into an uneasy silence as he neared the German soldiers, but they were so caught up in their own conversation that they barely glanced his way.

"I shouldn't have brought you outside with them around," the Dollmaker said to Karolina once they had passed the Germans. "We have to be careful."

"Why would they take a doll? That would be silly. There must be enough dolls in Germany for their sons and daughters to have," said Karolina. But she held on to the handle of the Dollmaker's wicker basket a little more

tightly so that she would not fall out. She didn't want to be taken away from her friend by a German.

"You're a very special doll. Even the Germans would see that," said the Dollmaker. His stomach growled as he neared the stalls. Karolina could smell cheeses, fruit jams, meat and fresh bread wafting through the square.

Karolina poked his belly. "I told you that you needed to go out and get food. You can't live on pickled cabbage for ever, not unless you want to become pickled yourself." Karolina hoped the Dollmaker would laugh at her joke, but he was too busy watching the stalls.

"There's not as much," he murmured.

"Not as much?" asked Karolina. "Not as much what?"

"Food. Cloth. There's not as much of anything as there usually is," the Dollmaker said softly. "Dombrowski was right. Things aren't making it into the city."

"Or they are, but the Germans are stealing it all," Karolina said. Her voice hinted at the scowl that would have turned her painted mouth downwards if she'd been a real girl. "Don't they have enough already?"

"Why bother to send food from Germany when they can take it from us?" the Dollmaker said. He sagged a little; he seemed more exhausted than angry. Karolina thought he might creep back to the shop in disgust if she allowed him to.

"Well, go on, then," Karolina said. "You need to get food before there's nothing left."

Shopping had never been exciting, not even for Karolina with her endless curiosity about her new world. But this trip was worse than normal. None of the merchants joked or smiled. Some glared at the Germans circling the square. Others refused to acknowledge their presence. Did they

think they could simply will the invaders away by acting like they were invisible?

The Dollmaker was walking back to the shop with his meagre purchases when he bumped into none other than Jozef Trzmiel. Rena's father looked as sleep-deprived as the Dollmaker himself. His jacket and trousers, usually so pristine, were badly rumpled. It was as if they were too exhausted to hold their shape in a time such as this.

The Dollmaker tipped his hat. "Jozef! Good morning! How are you?" he said, filling his voice with far more cheer than he actually felt.

Jozef usually greeted the Dollmaker with a handshake. But today he only nodded. "I'm ... fine," Jozef said. "Hungry. Like everyone else." He gave the bunch of carrots in his basket a shake. They were just as sad and brown as the cabbage the Dollmaker had just bought.

"I'm very glad to see you," said the Dollmaker. He lowered his voice and said, "It made me sick to see the Germans in the city. And Karolina and I were both worried about you and Rena." He pointed to Karolina, who nodded in vigorous agreement.

At long last, Jozef smiled. "I'm relieved to hear you say that. I thought maybe..." He sighed. "Cyryl, I thought that since your father was German, you would be happy about all of this. And things are worrying for Rena and me right now. Most of the Germans hate Jews. There have been stories – you must have heard. And even here in Poland, we're often blamed when things go wrong."

"Please, don't apologize. If I were you, I would have thought the same thing," said the Dollmaker. "But if Karolina and I can help you in any way... Rena's a wonderful girl. And you both have been extremely kind to us."

 81

Karolina could almost feel the other confessions building in his chest, namely how happy being friends with Rena and Jozef had made him. But instead, he swallowed, forcing the words down.

"It's all overwhelming. I... Cyryl, I've been made to leave the orchestra," Jozef blurted out.

The Dollmaker recoiled. "What?"

"Why?" said Karolina.

The look that stole over Jozef's face was cold and terrible. "According to the new government, Jews shouldn't be allowed to make art or play music," he said. "According to the new government, Jews shouldn't be allowed to do much of anything ... apart from work in the Germans' factories."

Karolina balled her hands into fists and saw the Dollmaker do the same. "They have no right," the Dollmaker said. In his anger, every word and syllable sounded like a crackling flame.

"But here they are, ruling us," Jozef said. "Rena says they're all witches. I laughed at first, but now ... who knows? They seem good at making people disappear, just like magic." Before the Dollmaker could ask exactly what Jozef meant, the other man said, "I'm sorry. I shouldn't be laying all this at your feet. I've found other work – a friend got me a position doing carpentry for a German company, so at least Rena and I can stay in Kraków. I still remember enough of my father's trade to be passable at it – although I wouldn't suggest hiring me for anything too important." He waited for some acknowledgement of the joke. But there was nothing funny in his vacant eyes.

To steal a man's music from him was a cruel thing indeed.

"You're not troubling us," the Dollmaker assured him.

"Thank you," Jozef said. He looked distractedly over the Dollmaker's shoulder. Both Karolina and her friend followed his gaze.

It was not difficult to spot Rena in her pale blue coat, even in the throng of people. Princess Wanda was cradled in her arms like an infant. The other doll's eyes were half shut, making her look thoroughly unimpressed with Kraków's current dreariness.

"The Germans are going to close Rena's school," Jozef said quietly. "And Jewish children aren't allowed in Gentile schools any more. I'm hoping I can find someone to teach her at home, but..." He pinched the bridge of his nose. "Rena loves school. She's going to be so upset when I tell her."

"I'm not a teacher," said the Dollmaker, "but I have quite a few books, and I'm not bad at maths. Perhaps I could help her with her studies while you are working."

"But you have the shop," said Jozef.

"There are plenty of times when no one comes in," Karolina said. She didn't want Rena to miss out on going to school, but she had to admit that she liked the idea of her friend being in the shop every day of the week.

The Dollmaker said, "Karolina is right. It wouldn't disrupt my day at all, Jozef. Maybe Rena could paint if I have a customer. It might distract her from..." He jerked his chin towards the German soldiers. "All *this*."

Jozef ran a hand through the coils of hair that were not hidden away beneath his hat as he considered this. "Only if it won't be an inconvenience," he said.

"It won't be," said the Dollmaker.

By now, Rena had turned away from the apples she

had been looking at, and spying her father, she slipped
between the housewives and glowering men to meet them.
She hugged Jozef and then looked up at the Dollmaker.
Normally, she would have hugged him too, but this time,
she stayed beside her father.

"Everything is fine," Jozef told her. "No one here is
happy about what's going on. Cyryl and Karolina don't
like it any more than we do. Isn't that right, Cyryl?"

"Absolutely," the Dollmaker said, answering for both
himself and Karolina. "Nothing will ever change that."

Rena stepped away from Jozef and gave the Dollmaker
a quick squeeze around his middle. "I'm glad," she whispered into the buttons of his coat, then drew back.

The Dollmaker twirled his cane in his hand, his sole
means of expressing his anxiety. "I... Jozef, if you want to
talk more, we could take a walk in the park. There will be
fewer people there – we could hear each other better in a
more, ah, quiet place."

Jozef glanced over at the soldiers, who were inspecting
the contents of an old woman's basket. "Yes," he said. "I
would like that."

CHAPTER 12

The Lakanica at the End of the World

The four of them made their way across the main square and through the yawning mouth of the Florian Gate, moving quickly to avoid the tram that passed by. There were no Germans to be seen once they crossed into Planty Park.

"What exactly was it that Florian did?" asked Jozef, craning his neck upwards so that he could see the saint's emblem on the gate. In the carving, a man hugging a red flag to his chest was borne up by a wisp of cloud. "I've always wondered, but I never had anyone to ask."

"He was a soldier who refused to hurt the Christians in the lands Rome conquered," the Dollmaker told him, motioning to Florian with his cane. "The other Romans

drowned him for it. I think that cloud is supposed to be taking him to Heaven after he died."

Rena peered up at Florian, frowning. "That story has a sad ending," she said.

The Dollmaker winced. "It's certainly not the happiest tale," he conceded.

"Florian's story seems appropriate now," said Jozef. "Or maybe it's just a coincidence. We're not the first people to be conquered by a foreign army – and we won't be the last." He bent down beside his daughter and tucked a stray lock of hair behind Rena's ears. "I'd like to talk to Mr Brzezick alone for a few minutes. Why don't you go and play with Wanda? We'll be with you soon."

"Karolina should go with you too," said the Dollmaker, taking her from the basket. "That way, you won't be alone."

"You won't be long?" Rena asked her father, and Jozef patted her head.

"No," he said. "We won't be more than fifteen minutes." This seemed to calm Rena. She accepted Karolina from the Dollmaker and, hugging her, set off down the path.

As they walked through the park, Karolina asked, "Why do you call the Germans witches?"

Rena's arms tightened around Karolina and Wanda, and she lowered her eyes to the dirt path. "Mama had a book of fairy stories that she used to read to me. I liked most of them, but I was frightened of the witches! They put spells on people and made them act strangely, like my friend Bianka. She said she won't play with me because I'm

Jewish. And the Germans made Zivia disappear, just like one of the witches in Mama's book would."

Rena had mentioned Bianka, the cello player's daughter, before. But Karolina did not recognize the other name. "Zivia?" she said. "Who is she?"

"The nice old lady who looked after me sometimes, if Papa's performances ran late. But then the Germans came and took her away. We don't know why," Rena explained. She kicked at the leaves in front of her; they were so deep that they lapped at her ankles like amber waves.

Karolina would feel awful if even grouchy Dombrowski were to vanish because of the Germans. She remembered how many of the dolls the rats had taken away – and she hadn't seen any of *them* ever again.

But maybe that wouldn't be the case in the human world.

"When the Germans lose the war, she'll come back," said Karolina, trying to make Rena feel better. "If she's an old woman, they wouldn't have any reason to hurt her."

"But what if no one beats the Germans?" Rena asked.

"I think they will," Karolina said. "France and Britain have already gone to war with them, and there are all sorts of heroic people who are still here in Poland. Like the Dollmaker!"

"Mr Brzezick?"

"Didn't you know? He used to be a soldier. He fought for Poland." Karolina thumped her fist against her chest, causing her heart to clink inside of it. "He even won medals. He keeps them in a box."

"But he only has one leg. He wouldn't be good at fighting now," said Rena. "Can he use his magic to fight instead?"

"His magic doesn't work like that," admitted Karolina after a pause. She hated to disappoint Rena. "But don't worry. He won't let the witches take you."

Some of the tension left Rena's face, and a smile – the first Karolina had seen all day – broke on her lips. "Maybe you're right," she said. "The Germans will lose, and then Papa can play the violin again. And we won't have to worry so much."

"The grown-ups will take care of it," said Karolina. The rats had been far smaller than the Germans, and they'd overrun her cottage in minutes with their hideous teeth and claws. She knew that on her own she had no hope of sending away the rats *or* the witches.

The more Karolina's thoughts lingered on the rats, however, the worse she felt. She couldn't stand to think about what was happening in her own country. But now that the Germans had come to Kraków, Karolina knew that this was not the right time to ask the Dollmaker to help her stop *her* war.

"What should we play?" Karolina said to Rena, turning the conversation to a far more pleasant topic.

Rena did not reply; she had stopped in the middle of the path. The toe of her shoe had brushed up against an apple. Its shimmering yellow skin seemed appropriate for autumn.

"I was just looking for an apple like this!" Rena said, bending down to pick it up. "It's our New Year soon, and it's our tradition to eat a sweet apple so we can have a sweet year. But all the ones in the market were nasty and brown. This is much better."

"I didn't know New Year started in the autumn," said Karolina. "It's not marked on the shop's calendar."

"Oh," said Rena. "It's a Jewish holiday that Papa and I celebrate. It's different from Mr Brzezick's."

"I see," said Karolina. She looked up, searching for the tree that must have dropped the apple. This was the right season for apples, but all the trees around them were alders like the one the Dollmaker had used to make Karolina. They only grew leaves and catkins, not fruit. "I've never seen an apple like that before," she said to Rena. "Have you?"

"I've had green apples before," said Rena. "But not a yellow one."

"It's a golden apple," a faint voice said. "A true one." The only person who could have spoken was the woman on the bench. Her hair was so red that it looked as if it had stolen all the colours of autumn, and twigs and leaves were artfully tangled in the locks. But it was not her hair that gave Karolina pause; it was her *scent*. Even from a distance, the woman smelled of damp earth and midsummer, aromas that Karolina did not associate even with the farmers who came to the city to sell their goods. The woman, she realized, wasn't human.

"Were you talking to me?" Rena said as she stood up.

"I was talking to you *and* to your friend," said the red-haired woman, crooking her finger at Karolina. Her smile was as soft as the clouds drifting above them. "You don't need to stay silent, little doll. You're alive – I can feel your heartbeat."

"You're like me?" said Karolina. "You're magical?" The Dollmaker had made Karolina's glass heart especially for her; it was a thing she alone possessed out of all the toys in the world. And only someone capable of doing magic would be able to sense it the way the woman claimed to.

"In a way," said the woman. "I can see traces of another

world on you, but I'm from a much more ordinary place," she said. "I come from a meadow in the west – I used to protect it."

"Oh! She's a Lakanica," Karolina said to Rena.

"A Lakanica?" asked Rena.

"The Dollmaker told me they're gentle spirits who rule over fields. They find lost people and bring them back home," Karolina explained. "Lakanicas are a little shy. They don't let humans see them very often." But that was the way of all magical creatures – Karolina included.

"I see," said Rena. She did not seem at all unsettled by encountering a spirit; it was almost as though she had expected it.

"Karolina and I haven't ever seen an apple like this before," Rena said to the meadow spirit as she walked towards her. "Is it special?"

"It's very special. It's the rarest and best kind of apple," said the Lakanica. "A firebird from a far-off country carried a magical seed all the way to my meadow and planted it in the very centre, hoping to share the magic of its world with the humans. A beautiful tree grew from it, and when the sun shone down on the tree, the golden apples appeared on the branches. They were so wonderful that one bite could keep a person full for an entire day."

"You said that the apples *were* wonderful," said Rena. "What happened to them?"

"The Germans rolled through my meadow in their tanks and burned everything, from the wildflowers to the tall grass," the Lakanica said. Her fingers twitched in her lap, as if they still recalled the feel of the flames lapping at them. "One of them shot the firebird with his rifle. And without the firebird to protect it, the golden apple tree

withered and died. I could only save a single apple – the one you're holding now."

"I knew they were witches," said Rena. "Only witches would shoot a magical bird."

"Are you going to live in the park now that your meadow is gone?" asked Karolina. The stretches of open grass between the trees and the path hardly seemed like proper fields to Karolina. Such a small space would not be right for the Lakanica.

"Yes," said the spirit. "I miss my meadow, but the Germans and their magic rule this part of the world now. There's nothing I can do to stop them."

"Their magic? Does that mean there are German magicians too?" Karolina said. "I know a magician. But he doesn't think he's a very good one."

"Yes, there are," said the Lakanica. "But I wouldn't go looking for them. The Germans tolerate only their own kind. You and I and the magician you speak of, we'd be wicked things to them. *Polish* things."

The idea was disconcerting, and Karolina leaned back in Rena's arms. She wanted to hug the little girl, but if she did, Rena would know that she was afraid. Then *she* might be afraid too. And Karolina didn't want that.

"The magician Karolina and I know is half German," said Rena.

"Then he should be even more careful," the Lakanica said. She leaned closer to Karolina and Rena. "This German magician would claim your friend as one of his own kind and force him to serve Germany."

Rena let the golden apple roll back and forth across her open palm. "Mr Brzezick wouldn't help the Germans, would he?" she asked Karolina.

 91

"No," said Karolina. She squeezed Rena's thumb. "He hates what they're doing. He's a Pole like you and wouldn't ever want to help the witches hurt more people." Then she asked the Lakanica, "How will the Dollmaker and I know who the other magician is?"

The meadow spirit took Karolina's wooden hand in her own. It felt like the mist that settled over the rivers just before dawn. "Most magicians smell like ink and starlight. The world bends around them."

Karolina had never thought of the Dollmaker like that; *he* smelled like the fire in a hearth at the end of a winter's day. But she supposed there had to be many different kinds of magicians, and some of them might be colder than her friend.

Rena glanced over her shoulder. "Papa and Mr Brzezick are coming," she said to the Lakanica. "Please, don't tell Papa about the German magician. He might get scared and not let me see Karolina and Mr Brzezick again if he thinks a witch is going to come looking for them."

"I won't," said the Lakanica.

"Thank you," said Rena. "I hope you find a safe home here in the park. Here's your apple back." She held the fruit out for the Lakanica to take, but the spirit folded the girl's fingers back over it.

"You should keep it," she said. "Keep it … and eat it for strength. You will need it."

The Lakanica remained on the bench for the space of a heartbeat. But as the wind picked up, it carried her away, her pale body losing its shape until Karolina could barely make out the brilliant red of her hair. All that was left behind was her warning about the German magician.

As Rena raced over to her father, Karolina noticed that

the Dollmaker was lagging a little behind Jozef. He looked as if he had grown years and years older in the last fifteen minutes. Karolina could not add to the worries she saw in the creases around his eyes and mouth by telling him about the other magician. What could the Dollmaker do?

Nothing.

CHAPTER 13

The Rat King

By the time the rats had rounded up all the dolls on the steps of the palace, they had devoured everything of value. Not a single candy-cane lamp post remained to guide weary travellers, and the roads were as splintered and uneven as the teeth of the rats.

The dolls gathered quietly; they could not risk disobeying the invaders. They journeyed from every corner of the kingdom, their path illuminated by fireflies, and Karolina was among them. They whispered fearfully as they approached the ivory palace. It was a far sadder place now. No stars shone upon it. What was there to look at but the ruins? Even the sky had changed; the clouds moved in sluggish, poppy-coloured wisps, and the air was thick with smoke.

When all the dolls had assembled, from the paper ballerinas to the wooden soldiers and the chubby porcelain girls, the Rat King appeared on the balcony where the true king and queen should have stood. The rat lord's presence seemed to mock the great monarchs. The curve of his belly glittered with the dozens of medals he had pinned to his waistcoat. Sickeningly, he'd jammed the queen's crown of crystal flowers onto his head. The circlet was so tight that it pinched his tattered ears together.

Karolina put a hand to her cheek. Every time she saw one of the rats, she felt pain bloom like thorny vines along the crack on her face.

"I am your new lord and sovereign. We rats rule the Land of the Dolls now," said the Rat King. "You will obey our new laws. You will bow to us when you see us. You will serve us. And if we ask anything of you, you will give it to us."

"Where are our king and queen?" one of the wooden soldiers yelled. "What have you done with them?"

Karolina expected the Rat King to rant and rave at the mention of the former monarchs, but he merely smiled, baring all of his ivory-yellow teeth. His tail curled upwards like a snake. "Do you see how red the sky is tonight?" he asked the crowd, craning over the balcony railing. It groaned beneath his unexpected weight. "Do you smell the smoke? Your old king and queen have been burned to ash – as you will be too, if you don't learn your place."

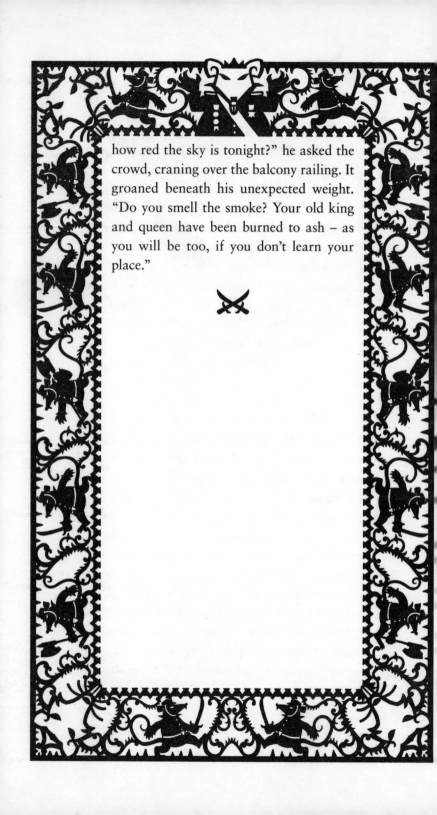

CHAPTER 14

Thievery

In October 1939, the Germans created a terrible new rule, one that allowed them to steal names.

Poland was now part of the *Generalne Gubernatorstwo* – the General Government, with Kraków as its capital. The main square was now called Adolf Hitler Platz, complete with a new sign. Its stark black lettering looked like the sort of brambles that would encircle a witch's poisonous garden.

Karolina hated the new sign, and she hated the new names. They were not Polish but German ones. Karolina felt that she had walked this path before … and knew where it led.

The Germans seemed intent on stealing the Dollmaker's name too. More and more often, he received post addressed

to Herr Birkholz. Who was Herr Birkholz? Certainly not her friend Mr Brzezick. Herr Birkholz was a man the invaders could call their own flesh and blood.

The Dollmaker set the first letter ablaze without reading it. The candle flame left the pads of his fingers blistered for three days. The second time, he actually bothered to open the letter – and read it with increasing anger. When he was finished, he tossed it aside. "They want me to register," he said.

Karolina, who had been working on the table with her needle and thread, asked, "Register for what?"

"As a *Volksdeutscher* – one of the German people," said the Dollmaker. "There's a list they want me to sign because my father was German. I'd receive more coupons for food by doing it. Many of the *Volksdeutsche* are actually happy the Germans are here. But if they think they can buy me off with extra rations, they're wrong." His lip curled.

The second letter went the way of the first, and the Dollmaker scattered the ashes out of the window.

The Dollmaker continued to feign ignorance when a German soldier addressed him in his father's language and eyed him as darkly as would any other citizen of Kraków. And, more importantly, he remained friends with the Trzmiels.

Karolina coaxed her friend into trying to do magic once or twice, but the pages of his books remained stubbornly still beneath his hands. The Dollmaker's heart must have hurt too much for him to be able to bring even the smallest amount of wonder into the world.

"I was never a good magician to begin with, Karolina. I'm sorry," the Dollmaker told her, wearily shaking his head in defeat.

Autumn gave way to winter. Each morning, when Jozef went to build shelves and tables and cabinets for the Germans, Rena came to the shop, wrapped in a scarf and a sweater, carrying her books. Between customers the Dollmaker taught her long division and multiplication. Karolina hovered over Rena as the girl studied the history of both Poland and the Jewish people, from their triumphs to their falls from greatness.

But the day Rena arrived wearing an armband marked with a blue star, she refused to look at her Polish history book. She closed it so quickly that she caught the hem of Karolina's skirts between the pages.

"I'm sorry," Rena said, lifting the cover long enough for Karolina to free herself.

"It's fine," said Karolina. She smoothed her skirts back into place, ignoring the rip along the hem. She could always mend the tear later. "Why didn't you finish that chapter?"

Rena pushed the book away. "I won't read this book any more. It's not telling the truth," she said. "It says that King Jan Olbracht was a great king, but he made all the Jews leave their homes and move to Kazimierz because people lied and said the Jews had set fire to their church. It's not true. And now the Germans are doing the same thing." She looked down at her armband. "They don't know any Jews, but they make up lies about how we want to hurt them and hurt Poland. Now we have to wear these stars on all our clothing to mark us out."

"I thought maybe the star was like the necklace you wear sometimes," said Karolina. "It has six points too, doesn't it?"

Rena shook her head. "My necklace is the Jewish star – the Magen David. It was Mama's. This star's different. We don't have a choice about wearing it. If we don't, the Germans will do something bad to us," she said. "Papa didn't say what, but he seemed scared. He looks so worried. He's too tired to play the violin any more." Rena folded her arms on the tabletop and rested her head with a great sigh.

Karolina wanted to reassure Rena that all would be well, but promising her that might make her a liar. She didn't know *what* would happen. Instead, Karolina said, "I'm sorry. I know what it feels like when your home turns into a bad place. The rats were terrible to the dolls after they took over."

"Someone must have rescued you from the rats then," said Rena. "Or else you wouldn't be here."

Karolina said, "A kind wind did. He brought me here so I could be with the Dollmaker."

"I wish a kind wind could blow me and Papa and all our friends far away from the Germans," Rena said. "Maybe you and Mr Brzezick could come too. We could go live in the firebird's magical country and eat golden apples all day."

Karolina knew that she would sew that wish into the next dress she made … but did anyone have the power to grant it?

As the snow melted into spring, Karolina read Rena's Polish history book, though now she knew better than to believe every word printed in it. She thought the secret to defeating one's enemies might lie between the pages, but

she could find no pattern to the Polish victories. Luck often seemed to play a part in which side won, but Karolina couldn't rely on luck to save the Land of the Dolls … or Poland. Both her country and the one she now resided in seemed to have little in the way of luck as it was.

"Soldiers and generals always talk about plots and strategies, but no one seems to really understand how to win a war," Karolina said to the Dollmaker.

"Most of it is up to chance," he replied.

"How did you fight your war?" Karolina asked. If she had not exhausted Rena's books, she never would have asked the question. The Dollmaker had never been the sort of man who liked telling stories about his glorious days as a soldier.

"By living to see the next day and the day after that – and by keeping a part of your heart sheltered from the bombs and the gunfire," the Dollmaker said quietly. "It's that part of your heart that will allow you to go on after it's over."

Karolina sat down with a sigh. "I'd rather win than just stay alive."

"At first, I wanted to be like Prince Krakus and end the fighting myself, even though I knew that I couldn't," said the Dollmaker. "But just because I couldn't help everyone didn't mean I couldn't help *someone*."

"What do you mean?" Karolina said.

"I lost my leg saving another man's life," said the Dollmaker. "I don't regret it. I cared for him, and I didn't want to see him hurt. Even helping one person is worthwhile, Karolina. And you can help Rena by being her good friend. Then she'll never be as frightened or lonely as you and I were in the past."

Was that true? Helping one little girl felt like a very small thing in the face of so much darkness. But Karolina didn't want Rena to ever feel the way she had before she'd come to Kraków.

"I wish I knew how we *could* help more," the Dollmaker said sadly. The light hit the lenses of his glasses as he shook his head, spreading rainbows on the walls of the shop.

Karolina remembered what Jozef had told them the day they celebrated Rena's birthday: that the Dollmaker might not understand the greater purpose of his magic, but that there must be one. Was the same true of Karolina's arrival in Kraków?

CHAPTER 15

The Story-Shaped Man

As the occupation continued, it seemed that the Germans had brought not only brutal laws with them but foul weather. The bitter spring gave way to an unbearable summer. Everywhere she looked, Karolina saw neighbours flushed with anger over a minor slight and labourers whose faces wept sweat as the heat crushed the city of Kraków.

Południca, Lady Midday, skulked among them in her dress of bridal white, causing men and women to faint from overwork and her burning touch. None of the humans noticed her, but to Karolina she was as real as the heat itself. She was like a wicked sister to the Lakanica, driven from her home in the fields just as the meadow spirit had been.

Inside the toyshop, however, it was dark and cool and

pleasant. And it was on a hot August day in 1940 that Rena acquired a new friend: a grey mouse seeking relief from the heat. The mouse had been coaxed from his hiding place in the wall by the smell of bread, and the butter the Dollmaker had slathered on top of it. The butter seemed like an excessive indulgence – or it would have if the Dollmaker hadn't presented two slices of bread to Rena for her lunch. He might go to bed with an empty belly, but at least Rena wouldn't. The Trzmiels and their Jewish neighbours received the smallest allocations of food now, and they had turned as pale as dust since the arrival of the Germans in Kraków.

Rena had just raised the slice of bread to her lips when she spied the mouse from the corner of her eye, its pink nose twitching. "Oh! Does he live here too?" she asked, pointing.

The Dollmaker looked up from the toy elephant he had been stitching a leg onto. "Not that I've noticed before," he said. "He must be a new addition to the shop."

"May I feed him?" asked Rena.

"If you feed him, he won't ever go away," Karolina said with a scowl. "Don't give up your bread for that thing."

"But he looks like a gentle mouse," Rena said. "Don't you think so, Karolina?"

Karolina could not pretend to coo over a *mouse*. It was far too close to being a rat, though at least the mouse was only as big as she was. "Awful creature," she said to Rena.

"Karolina doesn't particularly care for rodents," the Dollmaker said. "You can give the mouse a crumb if you'd like, Rena. But I'm afraid he can't bring along any friends. They'll nibble at the rocking horses and the dolls' dresses, and then I'll have to remake everything."

Rena nodded and slid off her stool. She pinched one

of the crumbs that had fallen from her piece of bread and went over to the mouse. Karolina thought the little creature would be frightened off by the *tap, tap, tap* of her red shoes, but it did not move as Rena set the crumb in front of it. "There you go, Mysz. You and I can have the exact same lunch."

"Mysz?" said Karolina. "You're going to name him *Mysz*?"

"Well, he *is* a mouse, isn't he?" said Rena, watching Mysz turn the crumb over in his paws. "It would be silly to give him a person's name."

"I suppose so," Karolina said. *She* had a person's name, but then again, Karolina looked far more human than Mysz.

"I think it's kind of you to feed him, Rena. I—" the Dollmaker began, but a resounding crash from outside cut his comment short. The shelves rattled, spilling a few dolls and stuffed animals onto the floor. The rocking horses reared back, as if they were trying to flee the source of the noise. And Mysz bolted back into his hole, taking his lunch with him.

"What was that?" Karolina cried.

"Nothing good," the Dollmaker said. He grabbed his cane from where it rested against the table and staggered across the floor, collecting the fallen toys as he went. There were so many of them that his arms were overflowing by the time he reached the window. "Oh my God," he whispered.

"What? What do you see?" said Karolina.

But the Dollmaker did not answer. He shoved the toys onto the nearest shelf and went outside, letting the door slam closed behind him.

"Mr Brzezick?" Rena called. She sprang off the floor and started after the Dollmaker.

"Don't leave me behind!" Karolina said, waving her arms to remind Rena that she was stranded atop the work table. The little girl doubled back and grabbed Karolina, clutching her against her chest as she followed the Dollmaker into the street.

At first, Karolina had no idea what had caused such a fuss. The only extraordinary thing she could see was the crowd growing in the spot where the towering statue of the poet Adam Mickiewicz stood. Or, she realized with horror, where the statue *had* stood.

Adam Mickiewicz was gone.

But the statue had not been spirited away – it had been torn down by force. Mr Mickiewicz lay on the cobblestones; his head and one hand had been severed from his bronze body. A few ropes were scattered around the base of the formerly grand monument. The German soldiers were admiring their handiwork.

The Dollmaker headed across the square, and he seemed too absorbed by the sight of the fallen statue to notice Rena or Karolina. His hand had tensed on the head of his cane, and his expression remained carefully blank, as if he too were a statue.

A smiling German private kicked Mr Mickiewicz's hand, passing it to his nearest comrade with a grunt. It was as if this – like the changing of the names – was all a delightful game. The Dollmaker drew back with a hiss.

"Barbarians," he whispered. An old woman standing nearby gave him an approving nod, her mouth pinched, as she turned back to the fallen statue. Karolina could not take her eyes off the young soldiers, sickened at the way it

 106

reminded her of the children who had played football in the square in the past.

All the soldiers here were boys, she thought, looking at their smooth faces. How could *boys* be so cruel?

Only one of the Germans, an officer, judging from the patches on his collar, had decided not to participate in the newly invented game. He looked a few years older than the other witches, and was tall and thin, with alabaster skin, and eyes the same piercing blue as Karolina's. But that was the only thing she had in common with him. She stared as the officer snarled at the crowd and shouted, "*Wracajcie do swoich domów.* Go back to your homes!" His Polish was barely passable, and many of the people exchanged puzzled looks, struggling to understand what he'd said. "Go home!" he repeated. "This is not your business. Go home, or you'll be arrested!"

He waved his hand, and at last, people seemed to understand him. They scattered, grumbling and cursing the curt man and his fellow Germans as they went.

Rena looked from the Dollmaker, who was still clutching his cane very tightly, to the fragments of Adam Mickiewicz strewn on the ground. She bent down and picked up several of the pieces, showing them to the Dollmaker. "The statue's not all gone, Mr Brzezick. See?" Rena said.

The Dollmaker turned and said, "Rena! What are you doing? You shouldn't be out here. There's too much..." He seemed unable to describe the strange violence that had overtaken the square.

"You were so upset! Karolina and I wanted to see what was wrong." Rena adjusted Karolina's red cap, which had fallen over one eye.

"I'm sorry," the Dollmaker said, drawing Rena up

against his side. "I should have told you where I was going. But I'm all right now. There's no need to worry." He shivered a little, although the day was sweltering.

Karolina looked back across the main square. She had hoped that the witches would move elsewhere, but they seemed determined to stay near the toyshop. Even from a distance, Karolina could see their sides shaking with laughter.

The Dollmaker seemed to have noticed the group of witches as well. "Why don't we go inside the church for a while?" he said to Rena, pointing to St Mary's Basilica with the tip of his cane.

Karolina was glad that the Dollmaker had made the suggestion. If he took Rena back to the shop, the Germans might see the blue star on Rena's armband. And if they did, they would say terrible things about her – and maybe even hurt her.

"No one will mind that I'm there?" Rena said. "And Papa won't mind?"

"You won't get in trouble," the Dollmaker said. "We're not going to pray." His hand tightened on Rena's shoulder as he escorted her across the remainder of the square. He slipped on the cobblestones several times. Karolina was glad when they reached the church.

Once they were inside, the Dollmaker uncurled his hand from around his cane, the joints in his fingers cracked. Karolina said, "I don't think bones are supposed to sound like that."

"I'm just a little stiff these days," said the Dollmaker. "That's all."

"Papa's hands click like that now," Rena said. "He says he's fine too."

The smile she received from the Dollmaker reminded Karolina of the wobbly smiles of the baby dolls in the shop, who always looked like they were about to burst into tears. But the Dollmaker did not cry; he turned his head towards the young priest who was holding Mass at the front of the church. The priest had lifted his hands up so that they too appeared to be climbing towards Heaven alongside the gilded saints depicted on the altarpiece. Karolina admired the fine details of the three wooden panels which rose far above the heads of even the tallest men.

The Dollmaker dipped three fingers into the basin of water beside the door and crossed himself. "In the name of the Father, the Son and the Holy Spirit," he murmured in prayer. "Amen."

"Does it look like the place where you go to pray?" Karolina whispered to Rena.

"Not really," said Rena, looking up. The ceiling formed a vault of blue and gold above them in an imitation of the summer sky. "We don't have many paintings on the walls at our synagogue. But there's lots of light and song. We can't pray or celebrate there any more, though. The Germans took it away. Papa says they store their guns in it now."

It seemed ironic that the witches had made a place of peace and contemplation into a shrine to war. The thought made Karolina all the more bitter.

"I'm sorry you had to see what happened outside," the Dollmaker said to Rena. "I just can't believe they destroyed the statue…"

"That's what *I* don't understand – it was just a statue. Why did they hate it so much?" said Karolina. "People can't fight with statues and poems."

"Adam Mickiewicz has always given us Poles hope. His

poems make us rise up and fight – they have for a hundred years. That's why the Germans want to remove any trace of him," said the Dollmaker. "You can destroy a person, Karolina, but destroying their story is far more difficult. No one is ever really lost as long as their story still exists."

Karolina thought about this and decided he was right. She held inside her the stories of everyone she'd known in the Land of the Dolls, even if they could no longer tell anyone those stories themselves. She might even carry the hidden tales of the Dollmaker's mother.

"What will happen to all the pieces of Mr Mickiewicz?" Rena asked.

"When the Germans are gone, we'll rebuild the statue," said the Dollmaker. "We must. Mickiewicz belongs to us – not them."

"Never them," Karolina said in agreement. "But we should be quiet – everyone else is praying."

But, she realized, that was not quite true. The two people huddled in a nearby corner – a man, and a boy about Rena's age – appeared to have little interest in the priest's sermon. The man was writing at a furious pace in a small leather book. His hair was the colour of the cherries the Dollmaker loved. And when he looked up from his notebook, Karolina saw that his eyes were as silver and round as coins.

She gasped, but the Dollmaker did not hear her. A choir had begun the day's selection of hymns, and their voices swelled to fill every hollow within the church. Her friend had closed his eyes to enjoy the music. And, Karolina thought, to forget the sound of the statue falling.

Rena, however, *did* notice that Karolina's gaze had been drawn to the whispering boy and the silver-eyed man. "Dawid?" she said.

"Who?" said Karolina.

"The boy is Dawid," Rena said. "He lives in the flat downstairs with his mother and little sister. We used to walk home from school together back when there was a school."

Karolina dimly recalled seeing Dawid the very first day she had met the Trzmiels. But the laughing boy who had raced into the parlour after Rena seemed a far cry from Dawid as he was now. He held himself stiffly, as though his own thoughts were almost too heavy for him to carry.

Rena walked over to him. "Hello, Dawid," she said quietly.

The boy whipped around, his eyes wide with fear. But that fear vanished as soon as he saw Rena. "Oh," he said. "Hello, Rena."

"What are you doing here?" Rena said.

The boy looked from Rena to the silver-eyed man, as if asking for permission. The man nodded, and Dawid said, "I was just ... getting some medicine. Mama ran out of ration coupons, and my sister's sick. So I came here."

"I hope Danuta feels better. But why are you buying medicine in a church?" asked Rena. Karolina had wondered that herself.

Dawid shrugged. "Because the Germans don't want us to have food or medicine, and this is the one place they don't think we'll ever go. People come here with the things we need, and we buy it from them," he replied.

"That's odd," Rena said.

Dawid did not have the opportunity to respond. The Dollmaker had joined them – and he was already apologizing. "I'm very sorry if we interrupted any ... transactions. Please don't mind us," he whispered to the silver-eyed man.

The Dollmaker seemed to have known what was happening even without Dawid's explanation.

"And I thought magicians were supposed to recognize magic when they saw it," said the man, sliding the notebook into his pocket with a snort. To Dawid, he said, "I'll have what you need by tomorrow. And don't worry about the money."

"Thank you, sir." Dawid bowed his head to the stranger and retreated towards the doors, but not before giving Rena a smile. "Bye," he said, then dashed away before Rena could bid him farewell. This, thought Karolina, seemed to be a pattern with Dawid.

The Dollmaker, meanwhile, had finally cobbled together a response to the stranger's accusation. "A magician? I have no idea what you're talking about," he said.

But the silver-eyed man did not relent. "You're the only magician in Kraków. Or even in all of Poland," he said. He raised a slender white hand and placed two fingers beneath the Dollmaker's chin, tilting it upwards.

"You've mistaken me for someone else," the Dollmaker said. He took a step back.

The silver-eyed man jammed his hands into the pockets of his coat. The fabric was glossy, making it look more like the pelt of an animal than velvet. "I can hear the heartbeat of the doll that little girl is holding, so let's not pretend to be anything but what we are," he said.

The Lakanica had been able to hear Karolina's glass heart too.

"And who are *you*?" Karolina snapped. Perhaps she shouldn't have spoken, but what use was there in pretending to be an ordinary toy when Kraków seemed to be filling up with magic?

"You'd call me a story," said the silver-eyed man.

"A story?" Rena asked. "What kind of story?"

"The kind everyone knows," the silver-eyed man replied. He leaned forwards. "The kind you've heard again and again. I used to be an outlaw from the countryside, but nowadays, it's not greedy barons I'm stealing from – it's the Germans."

The Dollmaker let out a choked laugh. "You can't honestly expect me to believe you're Juraj Jánošík," he said. "A Robin Hood figure who robbed from the rich and gave to the poor – a fairy tale."

"Juraj Jánošík? I read about him in one of the books you gave me," Rena said. "I didn't know he lived *outside* of the book, though."

"He doesn't," the Dollmaker said firmly. "There might have been such a person a long time ago, but he's been dead for more than two hundred years."

"No," said Jánošík. "That's where you're wrong. I'm a real man, who died and *became* a story. The more people tell a story, the more alive it becomes. And you're one to talk, Dollmaker! Have you ever heard of a sillier thing than a living doll?"

"Karolina's not silly!" Rena said. "She's my friend."

"Yes!" said Karolina. "It's not my fault I'm so much smaller than everyone in this world."

Jánošík chuckled. He was a myth; Rena and Karolina must have looked small to him indeed. "My apologies. I was just trying to make a point to your friend," he said. "We're all in this together, and he –" he gestured to the Dollmaker – "is wasting his talents. There's a war happening, in case no one bothered to tell you."

"I know that," said the Dollmaker. A snarl chased his

every syllable, as though he was speaking in the language of wolves rather than men. "I'm doing what I can."

"You'll have to do much more by the time all of this is over," Jánošík said.

"Have you been spying on us?" said Karolina, wriggling furiously in Rena's arms. If she had been as big as the Dollmaker, she would have borne down on Jánošík like a hawk.

"Your friend is a magician, and we're creatures of magic," said Jánošík. "Of course we pay attention to him … and what he's doing." He moved his long fingers through the air, outlining the Dollmaker. He may once have been human, thought Karolina, but now his flesh was as white as the paper his story had been recorded on.

"What do you expect me to do to help? Join the resistance and blow up Germans? I promised myself a long time ago I would never hurt another man," said the Dollmaker. His cane slipped from his hand, and he had to fumble for it so it didn't clatter to the marble floor.

"There are other ways of fighting," said Jánošík. "Look at me – I'm not fighting anyone with a fist or a blade."

The Dollmaker cast an anxious glance past Jánošík to Rena. "Then what do you suggest I do?" he asked.

"You have magic," said Jánošík. "Use it. I use trickery every day. How else could I avoid being caught by the Germans?" His eyes glittered.

"You think I can control what I do," said the Dollmaker. "But I can't."

"But you *are* a real magician," said Rena, giving the Dollmaker's coat a fierce tug. "We even met someone else who told me that you were. Didn't we, Karolina?"

 114

"We did," Karolina said. She knew that she should have told the Dollmaker before, but what good would it have done? He wouldn't have listened.

"Who else thinks I can do magic?" the Dollmaker asked. He fixed Karolina and Rena with a disapproving look. It was a look Karolina supposed she deserved.

"It was a meadow spirit who ran away from the Germans," Karolina said. "Rena and I talked to her that day you were in the park with Jozef. I'm sorry we didn't tell you about her."

"See?" said Jánošík, clapping the Dollmaker on the shoulder. "The doll is right: you *are* a magician. Why, you might be able to bring the statue of Mr Mickiewicz to life if you tried!"

"The Germans tore Mr Mickiewicz down," the Dollmaker said gloomily. "Or haven't *you* been outside today?"

"They played football with his hand," said Karolina, finding herself adopting the same melancholy tone as her friend.

"He'll be back," Jánošík said.

"That's what the Dollmaker told me," Rena said, grinning.

Jánošík reached into his pocket, and Karolina thought he was about to remove the notebook he had been scribbling in when they'd entered the church. But the object he took from it was a small cloth sack roughly the size of his fist. "It's sugar," he said, and dropped it into the Dollmaker's pocket. "Maybe you and Rena can have more than just bread tomorrow."

"I... Thank you," said the Dollmaker.

"Stay gentle. Be strong," Jánošík said. Then he spoke

to Karolina. "Stay with him. For as long as you can. It's important that you stay with him."

What was he talking about? Was this another cryptic warning, like the one the meadow spirit had given her? "Of course I will," said Karolina. "I'll take care of him too. It's what I always do."

"As well as you can," said the thief.

"As well as I can," Karolina said.

The sense that she had just made a solemn promise sent her heart rocking back and forth like the horses in the shop.

But Karolina knew it was a promise she had to make.

That evening, after Rena had left the shop, the Dollmaker sat in silence for a long time. He lit a candle on his work table, and Karolina sat near it, bathing in its glow.

At last, the Dollmaker spoke, saying something Karolina never expected to hear. "I'm going to register as one of the *Volksdeutsche*," he said. "I don't want to be seen as a German, and I don't need the extra rations, but we both know people who do."

"We do," Karolina agreed.

"But," the Dollmaker sighed, "the Trzmiels would be punished if anyone found out. *Severely* punished – even more than I would be."

"Then you can't get caught," said Karolina. She jerked her head towards the church, whose many windows were still lit. "Be clever like Jánošík."

"They hanged Jánošík, you know," the Dollmaker said thoughtfully. "In the end, they caught him and they hanged him. Yet somehow, he survived."

"We're magical. That means we're very good at sur-
viving," said Karolina, comforting both herself and
the Dollmaker. She knew that by signing the list, the
Dollmaker would forfeit his true name to the Germans.
But Karolina thought he was far cleverer than they were;
food was worth more than a name. Music, art, laughter –
each of those gifts sprung from a full belly.

And who better to give those gifts to than Jozef and
Rena?

CHAPTER 16

The Witches and the Mouse

Marzanna, the Lady of Winter, had no mercy in the months that spanned the end of 1940 to the beginning of 1941. She did not care that the people of Poland had far less coal and wood than ever before. She made frost flowers bloom on every windowpane and scattered so much snow over Kraków that it reached the Dollmaker's knees. The Lady of Winter turned away laughing as the people of the city sacrificed their tables and chairs and stately clocks to the fires that would keep them warm.

Even the Dollmaker's rooms above the shop were chilly; all his extra allotments of cooking oil and candles and coal had secretly been given to the Trzmiels. But the other shopkeepers did not know this. They looked at the swastika

 118

badge – the symbol of Nazi Germany – on the lapel of his jacket furiously whenever he went out to buy things with his many ration coupons.

"Greedy traitor!" they hissed.

Pride flared in Karolina each time the Dollmaker withstood these comments. She'd known her friend wouldn't abandon Rena and Jozef, no matter what anyone thought of him. Karolina couldn't always predict what the Dollmaker would do, but she understood his heart well; she felt as if she had a map of it inside her own. For it wasn't only the cobblestone streets of Kraków that needed to be navigated. People could be like labyrinths too.

Just as he had before the war, the Dollmaker went shopping once a week. He did not want to leave Karolina and Rena alone in the toyshop, so they came with him. But this presented an entirely different problem: Rena, with her blue-star armband, was not allowed inside many of the stores.

"Jews are only allowed here between three and four in the afternoon," Dombrowski told the Dollmaker after he and Rena had entered the bakery. "They can't come at any other time. That's what the Germans told me."

"Rena isn't going to buy anything," the Dollmaker said. His smile was as worn as the lettering in his well-loved books. "She's only here because I am. She's a child – I can't very well have her stay alone in the toyshop while I do my shopping."

Dombrowski leaned over the counter, his elbows leaving tracks in the light dusting of flour that covered it. "The girl is still a Jew. She's lucky to be in Kraków at all," he said. "You're going to get us both into trouble, Cyryl."

Karolina did not think the Dollmaker would have been

able to meet the long, dark look the baker gave him before he had become friends with the Trzmiels. But now he did, and calmly at that. "No one is going to get into trouble," the Dollmaker said.

"It's all right, Mr Brzezick. I can wait outside until you're done," said Rena, sliding back towards the door. "I'll be fine. I'm not alone." She held up Karolina, who let her head fall forwards in what she hoped the Dollmaker registered as a nod. Then the girl turned away from the two men and went back out onto the street, the smell of fresh bread following her, like an afterthought.

There was hardly anyone around. A group of young men stood at the mouth of the narrow street next to the bakery, arguing heatedly over the newspaper they held between them. On the other side of the road, a woman wearing a green headscarf rocked an infant back and forth in her arms.

Rena poked out her tongue to catch one of the snowflakes drifting down from the dense veil of clouds. When she realized Karolina was watching her, she said, "The snow doesn't really taste like anything, but I like to catch it anyway."

"The snow was sweet in the Land of the Dolls," Karolina said wistfully. She didn't want to be sad around Rena. But every so often, a vivid image of Karolina's home would sweep over her, and when that happened, she wanted to share it. If she shared it with someone, it would be more than a memory.

It would almost be real.

Rena stamped her feet together, trying to drive away the cold. "Sweet snow *would* be delicious. We could make doughnuts from it and put rose jelly inside." Now she too sounded wistful. "Was everything made of sweets in the Land of the Dolls?"

"Not *everything*," Karolina said. "The sugar flowers were pretty, but I wouldn't have tried to build a whole house from them."

Rena caught another snowflake on her tongue. "But the Land of the Dolls sounds too magical to be practical."

"Whoever said something can't be both?" Karolina said. "I like to think I'm a practical doll, even if I came to Kraków with the help of magic."

"That's true," said Rena. She looked over her shoulder and into the shop to where the Dollmaker had just finished paying Dombrowski. "Mr Brzezick isn't very practical, is he?"

Karolina wondered how long Rena had been thinking about this. "What makes you say that?" said Karolina.

"He's been giving Papa and me food," Rena said, lowering her voice to a whisper. "And I know he's not supposed to."

"It's the Dollmaker's food," Karolina said. "He can do whatever he wants with it. And what he wants is to give some of it to you and Jozef."

"But I don't want to get him into trouble," Rena said.

Karolina was about to tell Rena not to worry, but the Dollmaker's arrival stopped her. He adjusted the scarf knotted around his neck and said, "It's getting quite cold out here. Shall we go back to the shop?"

He offered Rena his hand, though Karolina never would know if she would have taken it. The sound of a whistle cut through the air like the shriek of a crow, causing Rena to jump back. The jarring noise was followed by the arrival of a grey truck with half a dozen *Wehrmacht* soldiers standing in the back. They leaped out as soon as the engine rumbled to a halt.

"Get in a line!" one of the witches shouted. "Hurry! Now!"

For one terrible moment, everyone remained where they were; they were too stunned to do anything else. Another blast from the whistle, however, forced them into motion. The woman with the baby rushed past the witches murmuring to her wailing child. The Dollmaker grabbed Rena's hand quickly and lined up beside the others.

The last German to leave the truck was the same officer who had threatened the crowd after his men had torn down the statue of Adam Mickiewicz on that terrible summer's day. Karolina would have remembered his piercing eyes anywhere. He adjusted his grey cap as he sauntered over to the frightened Poles. The skull badge affixed to it leered down at them.

It was a symbol that Karolina could hardly believe anyone would wear so proudly.

"Open your bags and empty your pockets. Now!" the witch barked at the people in line.

"Why?" the woman cried. "I was just going home. I haven't done anything wrong!"

The witch fingered the collar of his uniform. The fabric rustled, making it look as if the two lightning bolts stitched onto it were preparing to strike the woman. "I will decide that. And the next time you speak to me, you will address me as Hauptsturmführer Brandt," he said.

His voice was every bit as sharp as a rat's claws, which Karolina thought was appropriate. Both rats and pale men with ugly smiles seemed to possess the same awful ability: to make everyone do what they wanted with a harsh word and the threat of a sword behind it.

The Poles did as the witch captain ordered. The Dollmaker set his basket and cane down in the snow and turned out the pockets of his coat. Rena shifted Karolina from one hand to the other so that she could do the same.

Karolina wished that the star on Rena's armband could retreat behind the clouds the way stars did in the Land of the Dolls when they were frightened. No one else was wearing one, and that made Rena's all the more obvious.

The Dollmaker seemed to have the same thought. He put his arm around Rena's shoulder and fanned his hand out across her armband to hide it. "Everything is going to be all right," he told her quietly. "Don't say anything." Rena nodded, but Karolina could feel her shaking. She could not keep her eyes from the witch captain as he strode down the line, peeking into baskets and roughly grabbing at the coats of the people he had assembled.

Brandt stopped in front of a skinny young man with hair almost as red as the Dollmaker's. The witch captain grabbed his arm, causing the gold watch fastened around his bony wrist to jingle. "Where did you get this watch?" Brandt asked.

The young man jerked away. "It was my father's."

"And how did your father manage to afford such an expensive-looking watch?" Brandt said.

The young man stood up straighter. "He had a good job. He was a professor of mathematics at the university."

Karolina was glad that Brandt chose not to smile then; if he had, she thought his teeth would have been long and barbed just like a rat's. "Everyone knows that Poles are too stupid to be professors," the witch said, chuckling. "You're a liar and a thief."

The young man, who was beginning to look much more

like a young *boy*, swallowed. "My father had it for years. He *was* a professor. I—"

Brandt cocked his head towards the soldiers behind him, who came forwards to haul the young man roughly out of the line.

"Put him in the truck," Brandt said.

"I didn't steal it," the young man repeated. His heels left grooves in the snow as he tried in vain to wriggle away from the witches. "I swear that I didn't steal it!" But Brandt was not listening. His gaze swept over the people in the line once more. Karolina thought he lingered on the Dollmaker's face for a moment too long. Then at last, he said, "We're through here. Go!"

The witches hauled the still-protesting young man into the back of the truck and clambered into it themselves. The vehicle sputtered to life once more and went screeching down the street, bouncing this way and that on the cobblestones before disappearing around the corner.

Karolina did not think that Brandt's work for the day was finished. The rats, as she recalled, had never been satisfied with tormenting just one doll.

They had wanted to torment them *all*.

The group walked away slowly, as if they hoped that the last fifteen minutes were a nightmare they would soon wake from. How could they live in a world in which a young man could be arrested for the crime of wearing a gold watch?

The Dollmaker bent over and retrieved his cane and the basket of groceries. Karolina saw his expression shift from one of fury to deepest sorrow beneath the brim of his cap.

"Where are they taking that man?" Karolina asked.

"I don't know," said the Dollmaker.

It was then that Karolina understood that her friend

knew *exactly* where the witches had taken the boy – and that it was not a nice place. The Dollmaker had never been a good liar; his voice shivered and quaked … just as it was doing now.

Rena did not speak until they neared the end of the street. "I don't think he stole the watch."

"No," the Dollmaker said sadly. "I don't think he did either."

This awful truth hanging in the air, the three of them returned to the shop. But none of them spoke much for the rest of the afternoon.

The Dollmaker's decision to register as one of the German *Volk* had an unfortunate side effect: over the next few months the shop began to receive German visitors. But their patronage did not bring the Dollmaker any joy. These were true Germans, women and children who came with their fathers and husbands and brothers. The cheerful witch at the registration office had informed the Dollmaker that Kraków was to become a centre of *German* culture, and the sudden arrival of so many foreigners seemed to indicate that he was right.

The first of these unwelcome visitors came to the shop one afternoon, when the Dollmaker had put his lunch aside to work on a new toy, and Rena had lured Mysz from his hole to play. The newcomer looked no different from any other Pole. Her wheat-coloured hair was pulled into a taut bun that exposed her pale eyes and pink face. But she did not address the Dollmaker in Polish; she spoke to him in German.

Hearing it, Karolina wanted to spring from her place on the Dollmaker's table and hiss like a cat. Even the Dollmaker stiffened visibly as the woman said, "Pardon me, are you Herr Birkholz?"

A boy who looked about Rena's age peeked out from behind her, his hair mostly concealed beneath a black cap. He held a biscuit in one hand. Grains of sugar clung to his lips.

"Yes, I am. May I help you?" the Dollmaker asked. He was as mild and polite to the witch woman as he would have been to any other customer. But he had switched from Polish to German, and that alone seemed to change his demeanour. He sat a little straighter, and his words were sharper.

"I'm looking for a birthday present for a friend's daughter. She'll be three soon," the woman said, sounding relieved that she and the Dollmaker shared the same language. Was her husband an officer or one of the many German businessmen who had arrived in the city to start factories that made pots and pans and uniforms for the army?

But it hardly mattered why the woman was here. She and her son might not be proper invaders the way the soldiers were, but that didn't make them welcome in Kraków – or in the Dollmaker's shop.

"Look!" the boy cried, and pushed past his mother. He raced to the shelf full of stuffed toys. "Look, Mama! Animals!" The boy gave the lion's tail a fierce tug, as if he hoped this would somehow awaken it. Karolina grimaced. Rena would never have handled a toy in such a way, she thought.

"Yes, I can see that," his mother said, her smile pinched.

126

It was an expression that made Karolina wonder if this woman even liked her rough son in his black cap. Turning back to the Dollmaker, the woman asked, "Do you have anything for a younger girl?"

"I have a few cloth toys," the Dollmaker said. "Or rocking horses, if you think she'd prefer one of those."

The woman nodded her approval. "I was advised to come here. There are a few other shops, but their dolls are a little ... primitive for a good German girl," she said. "I suppose they must appeal to the locals. But surely you can't do much business with them nowadays."

The Dollmaker busied himself with his carving knife once more, the motions brusque. The doll he was crafting from this particular block of wood would be a warrior queen, shaped by his anger and his desire to see the witches expelled.

It was Karolina's duty as a doll to know even his most secret truths.

"The locals have been my customers for nearly twenty years," the Dollmaker said flatly. "And they'll continue to be in the future, I expect."

"I see," the woman said, her cheeks turning the same red as Karolina's hair ribbons. It was difficult not to feel smug about the witch's silent admission of guilt. She had been rude, and she deserved to be embarrassed by her behaviour.

As much as Karolina knew he would have liked to, the Dollmaker could not ignore her. The sooner the witch woman found a doll, the sooner she would leave. The Dollmaker set his knife aside with a sigh and went to help her.

Meanwhile, the witch's son was poking and prodding at

the animals, having jammed his biscuit into his mouth to free both his hands. He pitted one toy against another, enacting what must have been a great battle in his own mind.

"*Rar, rar!*" the boy said, forcing the lion captain to lunge at an anteater, which he flung against the wall.

Karolina slumped, her head falling forwards so that she could glare at the invaders through the curtain of her fringe. She wished the Dollmaker could throw them out!

But Rena did not seem bothered by the boy's roughness. She smiled at him and asked in broken German, "Do you like animals?"

The boy looked over his shoulder at her. "I suppose so," he said.

"My mouse just learned a new trick," said Rena. "He can dance now! Would you like to see?"

"Your *mouse*?" The boy dropped the lion on the floor and strode over to where Rena sat, his expression quizzical. Once he saw Mysz beside her, however, he recoiled. "I thought you were talking about a toy mouse, not a real one. Why are you playing with it? Don't you know that they're dirty?"

"Mysz isn't dirty," said Rena. "He keeps himself very clean." She brushed her finger against one of his pink ears. "See? He's soft too."

"Mice are vermin," the witch boy replied, like a tiny, red-faced general, barking out orders. "That's what my uncle says. They're as bad as cockroaches or lice. They spread disease and steal food." Then his gaze drifted to Rena's armband. He sneered. "But I guess you're vermin too."

"I'm not vermin," said Rena. "I'm a girl." She spoke firmly, but Karolina knew the boy's comment must have hurt her.

"No, you're a Jew," the boy said. His smile stretched wider and wider across his face, as jagged and sharp as barbed wire. "So you're no better than your nasty mouse. Neither of you belong here any more."

With this, he brought his foot down on Mysz. Rena screamed.

Karolina wanted to do the same as she watched the witch boy lift his foot.

Rena threw herself in front of Mysz, to shield him should the boy decide to stomp on him a second time. But the damage was already done: Mysz's back legs and soft, pink tail had been crushed by the boy's boot.

It took every ounce of willpower Karolina had to stay still and silent.

The Dollmaker, who had been showing the witch lady a baby doll, dropped the toy back into its cradle. "What happened?" he said. But no sooner had he asked the question than he looked down and saw Mysz – and Rena's tears.

"It was just a mouse," the witch boy said with a shrug. "And how can you be one of us when you've got Jews and mice in your shop? Aren't we supposed to get rid of things like them?"

The Dollmaker's face turned as pale as the snow, but it was rage that drained the colour from his cheeks. His hand shot out, and he grabbed the boy, pulling him away from Rena and her injured friend. "How *dare* you?" the Dollmaker snarled at him.

"Take your hands off my son!" the witch woman shrieked.

For an awful moment, Karolina thought the Dollmaker might slap the child instead of obeying the witch's command. She had never been able to connect the Dollmaker

to the soldier's uniform that was folded in the bottom of his wardrobe. But now, Karolina realized that he *could* be fierce when he wanted to. Perhaps he had to work very hard to be as gentle as he was.

Had the same been true of Fritz, the other soldier in Karolina's life?

She thought it might be.

"Your son is cruel," the Dollmaker said. "But he's also just a child. He does what the adults around him do, so the blame for his behaviour rests with you, Madam. Get out of my shop and don't come back." He let go of the little witch's shirt, and the boy scrambled back over to his mother.

"You needn't worry about that," said the woman. She turned her nose up. "And I promise, you'll lose business over this – if not more." The witch grabbed her son's hand and pulled him out of the shop.

With the witches gone, Karolina could speak once more. Leaning over the edge of the table, she whispered, "Rena!" Karolina did not ask if the little girl was all right; it would have been a foolish question.

The Dollmaker tried to bury his anger the best he could, but Karolina could still see embers of it burning brightly in his eyes as he knelt down beside Rena. "I'm so sorry," he said, and reached out to place a hand on her shoulder.

But Rena would not allow herself to be comforted by him. She had not looked up from Mysz, who was beginning to curl in on himself, as though he was trying to hold his broken pieces together.

"You fix toys all the time. Please, Mr Brzezick, you have to be able to fix Mysz!" The tears in Rena's eyes made them look like two jewels, though they owed their shimmer to pain. "Please!"

"Rena, Mysz is alive. The toys aren't. I wish I could help him – more than anything. But I can't," said the Dollmaker.

Karolina stepped off the work table and onto the Dollmaker's shoulder. "You made me a body so I could come and live with you," she whispered into his ear. "That was magic, wasn't it? You could do the same for the mouse, so he could keep living with Rena."

"It wasn't magic," the Dollmaker snapped at her. "It was an accident."

"You did it because you wanted it to happen," Karolina said. She decided to overlook the Dollmaker's curt tone; he was sad and afraid, and those feelings gave both people and dolls rough edges. "That's what magic is – making things happen because you want them to."

She waited for him to say something, but the only sound the Dollmaker made was a gasp as he watched poor Mysz's chest rise and fall. Soon it would be too late to help Rena's little friend.

Would he really sit by and do nothing?

The Dollmaker took Rena's hands away from Mysz and folded them in her lap. She looked up at him and, once again, made her plea. "Please help him."

"I'll try my best," the Dollmaker said, and kissed her forehead. He couldn't replace the thorny letters that had renamed the main square Adolf Hitler Platz or send the Germans away or bring back his lost friends from the last war.

But maybe he could fix a little mouse.

The Dollmaker placed his hands over Mysz, careful not to touch his injured legs, and closed his eyes. His grief seemed to rush over them all like rain, and Karolina knew

that it was rooted in something far larger than the fate of the mouse alone. It was sadness about the terrible things that were happening in the world they had to live in.

Just as Karolina was about to offer a word of comfort to her friend, the very texture of the air around them *changed*. She raised her head. The scent she caught was like that of the kind wind, as sweet as the roses winter had deprived them of.

Then the moment ended, and the world seemed to settle back into its bleak, grey state. The Dollmaker lifted his hands, though Karolina wished he wouldn't. She didn't want to see the injured mouse again – or hear Rena's tears when she realized there was nothing to be done for him.

"What in the world...?" the Dollmaker began, and blanched.

Mysz's legs were straight and whole, and his tail twitched happily as he stood up on his hind paws. He turned around in a circle, marvelling at his own recovery.

"You did it! You made him better, Mr Brzezick!" said Rena.

"Hooray!" Karolina said. She bounced up and down, skirts ballooning around her. She never thought she would be filled with joy about the rescue of such a close cousin of the terrible rats.

But their celebration was short-lived. As Rena went to scoop Mysz up, he raised his grey head and said to the Dollmaker, "Thank you."

It was then that Karolina realized Mysz had *not* been healed.

He had been *changed*.

Mysz's grey fur had become grey velvet that broke in waves over his body. His eyes were two black buttons that

glittered with merriment, and his whiskers had been transformed into little white strings that bobbed up and down when he moved.

The Dollmaker's mouth dropped open. "Oh. Oh no. That wasn't supposed to happen at all."

"Mysz?" Rena said.

Mysz bowed to her, sweeping one paw outwards. "Lady Rena," he said. It was the rich, deep voice of a gentleman; not the shrill tone Karolina had expected from a small animal. Had Mysz been a little prince or a duke all along, protecting his people from cats and traps set out by the other shopkeepers in the main square? From the way he was acting, Karolina thought that must have been the case.

"But … how is this possible?" The Dollmaker looked down at his hands, as though they might give up the secrets of the magic he had wielded. "I only wanted to heal Mysz. I didn't mean to turn him into a toy, let alone make him *speak*."

"Karolina could talk after you made her body," said Rena. "Mysz is a toy now, so that must be why he can talk to us." It was a child's way of looking at magic, and that made Rena's logic all the more sound to Karolina. And Mysz had not needed the Dollmaker to place a glass heart inside of *him*; even before his miraculous transformation, he already possessed a heart of his own. Still, Karolina watched the toy mouse warily as he hopped into Rena's outstretched hand. With his floppy pink ears and smile made of stitches, Mysz looked very little like the rats from the Land of the Dolls. But it had been one thing to be around a pet mouse; it was quite another to be around one who could walk and talk and perhaps wield a sword.

"She's exactly right," said Mysz. "I couldn't talk to any

 133

of you before – you don't speak Mouse. But toys always speak whatever language their owners do."

"I'm so sorry I let the boy hurt you," said Rena.

"It wasn't your fault, Lady Rena!" Mysz said. He nuzzled her cheek. "You couldn't have known. You've always been good to me. Why, you gave me bread when everyone else was driving me out of their homes and sending their cats after me!" He turned around so that he could address the Dollmaker. "And I can't thank you enough, sir. How can I ever repay you?"

"I... You're welcome," the Dollmaker said.

"What do you mean?" Karolina asked. "You're a toy mouse! How can you repay him?"

"I don't know yet," Mysz said, plucking at his whiskers. "But maybe I can one day."

"If you would look after Rena, I'd consider the debt paid," the Dollmaker said with a smile.

"Can Mysz really come home with me?" The thought of having the little mouse at her side made Rena glow; it was almost hard to believe that she had been on the brink of heartbreak only ten minutes before.

But, thought Karolina, hadn't life proven that a great deal could change in only a short period of time?

"I think that would be best," the Dollmaker said. "He was your pet to begin with."

"Can I show him to Dawid?" said Rena. "He was talking to Jánošík in the church. He must know a little about magic."

This was a far trickier question, but the Dollmaker did not hesitate to answer it for long. "Yes. You can show him to Dawid," he said, more generous with the secret than Karolina would have been.

Rena hugged Mysz against her, his button eyes clicking against her collarbone.

At least something had gone right, thought Karolina.

CHAPTER 17

Dancers and Walls

On days when Rena finished her schoolwork early, the girl busied herself with a new project: making a collection of paper dolls.

Like everything else, good sketchbooks were hard to come by that winter, but the Dollmaker had receipt paper for Rena to use. This paper was thin and cheap, but Rena didn't mind.

"The only paper in my house is Papa's sheet music or books. And I don't want to cut up those things," she said to Karolina and Mysz, who stood on either side of her.

Karolina was secretly grateful that she did not have to be *too* close to the toy mouse, especially when the Dollmaker had gone upstairs to find a new book for Rena.

But she was willing to put her concerns about Mysz aside for the moment to watch Rena guide the Dollmaker's big silver scissors across the yellow paper. Slowly but surely, a man's shape began to appear, and Karolina smiled to herself. She never tired of watching artists bring brand-new things into the world.

"Were there paper dolls in your country, Karolina?" Rena asked.

"A few," said Karolina. "The ones I remember best were the paper ballerinas. They were the best dancers and everyone loved to watch them."

Karolina wanted to describe them to Rena, but she knew no words could capture their art. The ballerinas had moved like dandelion seeds that had been caught by the wind. No doll ever giggled or spoke out of turn when the paper girls danced; they were too enchanted by the performance to disrupt it.

Karolina hoped that Rena's paper dolls wouldn't meet the same cruel end as the ballerinas. They had been more susceptible to the flames than most of the dolls, and, as far as she knew, none of them had survived.

Mysz scampered over to the pile of dolls Rena had already finished. He flicked his tail towards a paper man wearing a shirt streaked with blue and red. "He looks familiar," Mysz said.

"That's Mr Mikhel. He's the painter who lives across the street. He taught me a trick to draw hands better," said Rena.

Even though she had never met Mr Mikhel, Karolina felt a certain amount of admiration for the artist. She knew that hands were the hardest thing of all to draw.

Rena pointed her scissors towards another paper doll,

a girl with red shoes and two plaits that trailed behind her like dark clouds. "That's Helen. She used to dance everywhere instead of walking. Like this!"

The girl put down the scissors and slid off the Dollmaker's stool. She began to twirl across the room, moving her arms up and down, as if they were wings. When Rena stopped, she smiled sheepishly at Mysz and Karolina. "Helen was much better at dancing than I am," she said. "And her parents made clothes – like you, Karolina."

"You should take us with you next time you go to their shop," said Karolina. "Maybe I could learn something from them."

"And I'd like to see Helen dance," Mysz put in. "We mice used to hold dances in the main square at midsummer and have feasts of flowers. It was the only time the cats let us be."

But Rena did not respond to their eagerness, nor did she ask Mysz more about the tiny chapter of his history that he had shared. "I can't take you," Rena said quietly. "They're gone."

Gone.

It was such a small word, but it seemed ready to swallow up tailors and dancers and artists alike. Karolina imagined that if she had the Dollmaker write it out, the letters would look as ugly and gnarled as the new signs in the main square.

Mysz returned to Rena's side and asked, "Why are you making paper dolls of people you know, Lady Rena?"

"I got the idea from Little Kraków," said Rena. "Mr Brzezick made dolls of all the people in his neighbourhood, so I wanted to try doing the same thing. I'm making a paper Kazimierz."

Mysz rocked back on his haunches and whistled a few notes. Karolina assumed he had learned that from Jozef; no rodent she had ever met could make music.

"That's going to take a long time," Mysz said. "Kazimierz is even bigger than the main square – and the main square is *very* big. It used to take me a full day to cross it when I was an ordinary mouse."

"I don't mind that it will take lots of time," Rena said. "I like doing it. It helps me remember the way everything used to be when Kraków was a better place."

Karolina found it hard to recall that Kraków *had* been a nice place before it had been tarnished by war and pain. But then she remembered how the Land of the Dolls was her home – in spite of the misery the rats had brought to it. Was that so different from how Rena felt?

Karolina went and held the paper dolls of Mr Mikhel and Helen up. The shadows they cast on the wall of the toyshop wavered, as if they too were alive and wanted as badly as Rena herself to recreate the Kraków that had been.

"In my Kazimierz, it can always be summer," Rena went on. "The witches won't have come yet, so we can all be happy together. I can make a doll of Mama too. She can be alive in my paper Kazimierz, just like the prince and the dragon are in Little Kraków."

Mysz glanced towards Karolina. She met his black button eyes, and, for the very first time, she knew she had something in common with him. Karolina could almost see the thought they shared stretching between them like a length of red thread. They both knew that Rena's dream was a lovely one. But it was just that: a dream. And it was a rare dream that could blossom and thrive when Lady Marzanna and her army of frost had painted the world

white. Like the Germans, winter seemed to have no intention of leaving Kraków any time soon.

Rena ran her finger across the top of Mysz's head and asked, "Don't you miss your friends? The ones you used to dance with?"

"I do," he said. "But we mice know that a long time might pass before we can meet again. The world is a dangerous place for us. Every word a mouse exchanges with another mouse is a gift."

Was every conversation between friends a treasure? Karolina had never thought that the final time she talked to Marie or Pierrot *would* be the last time they spoke. She had saved too many words and stories for another day, assuming – wrongly – that she would have all the time in the world with her friends.

Karolina did not want to make that mistake again. She wanted to hear everything Rena had to say.

"Tell us more about the people in your paper Kazimierz," Karolina said to the little girl.

Rena was only too happy to oblige.

One evening as the ice and snow were beginning to thaw, Jozef came to the shop weighed down by a terrible burden – a burden that came in the form of a letter.

Rena's father stepped through the doorway, brushing off the dusting of snow that had formed on his shoulders. Rena sprang off the stool where she had been reading, leaving Mysz on the table next to Karolina. Usually, Jozef would pick his daughter up and swing her around and around, as if they too were snowflakes spinning through the air. But today, he

only hugged her against his chest for a long, long time.

That was when Karolina knew something was wrong. Rena also sensed that her father was distressed. "You look sad, Papa."

"I ... have some news," Jozef said, finally releasing her.

The Dollmaker went to pick Karolina up. "We can go upstairs."

"No, no. I think you all should hear this," Jozef said, guiding Rena to the back of the shop. The little girl scooped up Mysz, and he curled his tail around one of her fingers, as if trying to hold it.

As he folded his hands on top of the Dollmaker's work table, Karolina caught a glimpse of the blister forming on the left side of Jozef's palm. It was probably one of many. Jozef gathered his strength for a moment longer and then said, "Rena, we have to move."

"What?" Rena said. "Why?"

"I received a letter in the post." Jozef reached into the pocket of his coat and withdrew the letter in question. The stamp on the right-hand side showed Adolf Hitler's face, just like the letters that had demanded the Dollmaker acknowledge his German heritage. "The Germans want all Jews who are still living in Kraków to move to the Podgórze district on the other side of the river."

"And the Germans just announced this today? With no warning?" asked the Dollmaker. He sounded breathless, as if someone had kicked him squarely in the chest.

"A friend told me this was coming a few days ago," said Jozef. "He's good at finding out the things the Germans don't want us to know yet. I was hoping his information was wrong this time." He smiled grimly to himself. "The Germans have told us that the Christian Poles are angry

with us and that we need to move for our own protection. And who knows what they tell the Polish Christians?"

"It seems to me that the people you need protection from the most are the Germans," said Mysz.

Were Rena and Jozef really in danger from the Christians of Kraków? The only opinions Karolina ever heard, other than the Dollmaker's, were those of the baker (who despised almost everyone) and the newspapers (whose pages seemed to weep with the news they carried). But whether or not the Germans were lying, the law was the law, and Jozef had to make preparations to move.

"That doesn't seem fair at all," said Karolina. "Kraków is your city too."

Rena, meanwhile, seemed to be trying to understand what her father had told her. Karolina knew how confused and upset the little girl must have been. When the rats had thrown her out of her cottage, Karolina's emotions had run together like watercolours in a painting. Anger had bled into sadness, and sadness into helplessness.

"We have to leave our flat?" Rena said eventually. "I don't understand."

Jozef's smile turned as bitter as the black tea the Dollmaker drank. "I wish we didn't have to go, Rena. But we have no choice," he said. "And once we move, we won't be allowed to leave the new Jewish quarter without permission. They're building a wall around it."

"I ... I can help you move," said the Dollmaker. Karolina wondered if he was trying to distract the Trzmiels from their increasing losses, or himself from a future in which they were absent. She believed that it was both.

"You've done more than enough, Cyryl," Jozef said. "A man I work with has a cart. He said he can take some of our furniture and clothing. We might go to Podgórze and then be moved again – I don't know yet. The Germans are already forcing people out of Kraków to the countryside."

"But what do they do there?" the Dollmaker said.

"They grow food for the German army, maybe? We don't know." Jozef scratched his chin as he tried to come up with another idea. "What do you think, Rena? We could plant apple trees and carrots and have horses of our own if we lived in the country."

Rena, who had been toying with Mysz's tail, looked up. "I'd like a horse," she said cautiously. "But I hope it would be as beautiful as the ones Mr Brzezick makes."

The meadows and golden fields, like the ones the poor Lakanica had lived in, might suit Rena more than the streets of Kraków. And, Karolina thought grudgingly, Mysz would love it.

"If you're sure that we can't do anything..." the Dollmaker said.

"We'll be fine." Jozef reached out and took the Dollmaker's hand for a moment, as if he hoped to infuse this gesture with all the things he could not bring himself to say aloud.

The Dollmaker, having lost his parents so long ago, was now losing the only other family he'd ever had ... and they were losing him and Karolina too. A wall could keep love and friendship out more effectively than anything else in the world, thought Karolina.

She hoped the wall was only temporary, but didn't quite believe it was. The savagery of the rats had only increased as time passed. They had revelled in it.

What if the same were true of the German witches?

CHAPTER 18

The Other Magician

The morning the Jewish residents of Kraków packed up their lives to go across the river held the faint promise of springtime. It was a strange contrast to the gloomy proceedings in the city.

Karolina had expected the streets to be empty save for those who were moving; it was well before noon, and most people should have been at work. The business of living, however, seemed to have been put aside for the business of watching the banishment. Rows and rows of people lined the pavements. The Dollmaker had to dodge around them as he walked. Their comments were louder than the roar of the Vistula river. And worse, most of them were not Germans – they were Poles.

"I thought Jozef didn't want us to help him move," Karolina said as they moved through the crowd.

"He didn't," the Dollmaker said. "But we should say goodbye to him and Rena and Mysz. It might be ... quite a long time before we see them again." He looked away, as though the glare of the sunlight could mask the pain that tugged the corners of his mouth down.

"I'll hug Rena and Jozef all they want," said Karolina, "but I'm *not* hugging the mouse."

A group of cruel boys had begun pelting the Jewish people on the road with pebbles, melting snow, and fistfuls of mud. They cackled like crows on a line whenever they managed to hit their targets. Many of the crowd seemed pleased to see the departure of Kraków's Jewish residents. Some of these people would take over the homes the Jewish families had been ordered to leave behind.

Karolina tried to imagine the Dollmaker or Jozef throwing stones, but couldn't. The Dollmaker and Jozef were artists; the things they made were never hurtful.

The Dollmaker glared at the unruly boys and stalked over to them. Brandishing his cane, he said, "Enough. Let them be on their way and stop tormenting them."

"They're just Jews," a freckled boy said with a shrug. "They've never belonged in Kraków anyway." But any further argument on his part ended when the Dollmaker narrowed his eyes. The boy's face was burning as he muttered to his friends, "Come on."

"What brats!" said Karolina as the cluster of children retreated.

"They're only repeating what their parents tell them about Jozef and Rena and their people," said the Dollmaker.

Karolina was not as forgiving of their faults. "Well, maybe they should start thinking for themselves," she replied.

When Karolina saw the laden cart outside the Trzmiels' building, she was surprised. The objects she thought Jozef would value above all others were not the things he had chosen to pack. He had not packed his fine silver or his good cookware – those things had already been sold. He had not packed his degree in music from the Academy of Music in Kraków – the German witches did not care how well he could play his violin. He had not packed his watch – that, like the silver and the cookware, had been sold.

What Jozef Trzmiel had done was strip his home of photographs. He had wrapped in winter coats the candlesticks and chipped cups that his late wife had been fond of. He had filled the floors of Rena's doll's house with clothing that he folded into small squares. His pockets were brimming with books. The metal rectangle that the Dollmaker had bumped up against when he had delivered the doll's house – the *mezuzah*, which contained a sacred prayer – was stored carefully in a glove so that it would not fall out.

He had packed his memories as best he could.

Rena hoisted herself up onto the wagon and sat down on one of the chairs tied down to it. She reached up and stroked Mysz, who was peeking out from the collar of her jacket. His whiskers twitched in disapproval, but he cuddled up to her.

The Trzmiels deserved so much better, but the German laws were against them.

The Dollmaker's hand shot up in a wave, the abrupt movement drawing Jozef's gaze to him. Their eyes met, and Karolina thought that Jozef would greet him. She wouldn't have been able to contain herself if she had been in Jozef's position; Karolina knew she would have needed the comfort of a friend. But Jozef put his hand on Rena's shoulder, shifting her body in the opposite direction. Then he shook his head at the Dollmaker.

Would the Dollmaker listen to Jozef's silent plea not to approach him and Rena? Karolina didn't think so, and a moment later, the Dollmaker started across the street.

Never graceful on the best of days, he was made even clumsier by the sheer volume of people pulling carts, wheelbarrows and even prams piled high with their possessions past him.

He did not make it far. A German soldier, who had been lingering nearby to ensure that the soon-to-be exiles did not deviate from the road, stepped directly into the Dollmaker's path. "Where do you think you're going?"

Karolina froze in the Dollmaker's pocket.

"I'm trying to say goodbye to someone," her friend said.

"Are you a Jew?"

"No," said the Dollmaker. "But I need to get across the street."

"Give me your papers," the German said. He held out his hand.

The Dollmaker tried to look over the soldier's shoulder to the cart, which was being loaded with the last of the Trzmiels' things. "Please, I need to—"

The German placed his hands on the Dollmaker's chest and shoved him away. Karolina barely stopped herself from crying out in surprise. How dare he?

But the soldier seemed to think he had every right to push the Dollmaker around as much as he pleased. "I said, give me your papers," he repeated. This time, his hand went to the strap of the rifle slung over one shoulder.

Unable to argue, the Dollmaker reached into the pocket that did not contain Karolina and pulled out his passport, which was slightly bent from the number of times he had sat on it. The soldier snatched it from him and opened it. "You're a *Volksdeutscher*?" he asked.

"Yes," the Dollmaker said, though it was an admission he made through gritted teeth. The soldier was wasting precious seconds – and readily admitting that he shared a bond of any kind with this brutish young man must have left a sour taste in the Dollmaker's mouth.

The soldier closed the passport and placed it back into the Dollmaker's pocket. "Sir, go home," he said. "This isn't your business. You'd do well to stay away from it all." He did not sound angry but exasperated, like an adult warning a small child about a danger that should be obvious.

Neither Karolina nor the Dollmaker wanted to leave, but what choice did they have? They could not argue with a soldier who possessed a gun and the authority to use it. The Dollmaker returned to the side of the street they had come from, turning just in time to see the Trzmiels pass by.

Karolina waved to Rena so energetically that she thought her hand might fly free from her wrist. Mercifully, it stayed attached. The Dollmaker waved as well, though he was much more subdued.

Rena saw them and answered their farewell gestures with a small, melancholy smile. She did not look away from Karolina and the Dollmaker until the cart had rounded the corner and was out of sight.

"Why didn't Jozef let us say goodbye?" Karolina said. "Rena will think we don't care about her!"

The expression that crept across the Dollmaker's face was one Karolina had seen before in the Land of the Dolls, one of grief and the terrible *knowing*. "Saying goodbye is always difficult," the Dollmaker said. "Especially in wartime."

Remembering Fritz and Marie, Karolina said, "It is."

Karolina and the Dollmaker returned to the shop to find Mr Dombrowski smoking the stump of a cigarette outside the bakery and idly flipping through a newspaper that appeared to be several days old. Karolina hoped that the baker would finish his cigarette and go back inside without commenting on the day's events, but he'd never had a single thought that he did not launch off his tongue.

"They're gone, then, those friends of yours?" he asked as the Dollmaker took the shop key from his pocket. "The Jews?"

"All the Jews are gone," the Dollmaker said.

"It's probably for the best, Cyryl," Dombrowski said. "It wasn't natural, the way they kept to themselves, like they thought they were better than the rest of us. Well, now they can keep to themselves all they like." His laughter turned into a cough, and he hastily took another drag on his cigarette.

The Dollmaker practically stabbed his key into the shop's lock. "The Trzmiels are good people," he said.

"To you, maybe. But what did the Jews ever do for the rest of us?" said Dombrowski. He flicked his cigarette

onto the cobblestones and ground it out with the heel of his flour-dusted boot. "You're a strange man to have been friends with them to begin with."

"Why would you take joy in the misery and humiliation of people you don't even know?" the Dollmaker asked him. "These are people – people who have lived in Kraków for their entire lives. It's wrong that they're being told how and where to live. Can't you see that?"

"Every Jew is the same," said Dombrowski, flicking through his newspaper again. "Maybe now the Germans will leave the rest of us alone. It's the Jews they really hate. See? They're nothing but trouble." The baker held up a page and jabbed a finger at the grim, blocky letters at the top.

ANY POLE FOUND HELPING JEWS
OUTSIDE THE JEWISH QUARTER OR
ASSOCIATING WITH THEM IN ANY
OTHER WAY WILL BE SENTENCED.

Karolina felt the Dollmaker's heart wrench.

"What you do is your business," the baker went on, "but if they come for you because you were friends with those Jews, my family and I know nothing. Understand?" The Dollmaker did not reply. Instead, he stormed inside and slammed the door on Dombrowski.

"Why does he act like that?" said Karolina. "You've lived in the same city for ever. I don't understand."

"I don't think like other people, for better or for worse," the Dollmaker said quietly. Then he added, "And some people just don't think at all."

The insistent tick of the grandfather clock in the corner filled the silence for a few minutes. Karolina was the one to

break it, her rage fading into nothing more than a dreadful memory. She almost wished that she, like the Dollmaker, could cry; she thought it would be a far better use of her pain than shouting at the wrong person.

"I'm sorry," Karolina said. "I don't want to be cross all the time. But why do nasty creatures think they can take someone's home from them?" Karolina grabbed one of her plaits and twisted it around her hand.

"I'm upset too," said the Dollmaker. "I truly am, Karolina. No one had the right to take your home from you or do the same thing to the Trzmiels. I—"

The bell above the door rang, signalling the arrival of a customer and the end of their conversation. But the Dollmaker's greeting died on his lips when he saw who had entered the shop: the very same German officer who had arrested the young man with the gold watch last winter, Hauptsturmführer Brandt.

There were a thousand reasons why he might have come, and none of them were good.

What if the Germans had discovered what the Dollmaker had been doing with his extra rations? What if the soldier had seen the Dollmaker waving to Jozef?

"May I help you?" the Dollmaker asked in German. His voice was as strong and steady as the tree that Karolina's body had been carved from. He had had practice dealing with the witches now, and it showed.

"Are you Herr Birkholz? The owner of this shop?" Brandt asked, shutting the door behind him. He removed his cap, tucking it beneath his arm so that the grinning skull badge was hidden – as wicked intentions often are.

"Yes, that's me," said the Dollmaker. "Is something you need?" He returned Karolina to his pocket and

set his cane beside the stool. He needed the cane, just as he needed any other tool ... but Karolina understood that he did not want to appear vulnerable in front of the witch.

"My sister complained about you, Herr Birkholz," said Brandt. "She told me that you slapped my nephew. I've been meaning to visit you for a while now."

"Your sister?" the Dollmaker said. Karolina remembered the terrible witch woman all too well. She nudged him with her elbow, which seemed to jog his memory. "Oh! Yes. That was ages ago. I..."

But the witch captain no longer appeared to be listening. He had been distracted by the model of Kraków. Standing over it, Brandt could have been an ogre who wanted to grind the bones of the tiny Polish figures into flour for his bread. "This is an astounding piece of work," he said. "The details are incredible."

"Thank you," said the Dollmaker. This bit of praise had come unexpectedly, but he recovered from the shock swiftly enough. "As for the matter of your sister and her son ... I didn't hit him. I told him and his mother to leave the shop. He injured a pet that belongs to my friend's daughter." He stood up straighter as he added, "I didn't mean to frighten the boy, but he needed to be told that what he did was cruel."

"Ah," said Brandt. "I see. My dear sister seems to have left out several important details. But in the future, it might be wise not to make the children frightened of you. After all, I imagine they are your most important customers." In spite of how serious the conversation was, the witch captain was smiling. Karolina did not know what to make of him.

"I used to do woodwork myself. My father taught me

how. By the time I left home, I had entire regiments of toy soldiers in my room. They were very special to me as a boy, but my skills are nothing compared to yours," Brandt continued. He ran the tip of his finger along the top of the miniature Cloth Hall. "I'm Erich Brandt, by the way. It's a pleasure to meet you."

With no choice but to be polite, the Dollmaker crossed the shop to shake hands with the witch captain.

"Well, well," said Brandt, catching sight of Karolina in his pocket. "She's a marvel too. May I see her?"

The Dollmaker could not deny Brandt his request. His hand shaking a little, he gave Karolina to Brandt. "Please be gentle with her," he said. "She's a very special doll."

"I can see that," said Brandt. Karolina was careful not to stiffen in his hand or make eye contact with him as he held her up to the light. "Does she have a name?"

"No," the Dollmaker said, "she doesn't." Why had he lied? Was he afraid that Brandt would snatch Karolina away from him if he told the witch captain anything about her?

But as Brandt continued to handle her, Karolina felt his touch travelling through her little wooden limbs. He held her in the same way as the Dollmaker, as if he were conscious of her glass heart and all the dreams it contained, as if he knew she were alive. But how could he?

Remembering the Lakanica's words, Karolina inhaled as delicately as she could. She smelled leather and soap on Brandt's hands, but beneath that, the sharp aroma of gunpowder and ink. There was also the scent of the stars, ancient and sweet, which she had smelled before – when the kind wind had carried her to Kraków.

Could Brandt be the German magician who was looking

153

for the Dollmaker? If he was, Karolina's friend was in great danger indeed.

"You should name her," Brandt said as he gave Karolina back to the Dollmaker. The tips of their fingers brushed briefly in the exchange, and Karolina saw how the touch caused Brandt's eyes to light up. "Or rather, you should let her tell you her name."

"She's only a toy," the Dollmaker answered quickly. But unlike all the other lies he'd told to the witches, this one sounded flat and rehearsed.

Brandt grinned. The curve of his mouth reminded Karolina of his nephew, the little witch, when he'd started his game of war with the stuffed animals. It was pink and young and full of inner malice. "Of course she's a toy," Brandt said, though not harshly. "But everything in this shop ... it's quite lively, isn't it?"

The Dollmaker's grip around Karolina tightened. If they had been alone, she would have squeaked in protest. But she stayed silent, not even daring to peek up at Brandt through her feather lashes. "I've worked hard to make it that way. If you ever wanted to buy one of my toys, the shop is open every day," the Dollmaker said.

"Thank you, Herr Birkholz. I might need one." Brandt's boyishness emerged again. He seemed unsure of his footing in the shop ... and how to express whatever thought was building like a storm in the forefront of his mind. "I hope to see you again soon. Until then, you should be careful. It would be a great pity for anything to happen to someone as talented as you are."

With these cryptic words, he opened the door and departed from the shop.

"Thank St Stanislaus he's gone," the Dollmaker said,

watching through the window as Brandt strode briskly across the main square. "I thought he'd come to arrest me, Karolina! He's a member of the *Schutzstaffel*, the SS. They're the worst of the Germans in Kraków by far."

"He isn't just a member of the SS. He is a magician," Karolina said without hesitation. "He knew I was alive."

"He might just have been being poetic," the Dollmaker said. "He didn't look like a magician."

"Well, neither do you," Karolina said. "But that doesn't make you any less of one." She folded her arms over her chest, trying to think of a way to convince the Dollmaker that she was right about Brandt. "Do you remember the way everything smells when you open your window at night in midsummer?" she asked. "And how the world feels like it's holding its breath?"

"Yes," said the Dollmaker. "But what does that have to do with Brandt?"

"Being around a magician is like that," said Karolina. "Like everything is bending around them because they're brushing the stardust and raindrops from another world off their shoulders. That's what it felt like when Brandt held me – and when you hold me too."

The Dollmaker looked bemused. "That's difficult for me to imagine," he said. "I still believe you're mistaken about Brandt. I can't picture him doing magic. Can you?"

Karolina could imagine Brandt doing black magic all too well. And as for the Dollmaker, he could be as stubborn as she was sometimes.

"I hope you're right and I'm wrong," she said. Under her breath, she added, "For once."

"Don't worry," the Dollmaker said.

Karolina twisted one of her plaits back and forth,

unconvinced. When she released it, an unsettling number of strands were caught in her fist. The sight of them reminded her of a story the Dollmaker had told her about a man who might well have been a witch. He had spun straw into cloth of gold ... and asked for a child in return for his astonishing gift.

What did Brandt want from them? The witch had not told them, but the threat of what it might be loomed over them like the wall that now divided them from Jozef and Rena.

CHAPTER 19

The Dark Woods

Like many of the dolls, Karolina was put to work by the rats. They locked her behind the stone walls of a hideous building they had constructed. And day after day, she sewed for them under the watchful, beady eyes of a guard.

Karolina let out jackets for general rats who had eaten so many sugar flowers that they could not do up their buttons. She embroidered silk dresses for young rat lieutenants to send to their sweethearts over the sea. She stitched diamonds and sapphires onto the suits of the new rat nobility.

The rats never thanked Karolina for her beautiful work or apologized that it had made her fingers throb. She did not expect them to. They thought they had the right to order her about, and she couldn't change that. She was nothing to them but a prisoner.

Karolina worked quietly, but she thought her anger must have been glaringly obvious. She stabbed her needle through each piece of fabric as though it were a sword she was driving into a monster. And with each stitch Karolina made, she tried to curse the rats.

She wished that the gingerbread would rot their teeth and that the candy-cane lamp posts would give them stomach aches. She wished the rat lieutenants would miss their sweethearts so much that they would sail back over the sea to be with them, and that the rat generals would always lose their battles.

But magic did not work that way. Karolina could not use it to do the rats harm, and so all the wishes she made were in vain.

The rat guard never spoke to Karolina, and in the silence, her anger grew and grew like briars. The room where she worked had only a small window that was high above her, but Karolina could just make out the outline of the dark woods in the distance – and see the dolls who were dragged past her prison, wailing, to the pyres where they were burned. But she could do nothing for them in their final moments; she had no blessings or words of courage to give them.

After the sun set, Karolina's guard retired to bed along with the other rats, leaving her to curl up among the rolls of silk and the fat trunks of diamonds and opals. It was a prison, perhaps the most spectacular prison in the Land of the Dolls, but that did not change the fact that Karolina was kept there against her will.

The window tempted her every night, though from the ground it was difficult to judge whether it was large enough for her to slip through. Karolina thought she might go through all the trouble of scaling the wall and find that she was still trapped. And if the rats caught her trying to escape, they would not hesitate to burn her.

Where would she go if she did manage to escape?

The only place Karolina could think to go was the dark forest, and it had been known to swallow up anyone who stepped foot in it. Forests, she knew, were almost as ravenous as the invaders. But the trees might be kinder than the rats, and it was with this thought in mind that Karolina began her escape. She could not stand to sew another stitch for the rats, even if it cost her everything.

They did not deserve the beauty she created.

Karolina stacked the trunks of precious jewels one atop the other and scaled her newly made tower slowly to avoid making too much noise. Once she reached the top, she fumbled for the window ledge and hauled herself up onto it. It was a narrow window, much too small for any rat who had been gorging itself to squeeze through.

But it was the perfect size for a doll.

A group of rat soldiers passed by the window, marching in unison, and Karolina shrank back. She was so close! She couldn't be found out now. The rats lingered for an infuriating moment, one that felt like it spanned several lifetimes, before moving on. Karolina waited until she could no longer see them in the starless gloom before scrambling out of the window. She struck the ground with a soft grunt.

Gracelessly, Karolina twitched up her skirts and ran towards the dark woods.

Every time her foot struck the earth, it sounded as loud as the beat of a drum to her. But Karolina did not look back to see if her guard or the other rats were in pursuit.

She had to keep running.

The forest loomed like an open mouth before her, shadowy and no doubt full of teeth. Karolina did not care; she reached out to it, silently begging for the woods to engulf her.

As her fingers brushed against the first tall black tree, Karolina knew that her plea had been answered. If she kept running, she thought, the rats might never catch her.

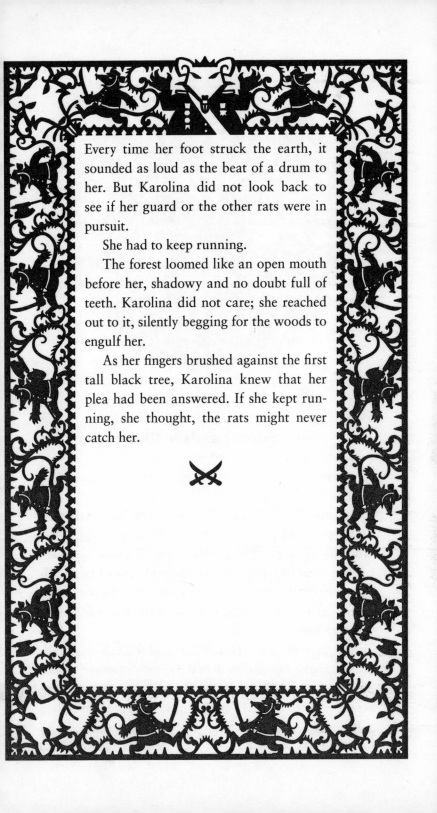

CHAPTER 20

The Violinist and the Butterfly

The German army seemed as unstoppable as the rats had appeared to Karolina.

She and the Dollmaker listened to the radio each day, dismayed as they heard how country after country had fallen to Hitler and his terrible vision of a thousand-year empire. As spring and summer changed places like guards of the watch, Germany even turned on its ally the Soviet Union – as a knife could turn on the hand that wielded it – and marched on Moscow.

The newspaper the Dollmaker read tried to justify the latest invasion, declaring that the German people needed more land and must take it by force. But Karolina did not believe a word of it. Using his armed forces, Hitler had

become the ruler – the *Führer* – of almost every country in Europe, from Denmark to Greece, within two years. No one could possibly need so much.

As time passed, more stories of unspeakable evil reached Karolina and the Dollmaker, though these were not printed in any newspaper. They were whispers that the Jewish people of Poland and the Soviet Union were being sent into the dark forests … and that they were never heard from again.

Karolina knew all too well how easy it was for a person or a doll to become lost in the shadows cast by trees, but she and the Dollmaker tried to ignore the rumours. To make a few people disappear was one thing; to make *all* of Rena and Jozef's people vanish, for ever, seemed beyond even the black hearts of the witches.

But Karolina was forced to remind herself, it had happened before.

Without Rena and Mysz in the shop, the winter of 1941 to 1942 felt even colder than the one that had come before it. Despite the Dollmaker's extra rations, there was little food or firewood to be had. Karolina's friend wandered around the shop trying to stay warm, increasingly restless as the war dragged on. He switched projects so regularly that the space by his work table was littered with half-finished rocking horses and even the skeletal framework of another doll's house.

Karolina thought the doll's house was rather uninspired compared to the one he had made for Rena, but she kept that opinion to herself. Not, she thought, that the Dollmaker would have asked for it in the first place; her friend talked to her less and less. But he spoke to *everyone* less and less, and she couldn't take it *too* personally. He

had even forgotten about his promise to do magic for her, but how could he when he moved about as if every breath he took pained him?

The Dollmaker lurked at the gates of the ghetto with a hidden parcel of food and a note many times, hoping to secretly pass them on to the Trzmiels. The entrance was shaped like the headstones in the cemetery where Rena's mother had been laid to rest, and Karolina could not comprehend hating *anyone* enough to make them live in a place whose boundaries were reminders of the dead.

The Dollmaker never managed to give his gifts to his friends; the entrance was guarded by too many Germans. It was as if a great sea separated Jozef and Rena from the rest of the world, one neither the Dollmaker's basket nor his letters could cross.

Karolina thought again and again of the conversation she and the Dollmaker had had, before darkness had crept back into his mind. If Rena – and the Dollmaker himself – needed her even more than the Land of the Dolls did, why wasn't she able to help them? It seemed so unfair to be thwarted at every turn and to meet with so much failure.

"Maybe Jánošík could pass a note to Rena and Jozef," Karolina said the night after another failed attempt to contact the Trzmiels. Rena's twelfth birthday had passed, and the card the Dollmaker had purchased for her sat unopened on his table. "He's probably good at sneaking in and out of places."

The Dollmaker ceased flipping between stations on the radio; all the news came from Germany anyway. The announcers had begun to be a little less confident about the supposedly inevitable victory against the Soviet Union. But who knew what was really happening?

"I would ask him to, but I've only ever seen him out of the corner of my eye." The Dollmaker took a sip of his tea, which had long since gone cold. He coughed as he swallowed it. "There are moments when I wonder if I actually spoke to him."

"We *did* speak to him, in the church that summer. Me and you and Rena," Karolina insisted. She picked up a sugar cube from the flowered dish in the centre of the table and plopped it into the Dollmaker's tea. With the Trzmiels gone, there was no one else who could benefit from it; the Dollmaker might as well use it himself. "He was real."

The Dollmaker raised the teacup to his lips. He did not thank her for adding the sugar, if he even noticed. "I suppose so," he said. "But his magic doesn't seem to be much use against the Germans. Neither is my magic, for that matter."

"But you saved Mysz's life after the witch boy hurt him," Karolina said. "Doing that made Rena so happy. That was important."

"Perhaps," said the Dollmaker, though he did not sound as if he believed her.

Little by little, the Dollmaker was returning to the man he had been before Karolina had arrived, one whose nightmares stalked him through the waking world.

Karolina was about to press him further when she looked down into the Dollmaker's cup … and saw the beginnings of a crack along her cheek. The mark was faint in the imperfect mirror, a ghost of the scar she had borne in the Land of the Dolls. But it was undeniably there.

Karolina's vision momentarily clouded over with fear. Why had the crack reappeared? She tried to tell herself that the Dollmaker would notice it soon enough and repair it.

But looking at him now, Karolina felt a prick of doubt.

What would happen to her – and to all of them – if the Dollmaker stopped believing in his magic? He was the only one who had the power to save them.

This world was marching into the dark, pulling Karolina along with it. And in the dark, she knew that she would know loss in whatever terrible form it took.

The great sadness and fear in Kraków did not prevent life from going on, however. The Dollmaker still had to buy food each week, and Karolina crawled into his basket to accompany him on his weekly trip.

By 1943, moving through Kraków took far longer than it had before the war. Whenever a German soldier passed by, all the Poles had to bow or salute him. Karolina knew that none of the witches were worthy of being treated like the glorious princes from the Dollmaker's books. But what could anyone do? It was the law.

Today, the traffic was particularly bad; the procession of people going to work and the market slowed to a crawl once the Dollmaker and Karolina left the main square. The reason for the delay was apparent soon enough: half the road was being dug up so that new cobblestones could be laid, forcing people on foot, horses and the odd car to compete for what little of the path remained.

Every single one of the exhausted workers was a Jewish man.

The blue stars on their armbands had faded to grey in the sun that beat like a hammer against their backs. A handful of Germans in crisp uniforms stood by watching

them with rifles in hand, disdain and loathing etched on their faces. They seemed angrier than ever, and Karolina thought she knew why. At long last, the tide of the war had turned against Germany. But that did not stop their cruelty towards the Poles. Occasionally, one of the soldiers would bark a command in mangled Polish at a worker who had dared to stop long enough to wipe his brow. Karolina was certain that few, if any, of the Jewish men had built roads or dug ditches before the war. But the Germans would not have given them a choice. Kraków had become a prison for all Jews, and Karolina's heart went out to them.

Most of the other people on the road paid no mind to the unfortunate workers, but the Dollmaker stopped to watch them. His eyes scanned across the faces of the men, and he uttered a terrible thing.

"Jozef..." Karolina wished he would take it back.

Jozef had never been a big man like the Dollmaker, but now he was as lean as a willow wand, and his eyes were glassy with exhaustion. He moved quickly, never even pausing for breath as he carried stone after stone from the back of a nearby cart. He reminded Karolina of the people the Dollmaker had made move about Little Kraków, for ever doomed to repeat the same action again and again.

"Don't admit that you know him," Karolina said, latching on to the Dollmaker's shirt. "They'll arrest you both!"

The Dollmaker did not respond. Instead, he pulled the clean, red handkerchief from his pocket and let the square of cloth be carried by the breeze.

It landed at Jozef's feet.

Had it been the kind wind who had dropped it in just the right place? As the Dollmaker walked towards his friend, his face as blank as any doll's, Karolina thought

that was the only explanation there could be.

Jozef, like the Dollmaker, kept his emotions buried as deeply as the stones he had laid. He bent down and picked up the handkerchief, his face vacant and polite.

"Thank you," said the Dollmaker. Slowly, he took the cloth from his friend, leaning in as he did so. "Jozef…"

"The Germans are putting all the people from the ghetto who can't work on trains that take them away. I don't know where to," Jozef said. His brave decision to speak allowed words to pour forth in a torrent, as if he had been saving them for just this moment. "No one comes back. Please, help me get Rena out of the ghetto before something terrible happens to her. Please, you—"

Neither Karolina nor the Dollmaker even had a chance to react to the horrifying news Jozef had passed on to them. One of the Germans had spotted the reunion and charged over, his hand already moving towards the pistol holstered at his side. "What are you doing?" he barked at the Dollmaker. "You're not allowed to talk to these workers!"

"I'm so sorry," the Dollmaker said in German. For once, Karolina was grateful that her friend could speak the language so fluently. "I dropped my handkerchief. This man was just giving it back to me. I'm leaving."

Rena's father turned back to the cart without a word of goodbye. He hoisted another stone up into his arms, as if to prove that he was as invested in the day's labours as the German seemed to be – and not at all distracted by the red-haired man who had wandered into the midst of the construction site.

"I will handle this."

Karolina had not recognized the officer who had

chastised Jozef and the Dollmaker and who had now departed, grumbling. But she *did* recognize the man who dismissed him.

It was Erich Brandt, the SS officer who had come to the shop.

Brandt did not yell at the Dollmaker as the other officer had, and he spoke in a way that struck Karolina as being nearly *friendly*. But his motives, like the Dollmaker's growing dread, were still invisible. "It's been a long time since I saw you last, Herr Birkholz," Brandt said. "What are you doing here?"

"I was just out buying food." The Dollmaker rattled the basket, almost sending Karolina spilling over its edge.

"I don't see anything in your basket," Brandt said, sliding closer.

"I was just on my way," said the Dollmaker. "I really should be going too. If I don't, all the shops will have run out of food by the time I get there."

Brandt shook his head. "You're in a hurry, and yet you had time to stop here and talk to a Jew. What business could you possibly have with him?"

The Dollmaker did not reply.

"If you don't answer me, I'll ask the Jew myself." The witch captain put his hand on the grip of his pistol. "Bring that Jew here!" Brandt shouted to a nearby witch, pointing to Jozef. He turned towards the Dollmaker, his look chilly. "You know what happens to people who help Jews."

If Brandt *was* the other magician, then he might feel a kind of kinship with something magical. And what was Karolina if not magical herself? She hastily decided that the only thing she could do to protect them all was to try to reason with him, as loath as she was to speak to the witch.

"The Dollmaker isn't lying." Karolina spoke up, raising her voice so Brandt would be sure to hear her above the workmen. "We *were* about to go shopping. I didn't think it was illegal to do that. Please just leave him alone."

Brandt's cheeks flushed rose red. He looked pleased to hear her voice. "I knew it!" he said. His grin was as frantic and greedy as the glint in his eyes. "I knew you were alive."

"Karolina," said the Dollmaker in warning. But it was too late now. Brandt had suspected the truth from the beginning, and there could be no denying it.

"So she does have a name!" Brandt's demeanour was positively jovial. Karolina did not know how he could be so pleased when the suffering around them was as thick as a cloud of smoke. The witch captain took the Dollmaker by the elbow.

"Come. Let's go back to your shop. We have a great deal to talk about."

"You aren't going to arrest him?" asked Karolina.

"Why would I? He said a few words to a Jew, that's all," said Brandt. "I only wanted to put pressure on Herr Birkholz in the hope that *you* would decide to reveal yourself. Toys like to protect their loved ones from dangers, real or imaginary, *ja*?"

Karolina's relief that the Dollmaker was safe was overwhelmed by the resentment that stirred inside her. Brandt wanted proof that the Dollmaker was a magician ... and *she* had given it to him. "You tricked me!" she said.

Brandt shrugged. His hand strayed towards her, and Karolina had to clench her little fists to keep herself from striking it. She didn't know what sort of penalty hitting a German officer carried, but she imagined the punishment would be hefty. "It was unpleasant but necessary," Brandt

replied, drawing a finger down the curve of her cheek.

The witch captain seemed to believe a great deal of unpleasant things were necessary.

But Karolina knew better than to say this aloud. She hoped she hadn't done something foolish.

The Dollmaker and Brandt entered the toyshop a few minutes later. Before the door closed, a butterfly that had been flitting through the main square followed them inside. Brandt batted it away; it was of no more concern to him than the Jewish men he had been overseeing.

The Dollmaker slipped away from Brandt and went to the work table, wincing as he did. He gave a sigh of relief as he sat down on his stool, rolling up the hem of his trousers so that he could adjust his wooden leg.

"That injury... If you don't mind me asking, how did it happen, Herr Birkholz?" asked Brandt.

"I fought in Warsaw in the last war," the Dollmaker said. Whatever shock he'd suffered at the exchange between Brandt and Karolina had passed now, and his tone was as smooth and brisk as the movements of a fox. "As you can see, it didn't end well for me."

"Then you fought alongside the German people," said Brandt.

Karolina wished the Dollmaker would make himself a little less *fascinating* to the witch.

"I suppose I did," the Dollmaker said. "But I've never lived in Germany. I've never even visited."

"You'll have to travel there," Brandt said. "When the war is over."

"Yes," the Dollmaker said. "When the war is over." Brandt would never know how differently he and the Dollmaker envisioned the end of the war, Karolina thought.

"You should have told me about your magic when we first met. I suspected that you were a magician, but you were so close-lipped about it that I thought perhaps I was wrong," said Brandt. He joined the Dollmaker across the room, making Karolina tense. It was one thing for Brandt to prowl around the shop as he had during his first visit, and another for him to make himself at home in it. "Karolina is an extraordinary creation."

"I didn't create her," the Dollmaker said. "I carved her body, but I had no part in crafting her soul."

"Maybe," said Brandt, "but she came to you, didn't she?" He ran his hand along the edge of the work table. "You're the only other person I've ever met who can do magic. I've looked for others. I've been to dozens of magic clubs, from Berlin to Cologne, but all they ever did were simple card tricks. And illusions aren't real magic."

"What kind of magic do you do?" Karolina asked.

"The same kind Birkholz did when he made you." Brandt nodded towards the Dollmaker and Karolina in turn. "I carved a wooden soldier, and later, he began to talk."

"When did you do this?" said Karolina, unsure of whether her interest in Brandt's abilities outweighed her revulsion. It was unsettling to think that not *every* magician was compassionate like her kind friend.

"Three years ago, give or take. It was just before the war began," said Brandt. "The soldier told me his name was Fritz and that he'd served a great queen who wore a crown of jewelled flowers in the Land of the Dolls."

"Fritz?" Karolina said with a gasp. "The soldier's name was Fritz?" Could it be her friend from the woods, the one she had travelled to the human world with?

She had always wondered where the kind wind had taken Fritz, but the idea that he had fallen into the hands of someone like Brandt made Karolina want to howl.

"Yes," Brandt said. "Fritz. It's a common name in my country, I assure you. He was a good friend for a time."

"Where is this Fritz now?" the Dollmaker asked.

"Not here," said Brandt, the answer both honest and evasive. He would not meet Karolina or the Dollmaker's gaze, and Karolina wondered what secrets lay curled inside of him like a serpent. "So, is Karolina the only thing you've brought to life? Or changed the shape of?"

The butterfly passed by his head again and landed on the work table. Even amid the richly coloured reams of cloth the Dollmaker had left out, its orange wings were striking. Karolina was grateful for the distraction the butterfly offered. Her temper had begun to unravel like the hem of an old shirt, and she was afraid of what she might say if she had to listen to Brandt much longer.

"Changing the shape of a thing?" the Dollmaker said. "That's an interesting idea." He affected a quizzical look, as if he had never done just that. He was getting better at lying.

"It's not difficult," said Brandt. He spied the butterfly tottering across the top of the work table and placed a finger on the corner of its left wing, dragging it down. The wing tore where it connected to the butterfly's torso, a horrid noise like ripping silk. The insect flopped uselessly from side to side as it tried to escape in its newly helpless state.

"Why did you do that?" Karolina exclaimed. "It wasn't hurting anyone."

"I need it to stay still," said Brandt, as if it should have been obvious. "Watch." He cupped his hands over the butterfly and closed his eyes. Something sharp crept into the air. To Karolina, it smelled of iron or autumn rain, harsh and unforgiving. Satisfied, Brandt drew his hands away.

The injured creature on the table was no longer a butterfly but a huge brown spider, three of its eight legs twisted and useless. Karolina squeaked in dismay. Did the butterfly know what it had become?

"Change it back," the Dollmaker said, his voice shaking. "It's still alive. It can still feel! Change it back."

Karolina thought of Mysz and how the little mouse would have felt if he had been transformed into something ugly and terrifying. The Dollmaker would never have done such a thing!

Brandt placed his hands over the spider again. He took them away an instant later, and Karolina was relieved to see that its monstrous transformation had been reversed: the little insect had returned to being a butterfly with a torn wing. "See? It's simple," said Brandt. "You should try it. I'd like to see what you could turn it into."

"It wasn't necessary to do that," the Dollmaker said. He curled a protective arm around the butterfly. Karolina remembered that Rena had tried to shield Mysz in much the same way after Brandt's nephew had stepped on him.

"You don't have to turn it into a spider," Brandt said, cackling. He was as literal as a child, Karolina thought. "It can become almost anything. You could even give it its old shape, the one it had before the wing was torn."

Karolina jumped out of the basket and went to stand

next to the Dollmaker's elbow. From there, she could just barely see the butterfly, which was still struggling to fly away. "The wing didn't tear on its own," she said.

Brandt gave her a dark look, but soon returned his attention to the Dollmaker. "Go on," he said. "Show me *your* magic."

Mimicking Brandt's earlier movements, the Dollmaker placed his hands over the butterfly, and his eyes fluttered closed. The air trembled as it had when he had healed Mysz, and Karolina held her breath. She pitied the butterfly in its sad state, but nonetheless, she thought it might be better if the Dollmaker's magic failed him. Then Brandt would leave, and his interest in her friend would be extinguished.

But the magic did not fail.

The Dollmaker took his hands away, and Karolina saw that both of the butterfly's wings were whole and dazzling. They beat so rapidly that they created a swathe of faint colour in the air, like a paintbrush. But those beautiful wings were now made of painted feathers, and the antennae that conveyed so much emotion had become thin lengths of wire, tipped with tiny glass beads.

Like Mysz before it, the butterfly had changed into a *toy*.

Brandt grinned. "I told you that you could do it," he said.

"Yes," the Dollmaker said, far less enthused than the other man. Had Brandt even noticed that the butterfly was no longer a *true* butterfly? Karolina doubted it. The witch saw the world exactly how he wanted to.

"I'm happy to have found someone like me at last," Brandt said to the Dollmaker, placing a hand on his shoulder and squeezing it. "I was afraid that if I *did* discover another magician here, they would be Polish. What good is a Polish magician?"

"Who cares which country the magic comes from?" said Karolina. "You'd have a lot in common with any magician."

"Magic shouldn't be wasted on inferior people like the Poles," Brandt said, scoffing. "And certainly not on the Jews. I saw enough of Polish magic when I first came here. It was hardly impressive."

Karolina could not help herself. "Like what?"

"I shot down a great red bird in the countryside far from Kraków, but it was a waste of a bullet," Brandt told her. "I thought it would grant me a wish if I spared its life, like in those silly stories, but all it did was offer me a measly apple. What good is that? In Germany, there are ghostly knights that race through the woods, and a king who rules every alder grove. They're strong – stronger than anything here."

Karolina put a hand over her heart, a chill working through her. *Brandt* was the one who had killed the firebird in the Lakanica's meadow. Rena had described to Karolina the taste of the very same apple the witch captain had refused; the way the sweetness of it spilled onto her tongue when she had first bitten into it. "It was like eating summer," Rena had sighed.

Now no one would be able to taste such wonder, all because of a single SS witch.

"You shouldn't have killed the bird," Karolina said. "It wasn't doing anything to you."

"It wasn't doing anything useful," Brandt retorted.

It was the Dollmaker who stopped the argument. "I would like to talk more, but unfortunately, I still need to

do my shopping and it will be time for the curfew soon."
His smile was like a single candle burning in a room that
seemed increasingly dark. Karolina didn't know how
he kept it so bright, but she was relieved when Brandt
accepted it as genuine.

"I'll come by tomorrow, and we can talk more," he
said.

In truth, Karolina knew that the Dollmaker had no intention of going to the market after the day's events, but the
excuse had worked. Brandt left the shop, whistling as he
did.

"You can talk to him all you like, but I won't," Karolina
said, glaring at the spot where he'd stood. The encounter
with Brandt had left her exhausted; she wanted nothing
more than to nestle up against the Dollmaker and allow
the steady melody of his breath to chase her down into
restful dark. There, she would not have to think about SS
witches or Jozef's terror ... or what her cracked and aching
face might mean for her and the Dollmaker.

"I don't have a choice about talking to him," the
Dollmaker replied. He pulled his glasses off, as if he could
no longer stand to see the shop and the square beyond with
any clarity. "Karolina, Brandt has to believe that we're
on his side. Now that he knows I'm a magician, he'll be
watching us. So as distasteful as it is, I have to be polite to
him ... at least for now."

The butterfly swooped down and settled on the
Dollmaker's finger. It rubbed its legs together, the sound of
the wood whispering against itself like Jozef's violin music.

Karolina thought that it must be trying to thank her friend; if it could not speak the way Mysz did, music might be its alternative.

The Dollmaker kept his hand so still that he reminded Karolina of the glass girls in the Land of the Dolls. Animals and insects were drawn to fragile things; it was those creatures alone who knew best how to handle everyone and everything with care. "You were not difficult to fix," the Dollmaker murmured to the butterfly. "It's too bad I can't fix this world in the same way."

CHAPTER 21

The Plan

The Dollmaker.

The butterfly.

Mysz.

Living toys.

The idea came to Karolina all at once, illuminating her mind and heart. She almost danced on the work table. Instead, her laughter filled the shop as her plan bloomed, startling the butterfly and causing it to fly away in the opposite direction. She had longed for inspiration like this in the Land of the Dolls, desperate for *something* that might allow her to fight back against the rats. And now that it had come to her in this world, Karolina spun around, mirroring the butterfly's unearthly dance with her own delicate steps.

"I know how you can do it," Karolina said. "I know how to help the Trzmiels."

The Dollmaker jammed his glasses back onto his nose and said, "Pardon me?"

"People can't go in and out of the ghetto," Karolina said. "But what about toys? You could turn Jozef and Rena into dolls, and dolls can fit in all kinds of places that humans can't." A soul was a soul, whether it belonged to a doll or to a person; all it needed was the right vessel to be carried in. The Dollmaker knew that.

The Dollmaker said, "I love Rena. I do. And Jozef is one of my dearest friends. But..."

"Are you afraid of getting caught?" Karolina said.

"It's not that," the Dollmaker said. "I'm afraid of making things worse. People are much larger than Mysz or the butterfly – and a mouse or a butterfly doesn't believe or disbelieve anything. I didn't feel them doubt the magic I was doing, and because of that, they didn't struggle against it." He thumbed his lip, following the butterfly's path with his gaze as it came to perch on top of the cash register.

"So you couldn't turn Jozef into a doll because he's a grown-up and he would have his doubts about your magic?" It was almost impossible for Karolina to imagine Rena without her father, but the Dollmaker *did* have a point. Jozef would never have believed in the Dollmaker's abilities if he hadn't seen evidence of them. But Rena and other children simply accepted that they lived in a universe full of miracles.

"I don't even know if I could turn *Rena* into a doll," the Dollmaker said, sinking down onto his stool.

"But you have to try," Karolina said, giving his sleeve a persistent tug. "Please, at least say that you'll try. You heard what Jozef said about what the Germans are doing. We can't

let anything happen to Rena." She waited, allowing the Dollmaker to consider her plan. Karolina could picture the clockwork of his mind turning the idea over and over again.

At long last, the Dollmaker said, "Brandt could probably get me into the ghetto, provided I come up with a plausible excuse about why I have to go there."

Karolina thought and thought. Then she said, "What about the doll's house?"

"Rena's doll's house?" asked the Dollmaker.

"No one remembers that Jozef was a violinist. All his work papers say he's a carpenter now," said Karolina. "Couldn't you say that he was making it for you, and he took it into the ghetto with him to finish and now you want it back? You could put Rena inside it and just carry her out. It's so big that you could probably fit a *dozen* dolls inside!"

"A dozen dolls," the Dollmaker repeated. He wrung his hands together. "Or a dozen children who had *become* dolls."

Karolina wished that she was big enough to put her arms all the way around the Dollmaker. She settled for hugging his wrist as hard as she could. The crack on her cheek throbbed a little as she tightened her hold, but she ignored it. "Yes," Karolina said. "See? Jánošík said you could save people, and now you really can."

"If it works," the Dollmaker said darkly.

"It will," Karolina said. "It just has to."

The butterfly had returned to the work table, and it seemed more than happy to trundle into the hand the Dollmaker stretched out towards it. "I would have to turn the children back *into* children once they're outside of the ghetto, though. They can't stay dolls for ever. They weren't meant to live their lives like that," he said.

"But they can't all live in the shop. There's not enough room here. Someone would see them."

"Father Karol at St Mary's Basilica turns a blind eye to people buying and trading food on the black market in his church, and I've listened to enough of his sermons to know that he doesn't approve of the way the Jewish people are treated. He probably would be able to help," said the Dollmaker. "If, that is, I can make him understand I haven't lost each and every one of my marbles." He tapped the side of his head with a chuckle as dry as kindling.

"If he watches you turn dolls back into children, he'll have to believe your magic exists," Karolina said.

"I'll see if I can turn this toy back into a *real* butterfly before I even think about speaking to Father Karol – or about going into the ghetto," said the Dollmaker. "I won't put Rena in danger unless I can be absolutely sure that I can help her."

With the utmost care, he cupped his free hand over the butterfly and squeezed his eyes shut so tightly that it looked almost painful. Karolina watched, her glass heart swinging wildly from side to side as she felt the magic building up around her. The Dollmaker took his hand away. The moment he did, Karolina saw plainly that the butterfly was not a toy any more, but the same small and lovely creature Brandt had almost destroyed.

"It worked!" said the Dollmaker. "It actually worked." He looked as if he were torn between laughing and shedding tears of relief, and Karolina felt the same way.

They had found a way to help their friends.

CHAPTER 22

The Silver Soldier

Day after day, Karolina huddled in trees and beneath bushes, wishing on the threads of her own torn skirts for the war to end. She had sunk so deeply into her unhappiness that she almost missed the sound of footsteps coming towards her … and the soldier in silver who they belonged to.

Karolina could not contain a gasp of surprise at the sight of the soldier. He was one of the queen's royal guards. His splendid silver doublet and trousers seemed to glow with a light all their own. It was a light Karolina would have recognized anywhere. Why wouldn't she? Karolina had made that uniform herself, though it was the stars that had gifted the queen with such radiant fabric. And the queen, in turn, had given it to her most loyal soldiers. These dolls had come to Karolina one by one, asking her to make fine uniforms for them to wear in the service of the queen and her husband. She had spent no more than an hour with each soldier, but it would have been impossible for Karolina to have forgotten any of them.

But whatever wishes were bound in the fabric, they had not helped protect the soldiers or the rulers of the Land of the Dolls from the rats.

At the thought of the invaders, Karolina touched her cracked cheek. The injury had stopped hurting long ago, but she had not been able to find anyone to mend it.

The soldier called out to her. "Hello?" She ducked into a log, but he crossed the clearing and bent down beside her. "I swear that I won't hurt you. I don't work for the rats."

"I know you're not going to hurt me," said Karolina. "No one wearing that uniform would ever bow to the Rat King after what he did to the real king and queen. But you startled me. It's been ages and ages since I've talked to anyone but the birds, and they don't answer back."

The soldier nodded. "I'm sorry I scared you," he said. "You're right:

I did serve the king and queen once. I miss them every day."

"I miss everyone every day," Karolina said quietly.

"I do too," said the soldier. He did not say more on the subject of the dolls who had been lost in the war, nor did Karolina. There were no words to describe exactly how it felt to know that so many of their friends would never laugh or dance again.

The soldier asked, "How long have you been in the woods?"

"I don't know," Karolina said, shrugging. "I feel like I've been running from the rats for a long time." She picked at the scab of mud on her knee.

"It does feel like it's been years since they came," said the soldier. "I think I remember you. You're the wishing seamstress, aren't you? You made my uniform." He tapped one of the pearl buttons on his doublet.

"I did," said Karolina. "And I remember the wish you made. You wanted to be brave."

The soldier said, "I don't know if I am. But I hope so." Then he asked, "What is your name?"

"I'm Karolina," she said. "What's yours?"

"Lieutenant Fritz," he said, "but you can call me Fritz. I don't even know if I am a lieutenant these days, now that there are no more royal guards."

"Well, there are," said Karolina, "but they're all rats serving the horrible new king." She shifted a little deeper inside the log, hoping the darkness would mask her shudder. Karolina had never considered herself a coward, but the Rat King terrified her.

"Are you planning to stay in this log, Karolina?" said Fritz.

"I will until tomorrow," said Karolina. "Then I'll move somewhere else. It's what we all have to do now, to keep ahead of the rats."

"Have you ever thought about leaving the woods?"

"Where would I go? The woods are the only place left that the rats haven't taken over."

"A friend of mine used to tell me about a kind wind named Dogoda who could carry the soul of a doll to wherever they needed to be," Fritz said. "The wind lives

186

at the top of a glass mountain. I'm travelling there to see if he will take me to a
place where I can discover a way to banish
the rats and end the war."

Karolina fiddled with the end of her
plait. "It sounds like a dangerous quest."

"It might be. But I have to try to do
something, even if I end up failing," said
Fritz. The soldier held out his hand for
Karolina. "It would be nice to have company on a journey like this. Please come
with me. We could help protect each
other."

Karolina hesitated. Could there really
be a way to save the Land of the Dolls?
She wanted desperately to believe that it
was possible. And Fritz seemed so determined. Together, they might be able to
fulfil the new wish that had been ignited
like a match in the dark of the forest.

"All right," said Karolina. She took
Fritz's hand quickly, afraid that if she
waited any longer, she would invent a
reason to stay. "I'll come with you."

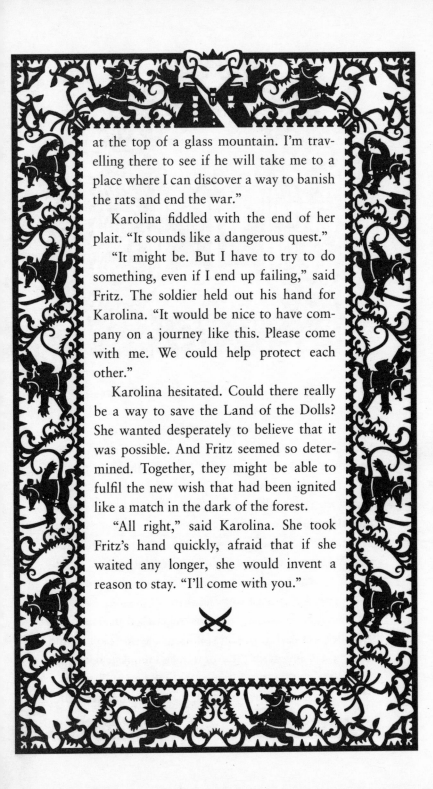

CHAPTER 23

Transformation

The Dollmaker spoke to Brandt the following morning as
they ate breakfast together at the café next to the shop.
Most of the other tables were empty. No one but a German
could afford to go to a café now. The poets and artists who
used to meet here had long since put their pens and paper
away. Many of them had been arrested for the extraordinary things they made. The Germans were determined to
crush anyone who tried to resist them.

"You want to go into the ghetto?" asked Brandt when
the Dollmaker had finished explaining the situation he and
Karolina had invented. "It's an unusual request, but I suppose it wouldn't be too difficult to allow you in."

"I'd be extremely grateful," the Dollmaker said.

"I really do want that doll's house back."

Brandt chuckled. It was not a particularly nice laugh, and Karolina sank deeper into the Dollmaker's pocket. "You take your craft much more seriously than I ever did. I admire your dedication." He picked up the tiny silver spoon beside his teacup and dipped it into the sugar bowl.

Karolina thought the worst part about Brandt was how his desire to be near the Dollmaker and his magic made him look *hungry*. She feared that, given enough time, the witch might become a fairy-tale witch and gobble up the Dollmaker. The amount of sugar Brandt was mixing into the Dollmaker's tea made Karolina believe the German might well be fattening her friend up to do just that.

"Then you'll help me?" asked the Dollmaker.

"Yes," Brandt said. "I can arrange it. After all, we're only talking about a doll's house. I don't mind doing you a favour. You and I ... I believe we're going to be good friends. It was practically destiny that we met each other." He gave the Dollmaker's upper arm a good-natured tap with his fist like a schoolboy. If Karolina hadn't known about the corrosive, black hatred that wove its way through each one of Brandt's thoughts and deeds, she would have felt guilty that the Dollmaker was deceiving him.

"Yes," the Dollmaker said. "It does feel like fate, doesn't it?"

The Dollmaker went for a walk every day after that, hoping to see Jozef among the workers laying the stones for the new road. On the fourth day, he was rewarded for

his efforts. This time, he removed his hat and let the wind take it to Jozef.

"We're coming for Rena," the Dollmaker said as he took the hat back from his friend, who looked as gaunt and weary as an old man. "And if you can convince any of your friends to let me take their children out of the ghetto, bring them to your flat on Thursday evening. I can help a dozen escape."

Jozef nodded, the bob of his head almost imperceptible.

But the Dollmaker's words made his eyes burn with hope, and for that, Karolina was glad.

Brandt arrived at the shop in a sleek black car on Thursday evening. It had been polished to a mirror gloss; he must have chosen it to impress the Dollmaker. Little did he know that no car, however well maintained, could alter the Dollmaker's opinion of him.

"Thank you again for helping me. I appreciate it," said the Dollmaker as Brandt drove through the city.

"I still wish you would have let *me* or one of my men retrieve the doll's house for you," Brandt said. "It's filthy in the ghetto. You shouldn't have to see how these Jews live. It's a disgrace."

Karolina placed her hands on her narrow hips. She'd decided on a pink dress for love and for luck that day, but now she regretted not choosing a fiercer colour. Who could be intimidating in a pink dress of all things? "You shouldn't blame them – they're not the ones who wanted to leave their old homes and go and live there," Karolina said tersely.

The Dollmaker placed a hand on Karolina's head. "Forgive Karolina – she doesn't mean it. As for the doll's house, I do need to speak to the carpenter in person," he said to Brandt. "It's been over a year since I commissioned it from him, and I don't want to wait any longer for it."

"You're a wise man," said Brandt. "Who knows how much longer there will even be Jews in Kraków?"

The car stopped in front of the ghetto's awful tomb-shaped gates, and Brandt stepped out, followed by the Dollmaker.

The German guards barely glanced at the papers the Dollmaker gave them. As Brandt's guest, there was no need.

Beyond the tombstone gates, the world seemed to dim. It was as if the sun itself had been ordered not to shine behind the ghetto walls.

As Brandt and the Dollmaker passed, a group of men and women who were roasting small, withered vegetables over an open flame drew away, hiding their meagre dinner behind their backs. Karolina remembered all too well what it was like to be afraid that what little she had would be ripped away from her. She had seen many dolls wear the same expressions as they'd struggled to survive beneath the iron rule of the rats.

A cluster of children so thin they made Karolina think of the strings on Jozef's violin sat on a nearby kerb, their gazes blank and unfocused. Only a few of them had shoes; the others had tied rags around their feet to protect the soles from the rough cobblestones. When was the last time they had eaten a warm meal? When did they last have the strength to play or laugh?

Karolina mouthed a hello at a girl a little older than

191

Rena, hoping to coax a smile from her. But the girl did not gasp in surprise or greet her; she only continued to stare at an unknown point in the distance, lost.

"The children look so hungry," Karolina said. "Where are their parents?"

"Most of them are orphans," Brandt said offhandedly as he continued to guide the Dollmaker through the streets. "We'll be sending them away shortly. They're a nuisance. The Jewish council constantly complains that there's not enough food for them. But then they're always complaining about something. The cold, the water, the sanitation... They should feel lucky we let them stay in Kraków at all."

The Dollmaker struggled not to let his distress over the state of the children show; he knew how avidly Brandt was watching him. But he was unable to hold his tongue entirely. "They're only children," he said. "What harm would there be in helping them?"

"They won't be children for ever," said Brandt. "One day, they'll be a threat to Germany, just like their parents were. They need to be dealt with. The Führer has a plan that will take care of the Jewish problem. The ghetto is already less crowded than it was."

Brandt took a pad of paper from the pocket of his uniform and flipped it open, scanning the words he had scrawled there. "Trzmiel ... Trzmiel..." He stopped in front of a building to the right, which leaned slightly to one side, as if the wind had forced it to bow to an invisible king. "Your Jewish carpenter lives on the third floor. Number Thirty-Two."

Karolina groaned. The third floor? She hadn't considered that the Dollmaker might have to carry the doll's house. The last time he'd made a climb like that, times

192

had been better – and he had been younger.

"Thank you," the Dollmaker said.

"You have twenty minutes," Brandt replied. "After that, you'll have to leave. I'm doing this as a personal favour. But even you must follow the rules."

The Dollmaker tensed. He and Karolina had known they wouldn't be allowed to stay in the ghetto for very long, but how could Brandt give them only twenty minutes? "I think I need more time than that to speak to Mr Trzmiel," the Dollmaker said.

"Why?" said Brandt. "You're going upstairs to get a doll's house from this Jew, not to build one." He smiled at his own joke, making Karolina loathe him all the more.

"I know, but—"

Brandt held up a hand. "If you continue to argue with me, I'll begin to think you aren't grateful," he said. "I can come upstairs to speed up the conversation if you prefer." His fingers brushed against his pistol.

The Dollmaker closed his mouth. "My apologies," he said. "I'm very grateful, and I don't want to make trouble for you. I'll see the man alone."

The argument was at an end, and Brandt had won. Karolina was afraid that twenty minutes was not enough time to accomplish a miracle. But it would have to do.

Her friend did not look back at Brandt as he walked inside the building and started up the stairs. As they climbed, the Dollmaker and Karolina passed a woman with night-dark eyes and rosy cheeks that were damp with tears. She did not look up as her shoulder brushed up against the Dollmaker's, nor did she greet him. Her thoughts were elsewhere, perhaps lingering on whatever had made her cry in the first place.

As she watched the woman, Karolina thought that everything in the ghetto seemed to be forged from pain.

The Trzmiels, who had once lived in an airy, open flat that always smelled of the flowers Rena brought home from the park, now shared a gloomy, cramped space with four other Jewish families. The main source of light was the single window overlooking the street; the other, which faced the city, had been bricked up. There were only two real beds and a few lumpy mattresses pushed up against the walls.

A number of children sat on the mattresses, all wearing the same strained and fearful expression. But two of them smiled at the Dollmaker as he nudged the door open: Rena and her friend Dawid.

"Mr Brzezick! Karolina!" Rena sprang up and raced across the room – which did not take her long, for there was not much to cross. She had lost weight, and with it the doll-like roundness of her face. She was much taller than she had been too. When she hugged the Dollmaker, she came almost to his shoulders.

How long had it been since they had last seen Rena? Almost two years? It hurt Karolina to think about the time they'd lost.

"Hello, Rena," said the Dollmaker. "You've grown so big, haven't you?" He swallowed, trying not to cry.

"I'm nearly thirteen now. Soon I'll be as tall as Papa," said Rena. "I'm so happy to see you!" She pulled Karolina out of the Dollmaker's pocket and whispered as reverently as if she were sharing her deepest secret, "I missed you, Karolina."

"I missed you too," said Karolina. For all she loved the

194

Dollmaker, he was still an adult. Being loved by a child like Rena was very different – and special.

"I couldn't keep her at home," said the Dollmaker, winking at Rena. "You know how she is."

"Mysz is the same way. He hates when I leave him here!" She reached into the pocket of her worn dress and pulled out the mouse toy.

Mysz stood up on the spread of her palm and saluted the Dollmaker. The mouse finally looked the part of a warrior; he wore an earth-coloured uniform whose brass buttons gleamed in the dull light and had a small leather scabbard hanging at his side. "Sir," Mysz said. "It's a pleasure to see you again."

"You're in a *real* army now?" asked Karolina as she looked over his uniform.

"Dawid gave the uniform to me. It used to belong to one of his toy soldiers," explained Mysz. He pulled a slim, silver sword from the scabbard and slashed at the air with it, sending his invisible enemies fleeing in all directions. "He duels with me too, so that I can practise."

"The sword is really a sewing needle," said Rena. "Dawid's sword is a pencil. Sometimes we have to use it to sew, just like we have to borrow the pencil to write with. But Mysz has got good at sword fighting."

Having heard the Dollmaker's arrival, Jozef appeared in the doorway leading to one of the adjacent rooms. He looked less frail than the last time Karolina had seen him, as if hope had strengthened him for the occasion.

"Cyryl," he said. This time, there was no handshake; he embraced the Dollmaker, thumping him on the back. "It's so good to see you again," he said. "How are you? How is Karolina?"

"Both of us are just fine," said the Dollmaker. "I only wish I could stay for longer."

"How long *do* you have?" Jozef asked him.

"Twenty minutes," the Dollmaker said. "Less by now." Jozef may have wished otherwise, but he must have known from the beginning how short the visit would be.

"What do you need?"

"You still have Rena's old doll's house, don't you?" asked Karolina.

It came as no surprise to her that Jozef asked, bewildered, "The doll's house?"

"I have to leave with it. Please say you still have it," said the Dollmaker.

"Yes, we've still got it. I thought about selling it, but no one has any money. We've been smuggling food in through the gaps in the ghetto wall just so we don't starve."

"Is that safe?" said Karolina.

"No," Jozef said quietly. "But what else can we do? There's no other way to survive." Not wanting to frighten Rena with tales of his dangerous exploits, he quickly said, "I'll get the doll's house for you."

That trust, Karolina thought, was more precious than any gold ring or fistful of jewels. Jozef was not just placing his own life in the Dollmaker's hands, but Rena's. And his beloved daughter was his most valuable treasure of all.

The children, who had been as timid as rabbits when the Dollmaker first entered, now looked almost eager to know what his plan was. Jozef and their parents would have told them that they were leaving the ghetto, but the smallest child – a boy no more than two, with a mop of corkscrew curls – was no doubt aware of the danger an escape posed.

"I remember you. You're the toymaker from the main square, aren't you?" a girl in a bold red cap said to the Dollmaker as Jozef retreated into the other room. Karolina flinched at the sight of the hat, thinking it made her a target for wolves. But it was the girl's dark eyes that struck her. They resembled the eyes of the crying woman on the staircase, and suddenly Karolina knew *why* the woman had been so upset. She was this girl's mother, and she had left her daughter with Rena in the hope that she'd find a new and safer home.

"I am," the Dollmaker said.

"Mr Trzmiel promised our parents you would take us somewhere safe," Dawid said. He was cradling a girl Karolina thought must be his younger sister, and she felt proud of him for being so calm.

"I'm going to keep that promise," the Dollmaker said. "But we need to move quickly if I'm to do that. First, I'm going to need to know your names."

None of the children rushed to provide him with one. Revealing one's name was dangerous for any Jewish child in Kraków; there was safety in silence. Karolina could sympathize, but she also knew how little time there was.

Dawid spoke up, saying, "I'm Dawid, and this is my sister, Danuta." He picked the little girl up and rested her on his hip. She waved shyly, and then her thumb returned to her mouth. She sucked at it aggressively.

The girl who had recognized the Dollmaker came next, emboldened and encouraged by Dawid. "I'm Roza," she said. "And this is my cousin Sara." She nudged the blonde girl, her hair in two plaits, beside her. Sara's lip jutted out in what looked like a permanent pout, and she crossed her arms over her chest in silent refusal to say more.

One by one, the rest of the children told the Dollmaker their names, laying them at his feet like the treasures they were. There was Eliaaz and Aron, Michel and Rubin, Razka and Leja, Perla and Gilta. Last came Rena – but of course, she needed no introduction.

Jozef returned with the doll's house in his arms just as the introductions were finishing up. He set it down on the floor and waited as the Dollmaker repeated the names of the children under his breath, again and again, until they sounded to Karolina like a poem.

Once he had memorized them, the Dollmaker rolled his sleeves up to his elbows and told the children, "You're going to leave the ghetto in the doll's house, and that means you are going to become very small and be very, very quiet."

Jozef raised a brow at this. "How will you do that, Cyryl?"

"Magicians can do lots of things, including making people the right shape to fit inside a doll's house," Karolina said.

"I believe you," said Jozef, bobbing his head in agreement.

Mysz leaped from Rena's hands onto the floor. It was a jump he could never have made as an everyday mouse, but he had been much more fragile in those days. The little soldier drew his sword and passed it to Karolina. "I don't want to scare them," he said. "Please keep it for now, Lady Karolina."

Karolina nodded and held on to it, keeping its sharp tip pointed downwards.

"Line up and stay totally still, please," Mysz said. He did not appear worried, and therefore neither did the

children; they followed his instructions swiftly and silently.

"You can do this," Karolina said to the Dollmaker, once the children were lined up.

"I hope to God that I can," the Dollmaker said, and closed his eyes.

Karolina tried not to think about how each second that crept by was a second that was lost to them for ever. Could the Dollmaker hurry up? Brandt might come charging up the stairs at any moment, and then what would happen to the children and Jozef?

"Please," the Dollmaker said as light engulfed the children. *"Please."* Was he asking his god to grant him power, or was he begging his own strength not to give out? Karolina thought he might be praying for both.

The light of the Dollmaker's magic grew brighter and brighter until Karolina had to narrow her eyes. Did the children feel any different? They had to, but none of them dared to open their eyes.

As the light finally receded, Karolina saw that the thirteen figures standing in the centre of the room were not children, but a set of little wooden dolls made of pine and yarn and cloth. Yet they looked remarkably like their human selves. The Dollmaker and his magic had captured the depth of Rena's eyes perfectly, and not a single strand of Sara's plaits had come undone during her transformation.

"Huzzah!" Mysz cried. "You did it!"

Panting, the Dollmaker slumped against the doorframe, trying to catch his breath. He dabbed at the sweat pouring from his brow with his sleeve, then crossed himself. "Thank God. Thank God, it worked," he whispered.

Jozef was at a complete loss for words. He stared first

at his daughter, then at the Dollmaker. It was Rena herself who spoke up.

"Look, Papa!" she said, holding her arms out to the sides. "I'm like Karolina now."

Jozef picked up his doll daughter, kissed Rena's wooden cheek twelve times and made twelve promises to find her. "Even if I'm so old that my bones are as brittle as chalk, I'll find you. Even if there is an ocean between us, I will find you," he told her.

The oaths he had sworn would be difficult to keep, but Rena showed no sign of disbelieving her father as she bade him farewell. If Jozef said he would come for her, then he would fight to do just that.

As Rena and Jozef said their goodbyes, the Dollmaker picked up each of the other children and put them inside the doll's house. Like Karolina, they were the perfect size for the little furniture, but it took them a moment to decide where to sit.

"Don't pose," Karolina advised them. "You'll get awfully stiff if you do, and then you'll end up moving."

"Yes. I need you all to move as little as possible," said the Dollmaker. "Our safety depends on it."

Mysz climbed up into the house and sat down beside Aron, the littlest boy. He put his fabric claw up against his own stitched smile, then gently placed it over Aron's mouth. The little boy nodded as Mysz withdrew his claw. Even he understood the need for silence.

Rena gave her father one final hug, then let him set her in the living room of the doll's house. She sat between Roza

and Sara, taking both their hands in her own. "You can't make any noises, even if you're scared," she reminded them.

"I'm not afraid," said Roza. Perhaps she was telling the truth, but Karolina noticed that she did not pull her hand away from Rena's.

As the Dollmaker prepared to leave, Jozef held the door to the flat open with his foot. His boot, like all of his clothing, had seen better days. "Let me help you down the stairs," he said.

"I'll manage," the Dollmaker insisted. "I don't want Brandt to see you."

"If you try to do it by yourself, you'll fall, and the doll's house will break, and that will be the end of the plan," said Karolina. She alone remained outside of the doll's house, poking out of the Dollmaker's pocket and clutching Mysz's sword against her chest.

The notion of failing Rena and the children made the Dollmaker relent. He allowed Jozef to take one side of the doll's house, and he took the other. The two men carefully manoeuvred it down the winding stairs, Karolina squirming inside the Dollmaker's pocket. They *must* have been in Jozef's flat for more than a quarter of an hour, and Brandt must be suspicious.

She was dismayed to find that she was correct. The witch captain met Jozef and the Dollmaker halfway down the stairs. "It's been twenty-five minutes. I was about to go upstairs and see if you were having any problems, Herr Birkholz," he said, pointing to a fine gold watch on his wrist.

Karolina was sorry to realize that she recognized that watch; it was the same one that Brandt had taken from the professor's son so long ago.

Brandt's blue eyes met Jozef's dark ones over the chimney, and there was no mistaking the mutual disgust that passed between them. Men like Brandt were the architects of Jozef's many sorrows. And Brandt, in turn, falsely believed that Rena's father and his people were the reason for Germany's past suffering.

"I'm sorry that it took me so long," the Dollmaker said, trying to dispel the tension. "My leg doesn't do very well with stairs, I'm afraid."

Brandt covered his wrist. In a tone that indicated he had been greatly inconvenienced by the extra five minutes, he said, "Pity." He jerked his head in Jozef's direction. "Give the doll's house to Herr Birkholz and get out of here. Now!"

"Yes, *Hauptsturmführer*," said Jozef.

Karolina felt a swell of anger rise up in her chest. How could Jozef bear it?

Karolina knew, however, that a loving father would do anything for his daughter.

Gingerly, Jozef adjusted the doll's house so that it rested in the Dollmaker's arms alone. Thirteen children and the tiny mouse inside held their breath.

Once his hands were free, Jozef stepped back and saluted Brandt, as he was required to do. He stared at the doll's house for a moment longer, then turned and marched back up the stairs.

Karolina wondered when Jozef would be able to see his daughter again ... or if he *ever* would. She did her best to cast the thought away.

But despite her efforts, it lurked in the back of Karolina's mind.

"I've seen toy animals in your shop that look a little like the mouse, but the clothes the dolls are wearing are shabby compared to your usual work," Brandt commented as he and the Dollmaker walked back through the ghetto. He reached inside the doll's house and fingered the corner of Sara's dress as he made this accusation.

"These are old dolls," the Dollmaker said quickly. "Karolina will help me make them new clothing. I can't really do the stitching any more – my hands are too stiff."

"She seems like a great help to you," Brandt said, though he did not take his eyes from the doll children.

What if one of them blinked? Karolina thought. "I am," she said, hoping to distract him.

Brandt grunted in acknowledgement and shoved Sara away. "I'm afraid I don't have time to drive you back to the shop. I've been called away," he said to the Dollmaker.

"It's quite all right," said the Dollmaker. Karolina hoped that his relief did not seem *too* obvious to the witch captain. "I can take the tram. Thank you for your help today."

"You're welcome," said Brandt. "I'm sure we'll be seeing more of each other. I would like to take a closer look at the house." He tipped down the peak of his cap, giving the Dollmaker and Karolina a clear view of the silver skull badge, and the Dollmaker smiled. Careful not to jostle the doll's house too much, the Dollmaker turned in the direction of the main square. But as he turned his back, Brandt reached out ... and plucked Karolina from his pocket.

She tried to cry out, but Brandt's thumb settled over her mouth before she could, and Karolina was forced to watch as the Dollmaker walked further and further away from her. The top of the doll's house bobbed up and down like a

white cork in the crowd of people returning to their homes after a long day of work.

"You," Brandt said to Karolina as the Dollmaker finally vanished from sight, "are coming with me."

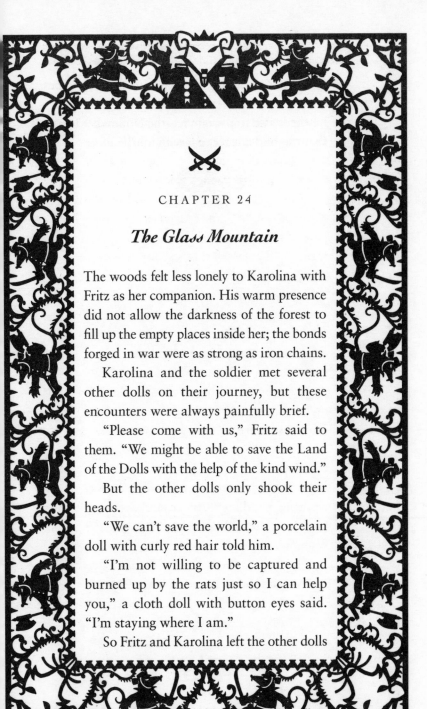

CHAPTER 24

The Glass Mountain

The woods felt less lonely to Karolina with Fritz as her companion. His warm presence did not allow the darkness of the forest to fill up the empty places inside her; the bonds forged in war were as strong as iron chains.

Karolina and the soldier met several other dolls on their journey, but these encounters were always painfully brief.

"Please come with us," Fritz said to them. "We might be able to save the Land of the Dolls with the help of the kind wind."

But the other dolls only shook their heads.

"We can't save the world," a porcelain doll with curly red hair told him.

"I'm not willing to be captured and burned up by the rats just so I can help you," a cloth doll with button eyes said. "I'm staying where I am."

So Fritz and Karolina left the other dolls

in the woods, though Karolina thought that the soldier's feet dragged a little more after each disappointment. She could not blame him for growing disheartened.

When they reached the foot of the great glass mountain at long last, Karolina paused to gaze up at its frosty peak. What if they had come all this way for nothing?

Noticing that she had stopped, Fritz said, "Karolina? Is something wrong?"

"It's just that I don't want to fail anyone," said Karolina. "Even if those other dolls didn't want to help us, I still want to help them. But what if we can't?"

"I swear on the queen's crown that I'll do everything I can to save the Land of the Dolls," said Fritz. "One way or another."

It was the most solemn promise he could have made to her, and although she was tired, Karolina felt a little better. Knotting her dirty skirts around her waist so that she would not trip over them, she began to walk once more.

Karolina had to believe in Fritz.

And she had to believe in herself too.

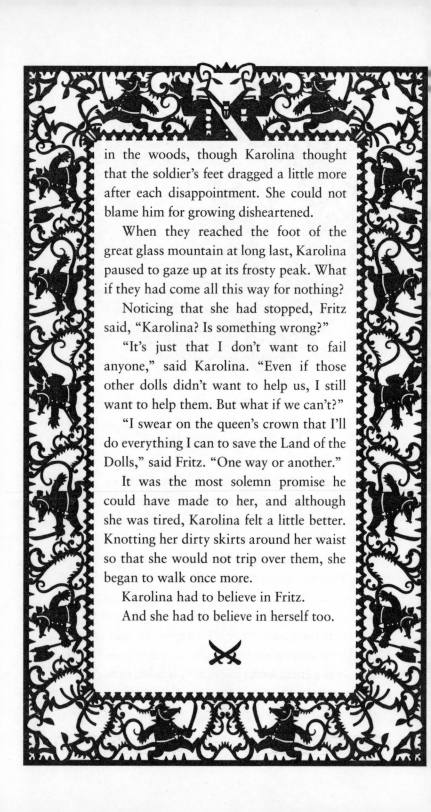

CHAPTER 25

The House of the Witch

Brandt removed Karolina from his pocket, and she discovered she had almost returned to the beginning of her own story: she was back in Jozef and Rena's old flat.

The witch had taken it over and filled it to the brim with his own possessions. But it felt hollow and empty nonetheless. The photographs of Rena and her mother had been replaced by pictures of Brandt's sister and nephew. A painting of Adolf Hitler was mounted in a place of honour above the mantelpiece, along with a rifle. Karolina thought how absurd and painful it was that Hitler now ruled so much of the human world but was so inhumane to those he had conquered.

Brandt dropped Karolina onto the table where Rena's

doll's house had once stood and went over to the fireplace. A huge German shepherd dog lay on the carpet beside it.

"That was the gun I used to bring down the red bird in the countryside," he said, turning his chin up to the rifle. "The bird fell like a star when I shot it. It may have been a pathetic thing, but in that moment, it was beautiful."

Karolina said nothing. What did he expect her to do – praise him for killing a living myth? She did not want to waste even a single word on Brandt.

"If you won't speak to me, then I have no more use for you, and I might as well use you for kindling," Brandt said as if he had read her thoughts. He took a match from his pocket, struck it and tossed it onto the pile of logs in the fireplace, which ignited almost instantly. "Or I could give you to my nephew when he gets home. He isn't exactly careful with toys."

Or with animals, Karolina thought grimly. But she couldn't be burned. That's what the rats did. She needed to escape – and get back to the Dollmaker. He would be worried when he discovered she was missing.

Karolina stood and pointed Mysz's sword at Brandt, though she did not know how much good the weapon would do her. "You shouldn't have stolen me," she said. "The Dollmaker is going to be angry with you. All he wants is to live in peace."

"You can't really expect that anyone with the talents Herr Birkholz has will be able to lead a quiet life, can you?" Brandt said with a smirk. "Magicians are called to be great and important people."

Karolina wanted to tell Brandt the truth: that however much he pretended, he would never be a true magician. He had stolen more magic from the world than he had

created. "People can always choose what they want to do," Karolina said instead. "And the Dollmaker has chosen to have a quiet, good life."

"And that doll's house? Is that part of this quiet life?" Brandt said. "I'm not an idiot. I know that Jew who helped Herr Birkholz carry the doll's house was the same one he was talking to on the street. Your friend is lying to me about something."

Karolina folded her arms over her chest. "So what if it was the same man?" she said. "The Dollmaker just wanted to talk to him so he could get the house he'd paid for. You thought that was fair this afternoon."

As clever as he was, Karolina didn't think that Brandt suspected who the doll children were, but if he examined them closely enough, he would discover what the Dollmaker had done. And Jewish children, whether they were human or doll-shaped, would not be treated well by the likes of Erich Brandt.

The witch captain seemed to accept Karolina's explanation for Jozef's reappearance, but that did not stop him from attacking her. "You think you're special, and yet Herr Birkholz didn't seem to notice when you were gone," Brandt said. "Maybe he's tired of you. I can't blame him. Who would want a mouthy little doll with a broken face?"

"The Dollmaker is my best friend. I was made to be with him," Karolina said. The way Brandt spoke about her made her feel as if he had stuck one of her sewing needles into her heart. But she wouldn't give the witch the satisfaction of seeing her react.

"People get bored with toys. They move on. Some people love their dogs more than their toys." Brandt got down on one knee to pet his own dog, who nosed at his

palm with unmistakable affection. Karolina hated the dog for it. It seemed impossible to her that any creature would care about a man as vicious as Brandt.

"He won't ever do that," Karolina said. "He wouldn't make dolls for a living if he was like other grown-ups."

"You're clever for a lump of wood," Brandt said. He removed a cigarette from his pocket and lit it over the flames. Smoke streamed from the corners of his mouth as he inhaled. Karolina wondered if another dragon had come to Kraków after all these years.

"And you're clever for a lump of skin and muscle," Karolina returned.

"I could throw you into the fire even now," Brandt said coolly. "You wouldn't be the first doll I've burned."

"The Dollmaker will know – and then he'll never speak to you again," said Karolina. She tried not to look at the flames.

"You're just like Fritz, you know," Brandt mused aloud. "You never know when to be quiet. That stupid soldier doll didn't approve of what Germany was doing. He said the rats must have flooded the human world and that the Führer was the greatest rat of all. He told me that he must have been called here to stop me from getting involved in the war. According to *him*, no war could ever be glorious.

"I believed him, for a while. I was too strange. Too..." He twirled his fingers, as if he intended to conjure the word. "Fritz was my only friend and I thought I needed him. I was a boy with only one foot planted in this world. But when I joined the SS, I finally became a part of something. It made me strong. I tried explaining to Fritz all the good I was doing for Germany, but he refused to listen."

 210

Karolina felt the ghost of the boy Brandt had been all around her, and in some ways, she could see how that boy resembled the Dollmaker. But the witch captain had chosen to behave viciously in the human world, whereas the Dollmaker had decided to be kind to those around him. And Karolina knew there was no way to resurrect the younger Brandt.

She was in the room with the monster he had become.

"Fritz wouldn't stop arguing with me, so I decided to put an end to it," Brandt continued. "That soldier was never supposed to be in this world in the first place. I tossed him into the fire one night. I showed him who was more powerful."

Rage took hold of Karolina with its crooked fingers. How could he do that to her friend? To *his* friend? "Fritz was good. He didn't do anything to hurt you. He was – " Brandt's hand flew out, and he stubbed his cigarette out on the table beside Karolina, the red-hot tip straying dangerously close to the hem of her dress.

"He was nothing," Brandt said. "He was trying to make me weak. Anyway, how do you know what he was like? You didn't know him."

"Yes, I did," said Karolina. She swept her dress away from the embers, but the act was almost unconscious; she was too angry to be overly concerned about her safety. "We left the Land of the Dolls at the same time."

"There were probably hundreds of dolls exactly like him in your country," Brandt said. "And they all probably had the same name."

"Fritz was one of a kind. He had skin that was as lovely and dark as midnight, and he wore a silver uniform," Karolina said. "He was brave, and he wanted to help the

Land of the Dolls. It sounds like he was trying to help you too."

Brandt's smile died away, just like the embers of his cigarette. "You're lying," he said. His voice quavered as if he had been rattled by an earthquake.

How stupid humans could be when they wanted to deny the truth. They struggled to grasp any excuse possible to keep their lies afloat. "You know I'm telling the truth," said Karolina.

"Whether or not you knew Fritz doesn't matter," Brandt said curtly. "You are both nothing to me. All you do is bring a little joy to a man who has lost all *other* joys in the world." He fired these words at Karolina, as if they were bullets. But she refused to be hurt by them.

"The Dollmaker was lonely when we first met," said Karolina, "but then he found people who made him happy."

"If you really want Birkholz to be happy, you should encourage him to work with me," said Brandt, his voice slick. "He could help me make Germany the greatest nation on Earth. And he isn't a Pole or a Jew. He is part German. Why help the weak? Isn't that what magic is for – making us strong?"

"Magic is supposed to help *everyone*," said Karolina, "not just certain people that you approve of."

Brandt sneered at her. "Are all dolls this naive? You don't understand the work I do, just as Fritz didn't."

"You destroy lives, hurt children and steal," Karolina said flatly. "Just like the rats Fritz wanted to defeat in our country."

The captain slammed the palm of his hand down onto the table, and Karolina lost her footing, going down hard

on her bottom. "Enough!" Brandt said. "I don't want to hear about Fritz or the Land of the Dolls or any of it. The magic belongs to me and to Birkholz; you're just the result of it."

"Believe that if you like," Karolina said, regal as the queen Fritz had pledged his body and soul to. "But deep down, you must know better, just like you must know what you're doing to the people in the ghetto is wrong."

"I'm following orders," Brandt said. "I'm a soldier. What do you expect?"

"The Dollmaker would tell you that you could fight against what's happening in Kraków," Karolina said. "He was a soldier too, and so was Fritz. But they wouldn't have hurt innocent people. You always have a choice."

Brandt picked his hat off the chair and jammed it upon his head. He reminded Karolina of a petulant child who had dressed up in his father's clothes. "If you mean so much to Birkholz, he'll gladly agree to help Germany in exchange for you. I'll phone him in the morning."

"I'll go back to him no matter what," said Karolina.

"And how do you intend to do that?" asked Brandt. "You're no bigger than a rat yourself. If you can leave on your own, please, feel free. You're no prisoner – I haven't arrested you."

"You'd look silly trying to arrest a doll," Karolina said tartly.

"Birkholz seems like such a peaceful man. I wonder who cursed you with that sharp tongue. You need to be taught a lesson." He started towards the front door, but he was not done with Karolina. "Soldat!" he barked, and the dog's ears twitched in response to his master's tone. "Attack!"

Distantly, Karolina heard the witch stride down the hallway and slam the front door, but she barely had time to comprehend what was happening before Soldat's teeth closed around her left arm. The wood did not snap neatly in two, but it splintered into a dozen pieces. Karolina cried out, more in alarm than in pain. Her good hand tightened around the hilt of Mysz's sword, but the dog's bite was brutal. What if Soldat destroyed so much of her body that she was sent back to the Land of the Dolls?

She wouldn't let that happen.

She wouldn't leave the Dollmaker alone.

"I'm not leaving this world! Not yet. I'm not ready!" Karolina shouted, and drove Mysz's needle-sword into Soldat's snout with all her might. The dog yelped, and Karolina tumbled to the carpet. Getting to her feet was a struggle with only one arm. Was this what the Dollmaker had felt like when he found out he'd lost his leg?

Karolina dived beneath the sofa just as Soldat lunged for her. Though his black nose brushed against the soles of her shoes, his sharp teeth could not reach her. How could she possibly get back to the Dollmaker with the dog guarding her?

If she waited until Soldat fell asleep in front of the fireplace again, Karolina thought, she might be able to sneak out before Brandt or one of his dreadful relatives came back. *Might*. But she couldn't hide under the sofa for ever, however appealing the idea might be.

Karolina wished that Fritz was here. He had been so calm in the face of horror.

Then Karolina heard the front door creak open, and she blanched. Had Brandt forgotten something, or had he returned in order to gloat over the damage Soldat

had inflicted? The footfalls that Karolina heard coming towards her were not those of Brandt's boots, however; they were as light as those of a dancer.

Who else would come into the flat?

Soldat uttered a single bark before someone said, "Down, boy. *Down*. I'm not here to hurt you." The voice rang like church bells in Karolina's mind, bright and inexplicably familiar.

Heart jangling inside her chest, Karolina peeked out from beneath the sofa, mindful that Soldat might still be lying in wait.

It was not Brandt's dog who greeted her.

"Jánošík!" Karolina cried. She thought she had never been so glad to see anyone in her entire life in either world.

"Hello, Karolina!" Jánošík said, plucking her off the carpet. "I was just about to rob this German captain blind, and here I've found you instead. The Dollmaker's been turning over every stone in the city looking for you. What are you doing here?"

He winked at her, and Karolina knew that she was finally, *finally* safe.

The thief and the doll hurriedly left Brandt's flat. With the curtains of every house drawn and the electric lights turned off in the shop windows, Karolina wondered how Jánošík managed to navigate the dark streets, let alone move so quickly that the heels of his boots couldn't possibly be touching the cobblestones.

When she and the Dollmaker had gone to visit Jozef and Rena in Kazimierz, the journey hadn't felt nearly so

long. "When will we be home?" Karolina asked Jánošík. She had rarely been outside the toyshop after dusk and recognized few of Kraków's landmarks now that they were draped in shadows.

"We're almost there," Jánošík whispered.

"We'd better be. Could you be a little gentler with me? I keep getting thrown around too!"

"I'm sorry it's a bit bumpy. But my feet can never quite meet with the ground," Jánošík said. He gave her plait a tweak. "It's a law we spirits can't break."

"It makes me glad I'm not a spirit," grumbled Karolina. As Jánošík had promised, the great tower of St Mary's Basilica appeared on the horizon shortly, sending a thrill through Karolina. She clung to Jánošík's sleeve, almost afraid that the tower would remain for ever out of reach.

The thief paused at the mouth of the main square. The Germans frequently patrolled the area at night, but knowing that didn't make Karolina less impatient. She could see the blue door of the shop, and still, she wasn't allowed to go to it.

Jánošík waited for several minutes before darting out into the square, staying beneath the lengthy shadows cast by the buildings.

The thief took the three steps up to the shop in a single bound and kicked the door. Jánošík wasted no time. "Magician! Come out here now! It's me, Jánošík," he hissed.

No one came. Where was the Dollmaker? What would happen to the doll children if he had been arrested? After what felt like an age, the doorknob rattled and the Dollmaker stepped out onto the step, framed by the muted glow of candlelight.

Jánošík placed Karolina in the circle of the stunned

Dollmaker's arms before he could speak. She turned and hugged him – a task that was far more difficult now that she only had one arm.

"Brandt took me," Karolina said, answering the question the Dollmaker was struggling to ask. "He picked your pocket when you were walking away with the doll's house. But it's all right – Jánošík found me and now I'm back."

"Brandt has stolen too many lives already," said Jánošík, his grin as sharp as the dagger he must have carried. "It was only right that I should take one back."

"I ... I can't thank you enough for bringing Karolina home—"

Jánošík cut off any further expressions of gratitude. "Go inside," the thief said. "You're out past curfew, and you need to be careful. Brandt will be looking for any excuse to make your life more complicated from now on." His eyes glowed, like an animal's. "I know what you did, and it's everything I hoped you *would* do. Take care of the children."

The story-shaped man melted into the darkness with a wave.

It was as if he'd never been there at all.

The Dollmaker moved back inside the shop and bolted the door firmly behind him.

The Dollmaker, Mysz and Karolina remained in the shop downstairs so they would not wake the doll children; even the oldest among them was fast asleep in the Dollmaker's bed. As remarkable as their day had been, it had not been a pleasant one.

"Are you sure it doesn't hurt?" the Dollmaker asked Karolina, fingers brushing against the stub of arm that protruded from her torn sleeve.

"It did, but not any more. You don't need to fuss over me so much," Karolina said, pushing the Dollmaker's hand away. "It's really not so bad. And we match now! You're missing a leg, and I'm missing an arm." She gave her empty sleeve a yank with her remaining hand.

"Not all dolls could survive battling a creature as big as a dog," Mysz said.

"I stabbed it with your sword to get away," Karolina said. "I wouldn't have been able to escape if you hadn't given it to me."

"Karolina, I'm so sorry that I lost you."

"It wasn't your fault," Karolina said. "But Brandt isn't going to be happy when he finds out I'm gone. If he comes here and searches the shop or your flat..." She didn't want to think about what would happen to all of them then.

Mysz scuttled up onto the Dollmaker's shoulder, and his tail moved back and forth against the small of his back like the pendulum of the old grandfather clock. "But Brandt must think the children are normal dolls," the mouse said. "He would have tried to take them too, if he'd realized who they were."

"That doesn't mean he won't work it out later," said the Dollmaker. "Did he say anything else to you, Karolina?"

For all her desire to tell the truth, Karolina's grief over Fritz was still too new and sharp for her to want to share his fate with Mysz and the Dollmaker. "Brandt thinks the two of you should bring glory to Germany together. But that's not a surprise," said Karolina. She wrapped her arm around the Dollmaker's wrist and settled her cheek against

it, his pulse as familiar to her as one of Jozef's songs.

"Whatever happens next, I'm thankful we rescued the children from the ghetto," the Dollmaker said.

"I am too," said Mysz.

Karolina settled back against the Dollmaker. This, she thought, was family. This was what it was like to be *home*. It was a different sort of family than most ... but it *was* a family nonetheless.

The Dollmaker picked Karolina up tenderly and said, "I will try to fix your arm soon – and the crack on your face. I'm sure I can do something to help you."

"Thank you," said Karolina.

CHAPTER 26

The Children in the Church

It was beneath the blue-and-gold ceiling of St Mary's that the Dollmaker told of all he had done, bent over his clasped hands in a confessional booth.

"Forgive me, Father, for I have sinned. It has been five days since my last confession," the Dollmaker said, far from prying eyes.

"Only five days?" Father Karol said. Through the wooden fretwork that separated the priest from the Dollmaker, Karolina could imagine how Father Karol's face must have crumpled like paper at the notion of anyone returning to him so soon. What, he must have wondered, could the Dollmaker have done to warrant an urgent visit?

Karolina climbed onto the Dollmaker's lap. Father

Karol could not see her, but she would need to greet him before the conversation was over.

"Yes," the Dollmaker said. "I've broken the law, you see. And I need your help to break it again." Lowering his voice further, he said, "There are many people who think that the Jews of Kraków are getting what they deserve. But I don't believe you're one of them."

"The Jewish people are our countrymen. They should be treated like it," Father Karol said softly. He was not agreeing with the Dollmaker, precisely. He was not foolish enough to do that when anyone could overhear their conversation. It was good to know that Father Karol valued the lives of the Trzmiels when so many others did not.

"Then help me to help them," the Dollmaker said.

"What is it that you intend to do?" Father Karol asked.

"I need a hiding place," the Dollmaker said. "For children who have..." He edged forwards on his seat and rested his forehead against the wooden latticework. "Well, they won't look like children when you first meet them."

"I'm not following," Father Karol said slowly, and he too shifted towards the thin barrier.

The Dollmaker lifted Karolina and Mysz up so that they could see and *be* seen through the little window. "They'll be like me," Karolina said to Father Karol. "Only they're human, and I've always been a doll."

Mysz crinkled his nose in agreement.

Father Karol's reaction was far more contemplative than either Jozef's panic or Brandt's greedy enthusiasm had been. He reached through the barrier, his fingers brushing the front of Karolina's red dress and Mysz's soft tail in turn. "How long have you been able to bring your toys to life?" the priest asked the Dollmaker.

"Years," the Dollmaker said. He lowered his gaze. Was he afraid that Father Karol would tell him that his gift was wicked? The Dollmaker had never meant any harm. "I know what you're thinking, but I promise you, I didn't begin to bring the toys to life on purpose. I wasn't studying black magic. I was simply—"

"He was lonely," Karolina said. "He needed me, and I needed him."

"Mr Brzezick, how many times have you confessed your sins to me?" said Father Karol. "I know you're not a bad man."

"Then will you help us?" Mysz said. He touched Father Karol's hand with his snout.

"If I can," Father Karol said, "I will. Tell me what needs to be done."

"A girl named Rena and twelve other Jewish children are living with us," Mysz said. "But they need to go somewhere safer."

"Rena?" Father Karol asked.

"She's the daughter of a Jewish friend," the Dollmaker said. "These two helped me smuggle her and the others out from behind the ghetto walls." He pointed to Karolina and Mysz.

"It was terrible," Karolina said. She gripped her left shoulder. "A German dog ripped part of my arm off. The Dollmaker says I'm as brave as any soldier. I should get a uniform like Mysz's."

"Unfortunately for us, the dog belongs to an SS officer named Brandt," the Dollmaker said.

"Ah, I know all about that one," Father Karol said, his tone turning outright frigid. "Brandt is as heartless as a child who doesn't see the pain of others."

"He's a magician too," said Mysz. "He wants the Dollmaker to help the Germans."

"As much as I wish it weren't true, it is," said the Dollmaker. "It's too dangerous to keep the children in my shop."

"I understand," Father Karol said. "As for the children, I would be happy to take them whenever you can bring them to me. I will relocate them where I can, outside of the city."

Karolina crossed the life line and love line of the Dollmaker's palm, careful not to tread on either of them; her friend had suffered enough broken hearts and ailments as it was. "I don't want Rena to get hurt if she stays with us," Karolina murmured. "But I'm going to miss her."

"I will too. But she'll be safer here with Father Karol," the Dollmaker said. "How long do you need, Father? I'm worried about keeping the children with me a moment longer than necessary."

"Come on Sunday after morning Mass and go down to the crypt," Father Karol said. "I'll have found places for the children to live in the countryside by then."

"I'll bring them," said the Dollmaker.

As he made to depart, the priest sketched a cross in the air. "Go with God," Father Karol said.

It was the most earnest blessing Karolina had ever heard.

That night, the tiny Rena and Dawid asked the Dollmaker to light two candles on his kitchen table in celebration of Shabbat. The familiarity and joy of the ritual seemed to

ease the minds of the children, who were very far from home and would be for a long time to come. As the oldest, it was up to Rena and Dawid to lead them in prayer. They covered their faces with their hands in reverence and prayed. *"Blessed are you, Lord, our God, sovereign of the universe, who has sanctified us with His commandments and commanded us to light the lights of Shabbat."*

"Amen," the children said in unison. Their prayers drifted up like fireflies, guiding them towards whatever would come next.

Karolina, Mysz and the Dollmaker stayed nearby, unwilling to interrupt the children's service. This was a moment that did not belong to them.

"I want to go with them to Father Karol," Mysz said quietly, so as not to disturb the doll children. "And stay with them."

"You may be a soldier, but you're not big enough to protect them from the Germans," Karolina said. "I could barely fight off a German *dog*, let alone an actual witch!"

"No," Mysz said, "but I'm not leaving Rena. I made a promise to the Dollmaker."

Yes, thought Karolina, he was right. That was important.

"I think that's a good idea," the Dollmaker said. "They will need someone there with them." Then, as if it were no more significant than an afterthought, he added, "You should go with them too, Karolina."

"Go with them?" asked Karolina. "But who will stay here with you?"

"I can manage on my own," the Dollmaker said, but Karolina thought he was straining to sound unconcerned. She remembered what he had been like before they'd become friends – and what *she* had been like.

"I'm not going," she said. "I love Rena, but I belong here with you."

The Dollmaker said, "Karolina—"

"I'm staying with you," said Karolina. "You can't make me leave."

Dawid turned, interrupting the argument before it could fully begin. "Please come and join us now," he said.

"All right," said the Dollmaker. He went to them, pulling a chair back from the table, and sat down. Rena immediately went to stand in the palm of his hand.

"Is the priest a nice man?" Rena said.

"Yes," the Dollmaker said. "He's extremely kind. He'll make sure that nothing bad will happen to you while you're in his care."

"What about later?" Sara asked. She'd been twirling one of her plaits and narrowly avoided smacking Roza in the face with it.

Karolina pressed a hand against her mouth to smother a giggle. Father Karol and Mysz really would have their hands full with her and her cousin!

"Later?" said Mysz.

"She means what comes next," Rena said. "We've all been talking about it, and we were wondering ... after we leave the church, what will happen to us?"

The Dollmaker removed his glasses, bending and unbending the wire ears as he thought. "I can't tell you for certain," he said at last. "But wherever you go, you'll remember your parents and your faith and Kraków. And when the war is over ... when the war is over, you'll make new friends. You'll have homes of your own. You'll start businesses or paint portraits. By the time all of that is done, you'll find that you've grown up, and, even as

adults, you'll remember your world before the war."

"That ... doesn't sound bad at all," Dawid said. His sister was dozing off beside him, her head bobbing up and down as she struggled to stay awake. It was difficult to believe that *anyone* so small could be so hated by the witches, just because she had been born a Jew.

"No, it doesn't," said Rena, smiling.

Karolina agreed with Rena, and she was glad Father Karol had been so hopeful. Secretly, however, she worried about Brandt. Now that Karolina had disappeared, the witch captain was sure to come to the shop soon, bringing his wrath with him. And she feared the witch captain as much as she feared any rat.

But fear would not protect her or the children. She had to have faith in the Dollmaker and Father Karol, and in the magic that had made so many impossible things come true.

On Sunday morning, the Dollmaker descended into the crypt of St Mary's Basilica with his satchel. Karolina, Mysz and the doll children bounced along inside it. They hadn't uttered so much as a word during Mass, though Karolina had felt their excitement and fear pressing up against her.

Father Karol was waiting for the Dollmaker at the bottom of the winding stairs. His black robe made him look as if he had been clothed in the shadows cast by the candles mounted on the walls. "We won't be seen here," he said. "Do you have...?"

The Dollmaker nodded and opened up the bag, setting it on the ground so that Karolina, Mysz and the thirteen children could scurry out of it. Father Karol did not gasp

or comment, but he pursed his lips so tightly that they resembled a line that had been drawn in chalk. The priest's imagination must have been vivid for him to believe in magic, or maybe for him it was God's will.

Karolina was accustomed to being around children. Brandt had been right about how they were always the toyshop's best customers. But being around children who were her *size* was still a new experience. Now that they did not have to stay quiet, the whispers and nervous giggles of Rena and her friends zipped through the air like the toy butterfly.

Little Aron immediately tried to wander away, and Mysz scooped him up. His arms were now full of a wiggling toddler who thought it was all a great game and tried to squirm away from the toy mouse whenever possible.

Eliaaz stood up on his toes and asked Karolina, "Is the magician going to turn you back into a person too?" He patted his yarn curls and then grasped both of her plaits.

"I've never been a human," said Karolina. The boy nodded.

Sara wasted no time in going to Father Karol and asking, "Are we going to have to stay in the church?"

The priest was not taken aback by her rapid approach or her question. "You won't be here for long," he said. "I've found somewhere for all of you to stay. You'll be well taken care of until the war is over and your parents can come for you."

"I hope the war is over soon, then," Perla said. "I miss my mama." She had yet to look up from the stone floor, where hundreds and hundreds of people must have walked since the construction of the basilica. Karolina felt as if they were surrounded by history and in the process of making it.

"She must also miss you," said Mysz, who had finally calmed Aron down. "So you'll have to be strong for her, and she'll be strong for you too."

Perla peeked up at the mouse. "I'll try," she said.

"We'll all try," said Dawid. He had not let go of either Rena's or his sister's hands, and Karolina could not see him doing it any time soon. She didn't know if they would all be sent away together. She hoped so, but kept silent.

The Dollmaker cleared his throat and said to the children, "I know that this is rather overwhelming, but I need to turn you back into your true selves now."

"Do we have to go back to being people?" asked Leja, a black-haired girl with a scar below her eye. "I like being a doll. It feels safe." She spun around in a circle.

"You'll want to grow up some day," the Dollmaker said. His voice was as soft as Mysz's velvet fur. "And you'll have to be human to do that."

"Maybe," Leja said, not sounding fully convinced. But she must have seen some wisdom in the Dollmaker's words. She lined up with the other children, swinging her arms as she did.

The Dollmaker held up his hands, and Karolina stood beside him, watching as the muscles of his hands and arms tensed. Once again, light surged around the doll children, distorting their shapes until Karolina could only make out their impressions. The glow faded gradually before dying out altogether, leaving thirteen human boys and girls standing in the middle of the room. They rubbed at their eyes and patted their arms and legs, trying to readjust to bodies that felt both new and familiar.

Karolina clapped her hands, but her celebration ended all too soon. The Dollmaker's legs suddenly gave out beneath

him. Father Karol, who had been staring unblinkingly at the children, broke free of his trance. He ran to the Dollmaker, catching him before he could collapse onto the floor.

Rena rushed to the Dollmaker's side and took his hand. "Mr Brzezick, are you hurt?" she asked. "Please say you're not hurt."

"Don't worry about me. I'm fine," the Dollmaker said. But the lines surrounding his eyes and mouth had become even more hollow, and his hair was marked with strands of frosty silver that had not been there before. The Dollmaker had grown older in the span of only a few minutes, and the thought of his heart gradually winding down like a watch created an unexpected ache in Karolina's chest. She had always assumed that she would leave this world first – not the Dollmaker.

Now she saw that might not be the case.

Karolina did not want to worry the children, however. They were watching him, tugging at their clothes and chewing their lips anxiously, and the Dollmaker forced a smile for their sakes. "I'm fine," he said again. "And you'll all be safe now. Won't they, Father Karol?"

"Yes," said the priest. "They will be."

Rena took the Dollmaker's hand and said, "When the war is over, you'll come and find me with Papa, won't you? Then everything can be the way it was before the Germans came."

"The summer I spent with you, your father and Karolina was the best time of my life. I'll carry it with me for ever," said the Dollmaker. Karolina's friend had finally spoken his truth, and all the love in it warmed her greatly. "I hope we can share that happiness again one day."

"We'll always be friends, no matter how much Kraków

changes. I promise." Rena threw herself into his arms. "Thank you. And thank you too, Karolina."

In that instant, Karolina could see a hint of the woman Rena would become in her profile. It made her feel as if she, like the Dollmaker, had grown older since they had entered the crypt.

"You don't have to thank us for anything," said the Dollmaker, embracing Rena.

"He's right," said Karolina. "We love you. We'd do anything for you."

Rena bent down and gave Karolina a final hug. "I love you too," she said.

One thought alone threatened to shatter Karolina's optimism: that the Dollmaker had *not* promised Rena that they would be reunited. Karolina remembered Jozef's own oath to his daughter and her grim certainty that it would be broken. Was that why the Dollmaker would not make a promise of his own? Was he afraid that he would not be able to keep it?

As the Dollmaker exchanged a last few words with Father Karol and the children, Karolina grabbed the strap of his satchel and tried to pull herself up into it. But it was a little too tall, and she fell backwards with a grunt.

Mysz saw her struggling and scampered over to her. "Do you need help, my lady?"

"Yes, please," said Karolina.

Mysz slipped one paw under her boot, allowing her to use it like a step to scale the side of the satchel. "Wouldn't you rather be in the Dollmaker's pocket?" he said as Karolina swung one leg over the lip of the bag so that she was straddling it.

"He wants me to stay with you and the children," said

Karolina. "I know he thinks I'll be safer, but I can't leave him all alone. He'll be too sad and too alone – and so will I."

"I understand," said Mysz. "It's how I feel about Rena. We've been through too much together."

"Yes, exactly." Karolina plucked at the corner of her skirts and then said, "I'm glad I met you, Mysz. You're not like other rodents."

The mouse took off his cap and bowed. "I'm glad I met you too."

After they had said their goodbyes, the Dollmaker plodded back up the stairs, Karolina riding in the otherwise empty satchel. He took the steps slowly and had to pause midway up to rest. The voices of the children below had faded, leaving them as alone as they had been at the very beginning of their time together.

"Are you sure you shouldn't stay?" asked the Dollmaker. "I could leave you with Father Karol and you would be safe."

"I've already told you that I'm staying with you. Don't argue with me – I can be just as stubborn as you are," Karolina said. Worriedly, she added, "You look tired. We should go home and rest."

"I feel as if I could sleep for a hundred years like someone in one of my books," the Dollmaker confessed, and bowed his head. Karolina thought he perhaps had dozed off, but he said quietly, "I think … I think that was the last bit of magic I'll ever do, Karolina. I've used up all of my miracles. I'm sorry. I wanted to help you and the Land of the Dolls. But I don't think I can now."

"We might not be able to save my people, but that doesn't mean that you've wasted your magic or that I've wasted my time in this world," said Karolina. The more she spoke, the truer each word felt to her. "You saved Rena and all those children, and I helped you do it. Maybe that's what we were supposed to do together."

The Dollmaker raised his head and laughed. It was a full, luminous sound that seemed to scorch through some of his exhaustion. "Magic is an odd thing," he said. "It never takes the form you'd expect."

CHAPTER 27

The Man Without Hands

Brandt came for them the day after the Dollmaker delivered the children safely to Father Karol.

"May I help you?" the Dollmaker asked. He had been in the middle of nailing a rocking horse onto its wooden base. But now, he put the hammer down on the table beside Karolina.

The Dollmaker did not try to disguise his weariness regarding Brandt. Karolina's friend and the witch captain had done this dance so many times that their words and steps were slow and tired; even Brandt himself looked worn out. What did he want from them now?

The grisly answer came a moment later.

"Herr Birkholz, you're under arrest for aiding and

abetting enemies of the German people," Brandt said, his judgment as swift as the fall of a gavel.

The announcement left Karolina stunned. But the Dollmaker managed to adopt his most befuddled smile. It was that of the simple neighbourhood eccentric he had been for so many years. "I'm afraid you've made a mistake," the Dollmaker said. "I haven't been helping Germany's enemies."

"There is no misunderstanding, Herr Birkholz," said Brandt. "I should have known that you were up to something when you wanted to go to the ghetto." He whistled, and the door flew open. Two soldiers marched inside, their features warped by their disgust.

They held Jozef Trzmiel between them.

Rena's father hung as limply as the rag dolls Karolina helped the Dollmaker stitch together, and both of his eyes were bruised so badly that they had almost swelled shut. But there was fierce anger in them as well, the kind that made soldiers draw their swords in the face of overwhelming odds. Karolina understood its nature, though she also knew that no one man – or one doll – could fight an entire army of witches or rats on his own.

"Cyryl, I'm so sorry," Jozef said.

"Jozef—" the Dollmaker began.

"I warned you not to take the wrong side in all of this," Brandt cut in. He came towards the Dollmaker, the fall of his heavy boots causing Karolina and the other items on the work table to shudder. "But you ignored me. This dirty Jew was caught trying to sneak food into the ghetto, and I know that you had something to do with that – if not more, Herr Birkholz. You used me to help *him*."

"Cyryl did nothing wrong," Jozef said. "He had no

idea. He just came to get the doll's house I made him, that's all."

Brandt barked a laugh. "Do you expect me to believe that Birkholz was not involved in your filthy dealings? That he just happened to go into the ghetto a handful of days before you were caught?" he said. "Lying is what you Jews do best. Not a single one of you is innocent, and you're finally going to get what you deserve."

The insult proved to be Jozef's breaking point, and Rena's father, weak as he was, lunged forwards. It happened so suddenly that the soldiers could not hold him. They watched as Jozef curled his hand into a fist and punched Brandt in the face. The witch captain cried out as a line of blood trickled from his nose. Then his expression darkened.

The blow must have hurt, but Karolina thought Brandt seemed more shocked than anything else.

One of the soldiers flanking Brandt swung his gun. It struck Jozef's cheek, sending him tumbling back into the Dollmaker's arms. The other officer raised his own weapon, his index finger curling around the trigger.

Brandt did not give the other soldier the opportunity to fire his gun. With breathless speed, he grabbed the Dollmaker's hammer from the table. Karolina saw every rat who had ever dragged a doll to the flames in Brandt's bloodshot eyes, but she could not think what to do.

In the face of her own history, she felt smaller and more helpless than she ever had before.

The Dollmaker flung himself between Jozef and Brandt. He raised his hands to shield his friend. "Stop!" he shouted.

Karolina did not see Brandt swing the hammer, but she *heard* it whistle through the air – and the crunch of bone

that followed as it struck the Dollmaker's hands – first one, then the other. The sound was like that of an icicle being snapped in two, hollow and gruesome, and the terrible noise pulled a scream from Karolina's throat.

Brandt dropped the hammer to the ground.

"Gott im Himmel," said the soldier who had hit Jozef. His grip on his gun slackened so much that Karolina thought he might drop it.

His comrade's eyes bulged in a particularly frog-like way. "It's a trick," the frightened soldier said, his gun shaking in his hand. "Dolls can't talk. The toymaker must know how to throw his voice."

"It's no trick," Brandt said flatly. "The doll can talk, just like you and I."

But he did not look at Karolina as he spoke; his attention was fixed on the Dollmaker's trembling broken hands. The expression of stunned dismay that spread across Brandt's pale face was like a sickness, causing his skin to flush.

Jozef turned his back to Brandt, heedless of his own safety, and gently lowered the Dollmaker's crushed hands. "Why? Why would you do this?" he said.

The Dollmaker was dazed with pain and perhaps all the more truthful for it. "I didn't want anyone else to get hurt," he said through clenched teeth.

"This," Brandt said, "is precisely why I warned you to stay away from the Jews, Herr Birkholz. You and the doll can't think clearly; you've been ... polluted. You could have been ... *we* could have been great together..." He flexed his hands.

"Brandt, please stop this," the Dollmaker tried again, but it was too late. The soldier who had lowered his gun grabbed Jozef and bound his hands behind his back.

Brandt grabbed the Dollmaker before he could reach Jozef, and Karolina shouted, "Don't touch them! Don't touch them, you witch!" She struck Brandt with the flat of her palm, but he picked her up off the table before she could hit him a second time.

"Don't," the Dollmaker said. "Brandt, please. Don't hurt Jozef and Karolina."

"The law is the law. I *have* to punish the Jew," Brandt said. "But you're a German. I'll have to bring you to the police station to be processed."

"Processed? You act like he's going to have a trial," Jozef growled. "There are never trials."

"Not for people like you," Brandt said. He would not look at Jozef.

Karolina could see that nothing about Jozef Trzmiel's life mattered to Erich Brandt.

The two soldiers dragged the Dollmaker and Jozef out of the shop. Brandt held Karolina wriggling in his grip. She caught a glimpse of Dombrowski's wide-eyed children through the bakery window on the corner, but it was brief. Then Dombrowski stormed over and drew the curtains across.

Karolina now wished that Mysz had not gone with Rena and the children. He would have stabbed Brandt with his sword and demanded that he surrender. But there was no Mysz and no kind wind to carry Jozef and the Dollmaker to safety. The magic was fading now, and soon, Karolina knew, it would be gone.

Brandt paused to close the door behind him, a gesture

of civility that baffled Karolina. "You can't hurt the Dollmaker," she said to Brandt, trying to appeal to him. "He's like you. You might be the only two magicians in this country. And Jozef is his friend!"

"As you pointed out, Birkholz and I are less alike than I originally thought," Brandt said curtly. He crooked his finger at the soldier currently holding the Dollmaker captive. "Bring the toymaker here. We're taking him to the headquarters at Montelupich."

The frightened soldier, the one pinning Jozef's shackled arms behind him, asked, "And the Jew?"

"You know the law," Brandt said. "He's a criminal."

The Dollmaker's expression crumbled like a ruin. "No," he said. "No, please."

But Jozef did not beg. His gaze travelled from Karolina, who had ceased flailing, to the Dollmaker. "Thank you for being my friends. Thank you for Rena," he said.

"Jozef, know that she is safe. I did everything I could to keep her safe," the Dollmaker said as Brandt pulled him towards the idling car parked in front of them. "I'll talk to Brandt. I can—"

"This wasn't your fault," Jozef called out as the distance between him and the Dollmaker grew and grew. "You helped my family, and I'm for ever grateful for that."

"Jozef—"

Brandt opened the car door, shoving the Dollmaker inside and tossing Karolina in after him.

The last thing Karolina saw before the car left the main square was the frightened soldier forcing Jozef down onto the rough cobblestones. Jozef's lips began to move, and Karolina knew he was not speaking to the soldier; he was praying.

Karolina would remember him beneath an ash-coloured sky, a kind and courageous man thanking his god for the world he had lived in and the daughter he loved.

The interrogation room where Brandt brought the Dollmaker was located in the basement of the grey prison. As they entered, the shadows swarmed Karolina and her friend like every hungry thing Karolina had ever seen.

The witch directed the Dollmaker towards the table and chairs that stood beneath the single lightbulb dangling by a thin wire from the ceiling. The Dollmaker sat down, and, strangely enough, Brandt placed Karolina in the injured man's lap. Even without the full use of his hands, the Dollmaker could not bear to let Karolina fall to the grimy concrete, and he coiled his arms around her protectively.

Brandt took a cigarette from the pack in his breast pocket before extending the packet to the Dollmaker. "I can light one for you, if you like," Brandt said. "It might help with the pain."

"How dare you speak to me like we're friends?" the Dollmaker said. His chest heaved as he struggled to breathe around the pain that was radiating out from his hands. "Jozef was a good man. You—"

"I never wanted this for you," Brandt interrupted. "But we live in a new world. There is no place for Jews and traitors here."

"Your wooden soldier would have told you otherwise," said the Dollmaker.

"Perhaps. But Fritz is gone, and the opinion of those who are gone hardly counts for anything," said Brandt. In

the gloom, the end of his cigarette glowed like the third eye of a monster. "I'm almost impressed. You tricked me! You managed to steal Karolina from my flat... *How* did you manage it?"

"Maybe Polish magic isn't as weak as you think," Karolina said tightly.

Brandt smiled thinly. "You claim it isn't, and yet you're *my* prisoners. You really are a fool." He turned to the Dollmaker and said, "I'll send in a doctor to look at your hands. Consider that a favour – I wouldn't do that for just anyone, you know."

There was no ceremony to his departure. He abandoned Karolina and the Dollmaker in the darkness, and soon enough, her friend gave in to his exhaustion. He rested his forehead against the uneven surface of the table, and by the time the physician arrived to dull his pain, he was asleep.

Karolina waited in the shadows and the cold until the Dollmaker awoke, still slumped across the table. In the dark room, it was difficult to tell how much time had passed. Had they been imprisoned for days or mere hours? Karolina could not say.

"Karolina?" the Dollmaker said groggily.

"Yes?" She placed her hand against the slope of his belly to affirm that she was still there.

"I'm glad Brandt didn't take you away," the Dollmaker said. Thanks to the doctor and his medicine, each word was as long and drawn out as a sigh. "I ... I don't want to be alone."

"I won't leave you," Karolina promised. This was what

she had been made for: to comfort a scared man, to lie and tell him she could do battle with whatever came for him. But as Brandt had proven, there was little she could protect the Dollmaker – or anyone else – from.

"Jozef is gone," the Dollmaker said bleakly. He began to weep then, but his tears were not a sign of weakness. Karolina's friend was no coward, for all his other virtues and vices, and she would have added her own tears to his if she could.

The loss of Jozef still did not yet feel real to Karolina; all she could see in the eye of her imagination was Jozef at his best, the Jozef whose music had been as beautiful as any king's or star's, who had come into the toyshop each evening, his frustration and sadness melting away the moment he saw Rena.

She hoped that Rena was far away – and safe.

"One day," said Karolina, "someone will make Brandt pay for what he did to Jozef."

"I wonder." The Dollmaker studied his broken hands with curiosity that seemed detached from the hot ache that was creeping up his arms. But Karolina thought she understood why. Her own splintered and aching face was a distant concern in their current circumstance.

"I once knew a story," the Dollmaker went on. "It was about a girl who loses her hands to a devil. I think it was German."

"Why did the devil want her hands?" Karolina asked him.

"You know, I can't remember." The Dollmaker smiled. "Perhaps he was scared that her hands would bring good into the world. But his plot failed in the end. The girl married a good-hearted king, who fashioned beautiful silver

hands for her. They lived out all their days together, surrounded by a ring of salt to protect them." Using the heel of his shoe, he drew a circle in the dust. "Like so."

"You've never told me that story before."

"I'd forgotten it myself," the Dollmaker said. "I'm sorry. I should have made you go with Mysz."

The heavy metal door creaked open, sending a beam of light knifing across the floor. A red-faced witch boy stepped inside. Karolina had not seen him before. "You're b-being relocated," he stammered, locking his hands behind his back in a false display of authority. This room was Brandt's kingdom; this boy was only a lowly foot soldier.

"Relocated?" Karolina asked. "Relocated where?"

"Hauptsturmführer Brandt didn't say," the soldier said. "Just that you – both of you – are going somewhere else."

The Dollmaker held his arms above his head as Karolina did when she wanted to be picked up. "Fine. You'll need to help me," the Dollmaker said. "I don't think I can stand up by myself. Put the doll in the breast pocket of my jacket. On the left side, by my heart."

The witch boy faltered in the doorway. "Can't … can't she climb in herself?"

Karolina realized he didn't want to touch them. In his eyes, she and the Dollmaker were the dangerous ones, not him and his fellow soldiers.

"Are you afraid of us?" the Dollmaker asked.

"Yes," the boy said plainly. "You're…"

"Witches?" Karolina said. She couldn't resist smirking at him. "You have it all wrong. It's Brandt who's the witch. Not me. Not the Dollmaker."

"She's right," said the Dollmaker. "I do magic, but that doesn't make me evil."

"You helped people you had no business helping," said the witch boy. "That *does* make you evil."

"I could say the same about you," the Dollmaker replied. "Now put Karolina in my pocket and we can go."

CHAPTER 28

The Land of the Birch Trees

Brandt insisted on accompanying Karolina and the Dollmaker to the train station that afternoon.

It was, Karolina thought, an act of cruelty packaged to look like an act of kindness.

Brandt kept the barrel of his pistol jammed into the Dollmaker's ribs as the car crept through the rainy streets of Kraków. Weren't the handcuffs enough to remind the Dollmaker that he could no longer walk those streets as a free man?

The Dollmaker watched the tall pink-and-yellow buildings creep by and the people racing through the downpour. He looked so focused that Karolina thought he must be trying to memorize all the winding roads and smiling faces,

 244

saving them for a time when he might need to remember them.

But if the Dollmaker wouldn't speak to Brandt, Karolina thought that she ought to. What if he accepted her friend's silence for defeat? "Where are you sending us?" she asked.

"To Auschwitz-Birkenau," said Brandt.

"And what will happen to us there?" Karolina said. She feared that Brandt might take her away from the Dollmaker and she made sure to keep herself as far from the witch captain as possible. He had taken everyone and everything they cared about: Jozef Trzmiel and the shop and now the Dollmaker's best and loveliest tools – his hands. What was to prevent Brandt from separating him from Karolina too?

"What happens to everyone at Auschwitz-Birkenau," Brandt said.

"No one ever comes back when they put them on the trains," Karolina murmured, remembering Jozef's frantic conversation with the Dollmaker.

"No," Brandt said, "they don't. They go somewhere else. Kraków isn't for Jews any more – or Jew lovers. The Jews who can work are making weapons on the outskirts of the city. Those who can't work..." The witch captain shrugged. "Well, you'll be joining them soon enough."

The car took a sharp turn and pulled up in front of the train station. There was no one waiting in line at the ticket window or selling radishes and carrots on the street beside it. There were only soldiers, their faces so twisted with hate they resembled the roots of an ancient, rotting tree.

Karolina peered out at them, hoping that Jánošík would be among them, stealing caps and pistols. But she saw no one who could help the Dollmaker.

The driver got out of the car and opened the door for

Brandt, who pulled the Dollmaker onto the street by his elbow. Karolina hissed when the rain struck her, but the Dollmaker only glanced over his shoulder to look at the street. His eyes moved over it, as a writer's pen would across the page.

He *was* trying to etch the sight of it into his heart … and that meant the Dollmaker didn't think that they would ever see Kraków again.

Karolina turned her head up and wished on every star currently cloaked by the rain clouds that he would.

The station may have been deserted outside, but inside it was so crowded that Brandt had to force his way through the masses. The coats and dresses of the people waiting on the platform were all marked by the star armband that identified them as Jewish. Like the Dollmaker, they were at the mercy of the Germans, who circled the crowd like pale vultures. Couldn't they see how frightened these people were?

Brandt pulled the Dollmaker along the platform, and the sea of people parted for him, as if the grinning skull on his cap held a magic all its own. He came to a halt in front of another German, this one a low-ranking *Schütze*, a private. As soon as the *Schütze* saw Brandt, he lowered the clipboard resting against his chest and saluted. *"Heil Hitler,"* he said in greeting.

"Oh, be quiet," Karolina said.

The *Schütze*'s head snapped from one side to the other. "Who said that?" he demanded.

"Ignore it," Brandt said. "This man needs to go on one of the trains. I apologize for the late notice. My name is

Erich Brandt. I've been helping with the Jewish problem."

The *Schütze* tapped his pen against the top of his clipboard, the sound alarmingly like gunfire. "I'm aware of who you are. But with all due respect, *Hauptsturmführer*, this is quite inconvenient," he said. "Our SS brothers at Auschwitz can only help us evacuate so many Jews at one time."

If the number of people on the trains was so important, it must mean that the witches in the country only had provisions for so many. Karolina tugged on her friend's coat and whispered, "We'll be all right; we'll get to stay together. And, at least, we'll be away from Brandt."

But the Dollmaker averted his eyes. Did he know something she didn't?

"This man needs to leave Kraków today," Brandt said to the *Schütze*.

The *Schütze* handed Brandt his clipboard and sighed. "One more will hardly make a difference, I suppose. Put his name at the bottom and sign. I hope he won't be difficult."

"His hands are broken," Brandt said as he began to write. "He won't be."

"Good," said the *Schütze*, taking his clipboard back. The formalities complete, Brandt pulled a small silver key from his pocket and inserted it into the side of the Dollmaker's handcuffs. With a twist, the cuffs fell away, and Brandt pocketed them.

"There are still people in this world who will defy you, even if I disappear into the belly of whatever monster lies at the end of these tracks," the Dollmaker said.

Brandt's face softened a little. "Maybe so," he murmured. "But it doesn't matter. No one will remember you or what you did in this city."

Thinking of Rena, the other children and the priest who had dared to believe in miracles, Karolina said, "No. That's not true!"

She felt a mean-spirited prick of joy as Brandt's expression turned as black as his coat. "I should take you," he said.

"If you do, I'll remind you every day of the Dollmaker and Fritz," Karolina said. "I'll stamp on your heart from morning until dusk. I swear I will."

To anyone else, the words might not have been intimidating, but Karolina had read Brandt well. He took a step back from her. He tipped the bill of his cap down so that it was not his eyes Karolina met, but the empty ones of the skull. It seemed fitting to her.

Desperate not to face his self-made ghosts, Brandt turned silently away. But the things that were unspoken between him and the Dollmaker were as loud as the whistle of the train that would soon be arriving.

"How many witches start out as princes and princesses?" Karolina said as she watched Brandt march back down the platform. This was one goodbye she was glad to make.

It was not until the Dollmaker replied that she knew she had spoken the question aloud. "More than anyone would like to think," he said.

"Why?" asked Karolina. "Why did Brandt hurt so many people with his own pain?"

"That's what weak people do," said the Dollmaker. "They're afraid, and hurt others with that fear. But there comes a point at which they don't deserve our pity any more."

The *Schütze* with the clipboard cupped his hand around his mouth and shouted into the crowd, "Leave your suitcases

here; do not take them on the train. You will be able to collect your belongings when you reach your new homes. Luggage that does not have a name on it will be confiscated. If you need something to mark it with, see me."

Several people did approach the *Schütze*, who gave them broken pieces of chalk. They printed their names with care on the sides of their suitcases, each letter thick and blocky so that it would be easy to read.

The children milling around their adults smiled at Karolina when they saw her looking out from the Dollmaker's waistcoat pocket. Some of them even greeted her with their wooden dolls and stuffed bears and soldiers that fit into the palms of their hands.

"You're all from the ghetto?" the Dollmaker asked one woman who had bent down beside him to write on her satchel. A dark-blue handkerchief was knotted beneath her chin, and when she raised her head, her wrinkles formed a map of all the places she had been.

"Yes," she said.

"Why are there so few of you here?" said the Dollmaker. "Where's everyone else from the ghetto?"

The old woman stood up, clutching her back as she did. The Dollmaker held out a hand to assist her and then withdrew quickly. His hands, Karolina thought, were not what they used to be.

"There is no one left in the ghetto," she said. "The Germans told us we're being sent out of the city."

Something about her tone made Karolina think the statement might be false. But she reminded herself that the witches wouldn't have cared who got on the train or whether anyone marked their luggage if they wanted to make all of these people disappear.

"What ... what happened in the ghetto?" the Dollmaker said.

"They made the young people march out of it one way and made the rest of us come here," the old woman said. "They hurt people, the SS, with their guns and their dogs. But I think you know what they are capable of, don't you?" she said, looking down at the Dollmaker's hands. Bruises the colour of raven's feathers had appeared along the lengths of his swollen fingers.

The Dollmaker did not have the opportunity to respond, for the long-awaited train had pulled into the station. It made Karolina think of a huge black animal, and she wished the Dollmaker could take them both as far away from it as possible.

When the train shuddered to a stop, the German soldiers opened the doors of the wagons that trailed behind it. They motioned for the people on the platform to climb aboard.

But no one rushed forwards to claim their seats because there *were* no seats inside. There was nothing at all – just a floor and a ceiling, all made of splintered, weather-beaten wood. Worse still, the cars looked far too small for more than a dozen people to fit comfortably inside.

"This isn't a real train," Karolina said.

"It *is* a real train," the Dollmaker said quietly. "Just not one that people should be riding in. A wagon like this is normally used for cows or sheep."

"But *we* aren't cows or sheep," Karolina said.

"To them," the Dollmaker said, "we are."

As Karolina had suspected, there was not enough room in the cattle wagon for the number of people crammed into it. The Dollmaker was forced to stand shoulder to shoulder with an old man and a woman whose son clung to her side. Sitting was impossible; the most anyone could do was bend their knees to relieve the ache or lean on a sympathetic neighbour for a moment or two.

The first hour inside the wagon was terrible. The second was nearly unbearable.

The world outside the two tiny windows on the side gave Karolina few hints as to where the train was taking them. Once it left Kraków, all she could see were brown fields, groves of pine trees and the bullet-coloured sky. Every so often, she spotted a farmer and his family working in the fields, but no one paid attention to the train.

Karolina had given up pretending to be an ordinary doll; so many of the Germans had seen her talking at the police station that there would probably be a newspaper headline about her shortly. She glanced around freely, even greeting the little boy beside the Dollmaker. He smiled back after a moment of due consideration.

"How much longer?" the little boy asked his mother, pulling at her dress.

"I don't know, Jakob," she said. "Hopefully, we'll be there soon."

"Where exactly is 'there'?" Karolina asked. "Does anyone know?"

"Maybe it's another ghetto," the old man standing beside the Dollmaker said.

"Another ghetto?" the elderly woman to his right said. "Haven't they forced us to live in enough horrible places already?"

"It might be better there," the little boy's mother said. She pursed her lips.

Karolina reached up and patted the Dollmaker's stubbled chin to rouse him from his thoughts. "What do you think?"

Before he could answer her, the old man asked, "Who is it that's speaking?"

"Me," Karolina said. She leaned out of the Dollmaker's pocket and poked the old man's shoulder.

"What a wonderful puppet," said the old man.

"She's not a puppet," Jakob said. "She's real. She said hello to me before."

"Yes, she *is* real," the Dollmaker said. It was the first time Karolina had heard him speak since they had boarded the train.

The old man's eyes grew as wide and round as the moon, but he did not say anything to dispute what the little boy had said. Instead, he said, "A magic doll! These really are strange times." Then he addressed the Dollmaker. "But you, sir... You're the only person here not wearing a star armband, and I never saw you in the ghetto. Are you not Jewish?"

"Why are you here, then?" asked Jakob's mother. She looked younger, as if the mention of magic had washed years of hardship away from her face.

The Dollmaker hunched his shoulders, but this was not the shop in the days before the war and the Trzmiels. He could not hide who he truly was behind his vacant smiles and polite words. "I helped a friend of mine and his daughter," the Dollmaker said. "That's all."

Karolina thought he had done so much more than that, but magicians were rarely ever the heroes of a tale. They

were forces of nature, and they faded out of history like the dew in the morning light.

Karolina gripped her skirts tightly. No. Surely that couldn't happen to the Dollmaker. It just couldn't.

"How did *you* come here?" Jakob asked Karolina. Some of his fatigue seemed to have left him, but Karolina knew that it was temporary. There was only so much a body, especially a little body, could endure without complaint.

"The Dollmaker brought me here from far away," said Karolina. "It's a long story."

"You ought to tell us," said the Dollmaker.

Karolina tried – and failed – to keep the weariness from her voice as she asked, "What good is a story now?"

"It will help to pass the time at the very least," the Dollmaker said. "Tell us about the Land of the Dolls."

Karolina almost refused him again. Then she realized that her friend needed her to tell a tale.

"There once was a little doll named Karolina," she began slowly, "who lived in a country far from the human world…"

The story bore them away from the cattle wagon as Dogoda, the kind wind, had once carried Karolina. When she paused for breath midway through the tale, the Dollmaker whispered to her, "This is the first time you've told me everything that happened to you in the Land of the Dolls."

"It used to hurt too much to talk about, but it doesn't any more. I have a new home with you," Karolina whispered back. "It's what your mother must have wanted. She brought us together, even after she was gone."

"Yes," the Dollmaker said. "Of course."

As Karolina resumed her tale, she felt one of the Dollmaker's tears splash onto her lace apron. She began to

speak more quickly then, knowing that she had to finish the story for her friend before the end of their journey. Karolina *needed* to give him the memory of the sunny afternoons by the laughing brook and the gentle lullabies of the stars and the brave deeds performed by her people.

Because if she gave these beautiful parts of herself to the Dollmaker, she would always be close to him, and it would not matter how much distance separated them otherwise.

Hours later, when the train ground to a halt and the door to the cattle wagon was opened, the Dollmaker and the other passengers were pushed outside by two SS officers holding rifles.

"Out! Out! Hurry!" the witches shouted.

Dogs like the fearsome Soldat snapped at the heels of the people as they left the train. A number of men wearing blue-striped uniforms stood nearby. Each had a six-pointed star on the front of his shirt and looked as thin as a paper doll.

The sun was dipping below the horizon now, painting the long, dusty stretch of packed earth laid out before them in glaring orange light. The sound of the electricity carried by the barbed-wire fences around them was sinister and unwavering. Karolina's gaze travelled up the gravel path to where the railway tracks ended and two red-brick buildings with huge chimneys stood. Each was fringed by clusters of spindly trees whose leaves whispered in welcome.

Why would there be such beautiful trees if this was an evil place?

"Birches," the Dollmaker said, more to himself than Karolina. "Birkenau. The land of the birch trees."

"What are you talking about?" said Karolina.

"My family's name," the Dollmaker said. "This place has my family's name. *Birkholz* and *Brzezick* both mean 'by the birch woods'."

A piercing whistle rose above the crowd. The old men, women and children of Kraków all looked towards its origin, a smartly dressed SS officer. He carried a baton and wore a pair of white gloves, as if he intended to draw one of the women into a waltz down the gravel path.

"Welcome to Auschwitz-Birkenau," the officer said, smiling at the group. But that smile made Karolina's glass heart grow cold. It made her think of Erich Brandt's empty grin. "I know you have all had a long and uncomfortable journey, but things will be better. Form two lines, women in one, men in the other. I am going to divide you up so that we can assign you appropriate work."

The Dollmaker fell into line with the others. Then he leaned down and planted a kiss on Karolina's forehead. It was, she sensed, both the first kiss and the last kiss he would ever give her. "I love you, Karolina," said the Dollmaker. "Before you came to me, I'd been afraid to go out into the world for so long, but you gave me the courage I needed. And if you hadn't spoken up, I would never have got to know Jozef and Rena. You saved me."

"I'm not saying goodbye to you," Karolina said. "I refuse! We're supposed to stay together."

"I wish that we could," the Dollmaker said. "You were the best friend I could have possibly asked for. I don't know what I would have done without you."

Karolina grabbed a tiny fistful of the Dollmaker's jacket,

trying to anchor him to her. "Stop talking like you're going to leave me alone! You can't."

The more she babbled, the hazier her friend's face became, as if he was already beginning to fade away from her. Karolina blinked. She wanted so badly to store the Dollmaker up in her memory, as he had done with the city of Kraków. But why couldn't she see him clearly?

"Karolina," the Dollmaker said. "You're..." He gestured to her and panicked. Karolina raised her hand to her face. She felt a bead of moisture working its way down her cheek, causing the crack to sting.

She was crying.

Karolina had learned the trick of tears at last, but what good did it do? She'd wanted to be brave for the Dollmaker, and instead, he was the one comforting her.

"I'm so sorry," the Dollmaker said.

Karolina wiped her eyes. There had been so many times when she'd wanted to cry, but now that she'd got her wish, she only wanted to be rid of her tears. Wasn't that the way it always went with wishes?

A sob gathered in Karolina's throat, ready to take flight. But she swallowed it as she threw her arm around the Dollmaker. "I love you more than anyone," Karolina said. "I'll always love you more than anyone. No matter what happens—"

But Karolina's goodbye was cut short by one of the soldiers standing nearby. "Is that a *doll*?" he said. The soldier grabbed Karolina from the Dollmaker's pocket. The world flickered from dark to light as her eyes closed, then snapped open again like shades as the witch righted her once more. "You have to be joking. What have you got in your other pocket, your teddy bear?" He waved at

the man with the white gloves. "*Doktor*, look! A grown man is carrying this around. Can you believe it?"

The man in the white gloves – the doctor, apparently – did look towards Karolina and the Dollmaker, but he did not join in the other soldier's laughter. He rolled his eyes and, using his baton, lifted the hem of the Dollmaker's trousers to expose his wooden leg. "Ah, yes. I see," said the doctor. "Go into the left line."

His fun spoiled, the other soldier shoved the Dollmaker back into the column of people filing towards the red-brick building. "Go on," he commanded.

"Wait," said the Dollmaker. He reached for Karolina, and she found her own fingers straining to meet with his. Who cared if anyone saw her move now? She had to go with him! "The doll—"

"You can get it back after you shower," snapped the soldier. Karolina swung back and forth at his side, brushing up against his gun as she moved. It was as cold as one of Lady Marzanna's frosty kisses. "Now get going or I'll make you."

The depth of the look that passed between the Dollmaker and Karolina could not be conveyed in a single word; it was too full of every story and victory they had shared with each other. It was too full of love. And so the Dollmaker chose not one word but two. "Live well," he told her.

A moment later, he was gone, carried away by the crowd being herded forwards.

"What an idiot," the soldier said, sneering. He scoured the platform until he found one of the thin men in the striped uniforms. "Put this doll with the other things and be quick about it," he barked, shoving Karolina at the

other man. "We've got another shipment coming in."

The thin man's eyes were full of cinders and ghosts as he stared at her, and Karolina could feel each and every one of the bones in his wiry hands. Would the Dollmaker end up like this poor man?

The witch cuffed the thin man on the back of his head hard enough to make him stumble. "Don't make me tell you again!"

"Yes sir," the thin man said quietly. Still holding Karolina, he plodded towards the odd array of items that had been left on the platform in the wake of the disappearing crowd. Each was a fragment of a life Karolina knew nothing about, from the crutches to the prayer shawls to the hats. The thin man collected all of them until his arms were almost overflowing and then deposited Karolina and the other objects into a pram that had tipped over into the dirt. He wiped his brow and then his eyes with the sleeve of his dirty shirt. But he made no sound at all.

The thin man did not take Karolina to the red-brick building the Dollmaker had vanished into as she had both hoped and feared he would. Rather, he wheeled the pram over to a series of long wooden huts. No one had bothered to plant trees around these buildings, and their windows had been boarded over, making them look like sleeping beasts.

When the thin man came to the first of the sheds, he pushed open the door using his shoulder, grunting as he did. Karolina had not known what she had expected to see inside, but she was stunned by what loomed before her.

There was a mountain of shoes, the laces tied together

to keep the pairs matched. There was a mountain of spectacles, their ears tangled. There were mountains of dresses and rings, and even a small hill of toothbrushes, which a few young women were sifting through. Their eyes had the same dark, pained look as the thin man's.

The man wove between the strange mountains, dropping the hats into one pile and the crutches in another. He did not greet the women, nor did they look up from their work to greet him.

Finally, the thin man picked Karolina up. "You must have been very loved by the person you belonged to," he said quietly.

Karolina wanted to tell him that she *still* belonged to the Dollmaker and that he belonged to her, but she could not find her voice; it was trapped inside her aching chest. This new pain was far greater than even the loss of her arm had been, but she could not explain *why* it hurt so much. What had the witches done to her?

The thin man set Karolina down at the foot of one of the mountains. She slumped between a teddy bear with one eye and another doll who was missing one of her glass eyes. As her head lolled backwards, Karolina could see dozens of other dolls and stuffed animals, one stacked atop the other in a great heap.

Who had these toys belonged to? Didn't they have anyone who loved them enough to take proper care of them?

But as the thin man left the shed, Karolina thought she knew the answer to all her terrible questions. The toys had been loved just as she was, but the humans who cared for them had not been able to keep them. The toys had been left all alone … and now, so had Karolina.

The Dollmaker was not coming back for her.

And if the Dollmaker did not come back for her, it could mean only one thing: that he, like Jozef Trzmiel, was gone for ever.

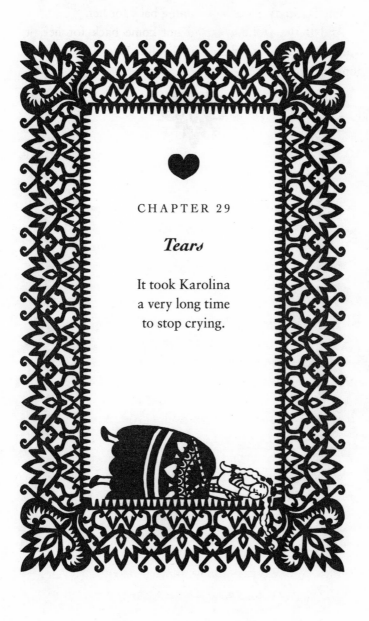

CHAPTER 29

Tears

It took Karolina
a very long time
to stop crying.

CHAPTER 30

The Kind Wind

Karolina and Fritz reached the summit of the glass mountain as the sun dipped down into the dreadful sea the rats had come from. The snow around them was not real snow, but a layer of powdered sugar. However, it was cold so high above the Land of the Dolls, and Karolina shivered when she leaned over to fill her palms with the snow.

"Have you ever seen anything like it?" asked Karolina.

"Once," Fritz said. "An explorer brought the king and queen a jar of this snow. He said his next trip would be to the moon." His smile was as soft as the sweet frost around them. "I wonder if he ever made it."

"I'd like to visit the moon one day," said Karolina.

"We can almost touch it from here,"

said Fritz, waving his dark hand at the sky above them.

"Almost," Karolina said with a sigh. She glanced around at the barren mountaintop. She didn't know what she had expected, but the emptiness of the place was doing its best to squash the last threads of her optimism. "What do we do now?" she asked Fritz. "I don't even feel any wind here, and I certainly don't see anyone else who could help us." Karolina slumped to the ground.

"I refuse to believe that my friend wasn't telling the truth about the wind," Fritz said. "I need to help our people. And I want to help you. I see your face, Karolina. You didn't deserve that."

Karolina refused to give in and touch her splintered cheek. The last thing she wanted from Fritz was pity. "No doll did," she said.

"No, they didn't," agreed a sighing voice. This voice was accompanied by the strongest wind Karolina had ever felt. His fingers tangled in her hair, blowing it back from her temples, and her carefully knotted skirts came undone so that they flapped around her.

Fritz laughed. "You see?" he said to Karolina. "The wind really does exist!"

After so many stories had been tragically wrong, Karolina could hardly believe that any story had the audacity to be true. "Are you Dogoda?" she asked the wind. She had expected it to be as cool as the air around them, but it was as mild and warm as sun-kissed earth.

"Yes," said the wind. "I know who you are too, little dolls. Two human beings have called out to you, and I am here to take you to them."

"Two humans?" asked Fritz. He slapped a hand on top of his head to prevent his cap from blowing away.

"Yes," said Dogoda.

Karolina recoiled. "But we didn't come here to go to the human world. What's the point in going there?"

"When a human cries out for a doll, there is always a reason," said the kind wind. "They need you … and you may find that they have what you need too."

"I'm not running away from the Land of the Dolls," Karolina said firmly.

"We wanted to find a way to help our people," Fritz said. "Maybe this is how we will do it – even if it's not what we expected."

"Fritz..." Karolina began. Could he be right?

"You don't have to come," Fritz said, "but I want to make this journey." He stretched his arms out to either side and let the wind carry him higher and higher until the soles of his boots left the snow.

The mist around them began to take shape, forming enormous wings that seemed to stretch from one end of the darkening sky to the other. Dogoda's face appeared between them. It was youthful and glad, framed by curls the cheerful colour of sunflowers.

"And you, little doll?" he asked Karolina. "Are you ready?"

Fritz's face shone expectantly, and gazing into his eyes, Karolina knew what her decision would be. "Yes," she said. "I'll come with you."

The wind took Karolina up into his arms, and together with Fritz, they flew.

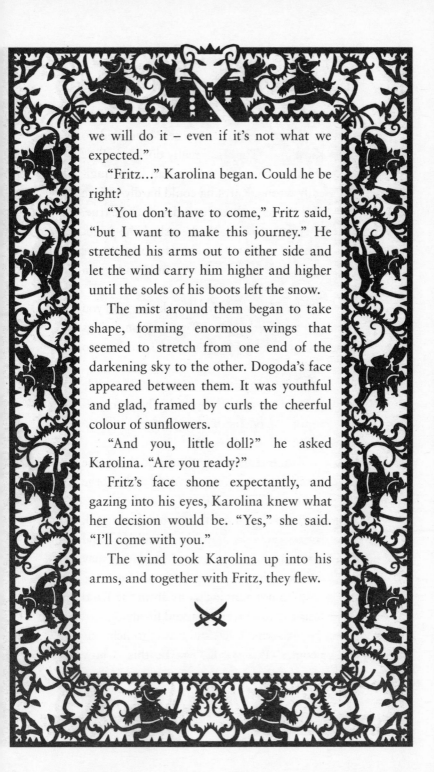

CHAPTER 31

The Last Journey

The last creature Karolina had expected to appear in the shed was the Lakanica.

The meadow spirit had changed since she and Karolina had last spoken in Planty Park. Her brilliant red hair had turned ash grey, and the flowers twined in it were now brittle and withered.

"Hello, little doll," said the Lakanica. Her voice was choked by smoke, and she coughed delicately into her fist.

"What are you doing here?" asked Karolina. "I thought you were going to stay in Kraków!"

The Lakanica sat down next to Karolina and tried to stroke one of her plaits. But her fingers passed through it. "I thought that I could," she said. "I tried to make a new

home there. But I couldn't forget my meadow."

"*This* is your meadow?" Karolina said. When she had first met the spirit, the Lakanica had been beautiful and alive, and this place was neither.

Auschwitz-Birkenau was where dreams went to die.

"It was mine," said the Lakanica. "But not any more. It belongs to the ghosts now, and I have no power here any longer. I cannot make flowers blossom or trees grow. I cannot guide anyone out of the darkness."

"Please," Karolina said. "Please, tell me where everyone went. The Dollmaker said goodbye to me before the witches took me away from him, but he can't be gone." She began to cry again, though this time she was too exhausted to resent her tears.

"The Germans have taken him and all those people from that train to a place where neither you nor I can follow," said the Lakanica. "I am sorry for the loss of your friend." The meadow spirit went to embrace her, and Karolina batted her hand away. She did not want to be comforted. She wanted to run so fast that she could shed her grief as a snake might shed its skin.

But there was nowhere to go.

"Leave me alone!" Karolina shouted. She yanked her cap from her head and hurled it at the Lakanica. "You're useless. What good is your magic if you couldn't help the people on the train or the Dollmaker? You can't even help *me*."

The cap floated harmlessly through the Lakanica's chest, but she obeyed Karolina's order nonetheless, gliding backwards. "I am sorry," she said again. "I know what your magician did for the children. All the spirits of Kraków do. We—"

"Go away," Karolina said. "If you knew, you should have stopped Brandt from taking him and Jozef. They'd still be here if you had helped!"

"I wish we could have, but we don't have that kind of power. We are creatures of dreams," the Lakanica said. "But know that the children your friend saved will be safe. They will never see what my meadow has become. They will all grow up. Some of their parents may even find them again."

Karolina wanted to believe her. She had thought that growing up would be a terrible thing until she'd watched Rena do it, little by little. Now she had come to realize that it was the most important thing in the world. "I'm sorry I shouted at you," said Karolina. "But it hurts so much."

"Broken hearts hurt more than anything," said the Lakanica.

"But I don't have a broken heart," said Karolina.

"Oh, but you do," the Lakanica said. "Can't you feel it?" Karolina was about to deny it again, but she could not lie about the pain in her chest. Where before her heart had been so solid, now she could feel how the two sides of it met. "Can I mend it?" Karolina said.

"I'm afraid you can't," the Lakanica said. "But it will hurt less as time goes on. Your happy memories will soothe it, little doll." This last word was almost a sigh, and Karolina watched as the meadow spirit began to shimmer and lose her shape.

"Wait," she said. "What do I do now?"

"Eventually, someone will come for you," the Lakanica said.

"And then?" said Karolina.

"And then you will go home." The Lakanica's eyes

fluttered closed, and her shape abandoned her entirely. Karolina was alone in the shed once more.

Karolina did not know exactly how long she stayed among the lost toys.

In winter, the women who sorted through the mountains of clothing and memories were chased inside the shed by the bitter wind. In summer, they rolled up their sleeves to expose arms scalded red by the sun. But in all seasons, they traded rumours and poetry and recipes under their breath as they pored over the belongings of the lost.

They vowed to love.

They vowed to get revenge.

They vowed to remember.

Karolina listened, but she never spoke to them.

Little by little, she felt her time in the human world was coming to an end. Her hair crumbled first, falling out in clumps that were no longer gold but grey and filthy. Her dress unravelled thread by thread, as if invisible fingers were pulling it apart. The wood of her face puckered and warped as droplets of rain and snow blew inside the shed, and the crack on her cheek spread in all directions like a spiderweb.

In the moments when Karolina could not bear to be surrounded by so much sorrow, she let her memories return her to the life she had known in Kraków. She would smell the dumplings the Dollmaker liked to fry, and listen to Jozef play his violin. She would see herself back in Rena's beloved doll's house with Mysz and envision all the many games they would play together.

Then one day, the door to the shed opened and Dogoda entered. His cloud wings beat slowly, disturbing the hair and skirts of the working women, though they did not see him. Karolina wished that they could. His crown of flowers was still fresh and lovely. It was a tiny reminder of the beauty that had once existed in this world, and so many others.

The sight of the kind wind only made Karolina hurt more. The last time they'd been together, she was about to meet the Dollmaker.

"Hello again," the Dogoda said.

Karolina tried to sit up, but her legs were too loose and wobbly. "Please, take me to where the Dollmaker is now," she said to Dogoda. "You took me to him before. Can't you do it again? We still need each other."

"I cannot cross into the place where human souls go when they leave this world," Dogoda said. Each word he spoke sounded weighed down with pain. "There are other winds and other spirits for that. All I can do is take you back to the Land of the Dolls."

"There's nothing for me in the Land of the Dolls," Karolina spat. "Only another war I can't stop." She felt cruel like a knife hungry to bury itself in someone's heart; she wanted to make someone else hurt as she did. And if that someone else was the wind, so be it.

"All wars end, Karolina. Didn't the Dollmaker tell you that?" said Dogoda. He knelt down beside her. "The body he made for you cannot hold your soul any longer. It's time for you to leave this world."

Karolina bowed her head. If the Dollmaker had still been with her, he could have mended her hair and her face and her legs. His clever hands might have even been able

to fix her heart. But his soul had been blown far, far away too.

Fighting to keep her voice steady, Karolina asked, "Does it hurt to lose your body?"

"It does for a moment," said Dogoda. "And then it won't."

It sounded so much like something the Dollmaker would have said that Karolina believed him.

"Are you ready?" asked Dogoda.

"Yes," Karolina said. She closed her eyes and let Dogoda pull her into his misty embrace. For one terrible instant, she felt as if she were being torn from the Dollmaker's arms all over again.

As Karolina and Dogoda rose up, he said, "I want to show you something before we leave the human world." With some effort, Karolina prised her eyes open. The dreaded landscape of Auschwitz-Birkenau, the place that had wrongly borne the Dollmaker's name, had fallen behind them. She and Dogoda were moving quickly now, not just over the fields and rivers, but across time itself. Below them, irises and crocuses bloomed in the full glory of summer only to wilt and be buried beneath a thick mantle of snow. The streams froze and melted and froze, and the sun swung from east to west like the pendulum of a great clock.

When Karolina and the wind reached Kraków, spring had come again. But the enormous black-and-red flags of Germany were gone from the Cloth Hall. Could this really be Kraków? Karolina saw no one with a star armband or a grinning skull-adorned cap as Dogoda drifted through the main square, stirring the peonies in the flower boxes lining the windows of stores and flats alike. The wind slowed his

271

pace as they reached the blue, blue door of a shop across from St Mary's Basilica. But this was not just *any* shop.

It was the Dollmaker's shop.

A teenage girl and boy stood in front of it, peering in at the abandoned rows of dolls and stuffed animals. It was obvious that no one had taken care of the shop in many years; the floor and the shelves were all covered in a veil of dust that looked to Karolina like lace. The rocking horse the Dollmaker had been carving when Brandt had come to arrest him was still sitting on the work table. At the sight of it, Karolina felt fresh tears threaten ... until the young woman brushed her dark curls back from her luminous eyes – one green and one blue.

It was Rena. And the boy – the young man – beside her was Dawid.

They had both survived.

Mysz was there too, perched on Rena's shoulder. His velvet fur was a little sparse in places, but he still seemed as lively as ever. The Dollmaker had left both Kraków and the human world behind, but the magic he had done remained strong.

"We're home," Mysz said.

"Are we?" Dawid asked. "Kraków feels different, even though the Germans are gone."

Rena continued to look intently through the dirty glass. "Maybe it isn't home," she said quietly. "Maybe it can't ever be again. But I wanted to see it one more time." She took Dawid's hand in her own and squeezed it.

Rena's heart, like Karolina's, seemed to be full of little cracks where the memories of her father and mother, the Dollmaker and all the people who had been taken from her resided. But Karolina hoped that Rena *could* make another

home for herself in the future, and that Dawid and Mysz would be a part of it.

And now it was time for Karolina herself to bid farewell to Kraków and allow the kind wind to take her home as he had promised.

She thought it was what Rena would have wanted.

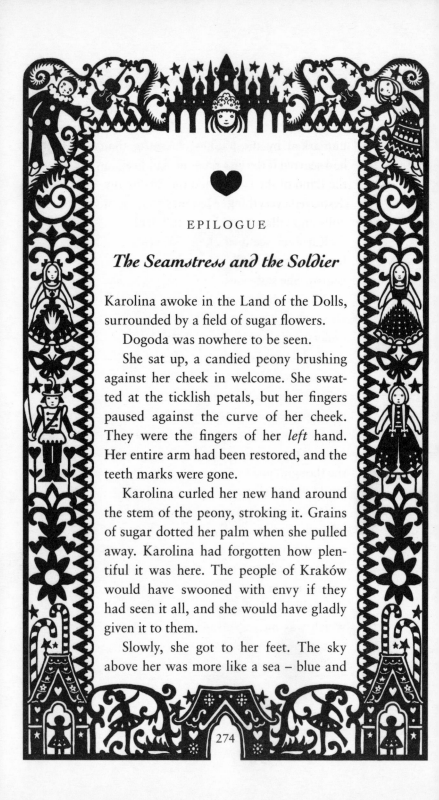

EPILOGUE

The Seamstress and the Soldier

Karolina awoke in the Land of the Dolls, surrounded by a field of sugar flowers.

Dogoda was nowhere to be seen.

She sat up, a candied peony brushing against her cheek in welcome. She swatted at the ticklish petals, but her fingers paused against the curve of her cheek. They were the fingers of her *left* hand. Her entire arm had been restored, and the teeth marks were gone.

Karolina curled her new hand around the stem of the peony, stroking it. Grains of sugar dotted her palm when she pulled away. Karolina had forgotten how plentiful it was here. The people of Kraków would have swooned with envy if they had seen it all, and she would have gladly given it to them.

Slowly, she got to her feet. The sky above her was more like a sea – blue and

274

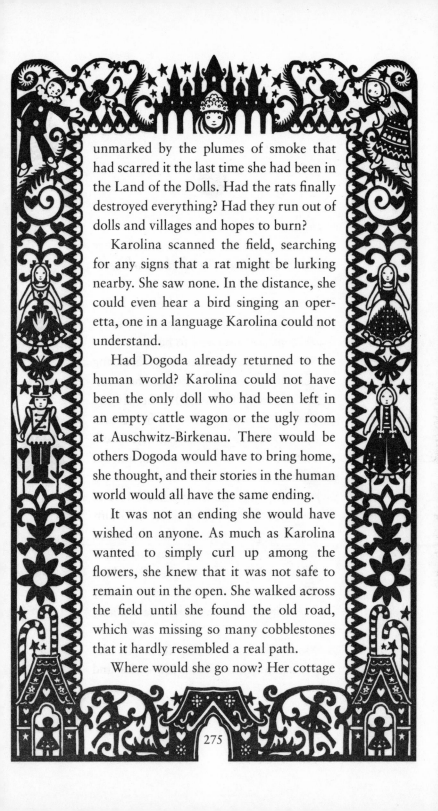

unmarked by the plumes of smoke that had scarred it the last time she had been in the Land of the Dolls. Had the rats finally destroyed everything? Had they run out of dolls and villages and hopes to burn?

Karolina scanned the field, searching for any signs that a rat might be lurking nearby. She saw none. In the distance, she could even hear a bird singing an operetta, one in a language Karolina could not understand.

Had Dogoda already returned to the human world? Karolina could not have been the only doll who had been left in an empty cattle wagon or the ugly room at Auschwitz-Birkenau. There would be others Dogoda would have to bring home, she thought, and their stories in the human world would all have the same ending.

It was not an ending she would have wished on anyone. As much as Karolina wanted to simply curl up among the flowers, she knew that it was not safe to remain out in the open. She walked across the field until she found the old road, which was missing so many cobblestones that it hardly resembled a real path.

Where would she go now? Her cottage

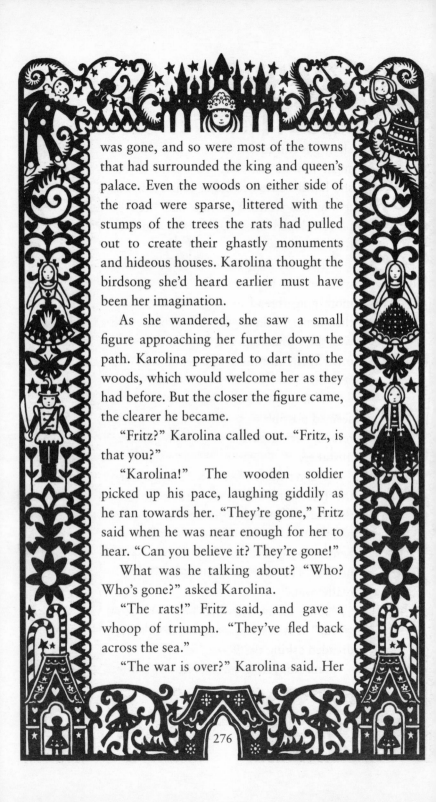

was gone, and so were most of the towns that had surrounded the king and queen's palace. Even the woods on either side of the road were sparse, littered with the stumps of the trees the rats had pulled out to create their ghastly monuments and hideous houses. Karolina thought the birdsong she'd heard earlier must have been her imagination.

As she wandered, she saw a small figure approaching her further down the path. Karolina prepared to dart into the woods, which would welcome her as they had before. But the closer the figure came, the clearer he became.

"Fritz?" Karolina called out. "Fritz, is that you?"

"Karolina!" The wooden soldier picked up his pace, laughing giddily as he ran towards her. "They're gone," Fritz said when he was near enough for her to hear. "Can you believe it? They're gone!"

What was he talking about? "Who? Who's gone?" asked Karolina.

"The rats!" Fritz said, and gave a whoop of triumph. "They've fled back across the sea."

"The war is over?" Karolina said. Her

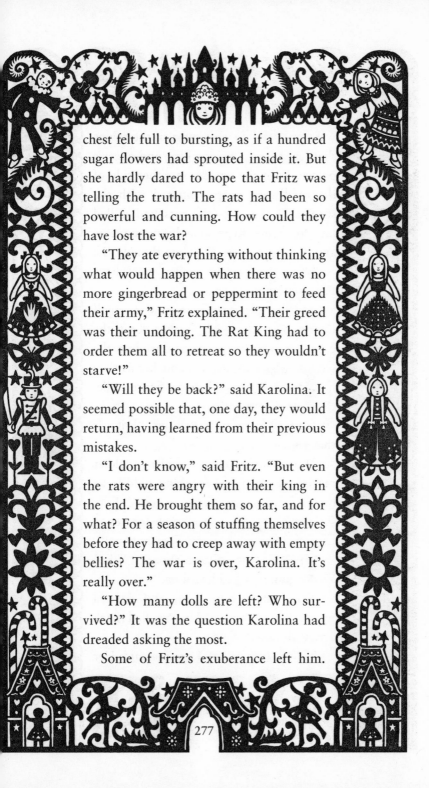

chest felt full to bursting, as if a hundred sugar flowers had sprouted inside it. But she hardly dared to hope that Fritz was telling the truth. The rats had been so powerful and cunning. How could they have lost the war?

"They ate everything without thinking what would happen when there was no more gingerbread or peppermint to feed their army," Fritz explained. "Their greed was their undoing. The Rat King had to order them all to retreat so they wouldn't starve!"

"Will they be back?" said Karolina. It seemed possible that, one day, they would return, having learned from their previous mistakes.

"I don't know," said Fritz. "But even the rats were angry with their king in the end. He brought them so far, and for what? For a season of stuffing themselves before they had to creep away with empty bellies? The war is over, Karolina. It's really over."

"How many dolls are left? Who survived?" It was the question Karolina had dreaded asking the most.

Some of Fritz's exuberance left him.

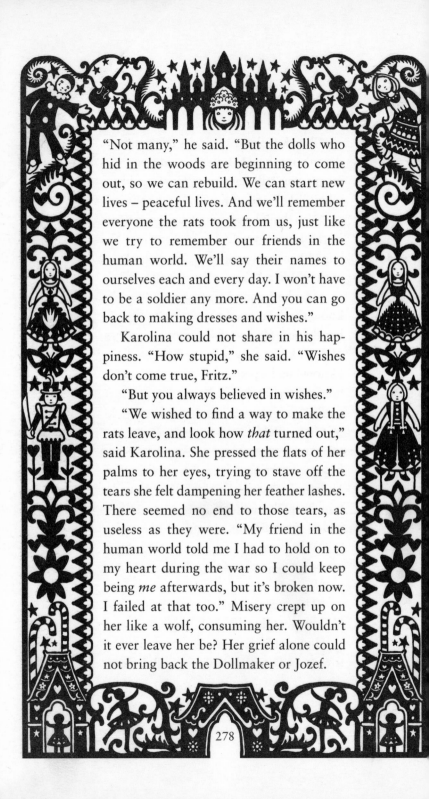

"Not many," he said. "But the dolls who hid in the woods are beginning to come out, so we can rebuild. We can start new lives – peaceful lives. And we'll remember everyone the rats took from us, just like we try to remember our friends in the human world. We'll say their names to ourselves each and every day. I won't have to be a soldier any more. And you can go back to making dresses and wishes."

Karolina could not share in his happiness. "How stupid," she said. "Wishes don't come true, Fritz."

"But you always believed in wishes."

"We wished to find a way to make the rats leave, and look how *that* turned out," said Karolina. She pressed the flats of her palms to her eyes, trying to stave off the tears she felt dampening her feather lashes. There seemed no end to those tears, as useless as they were. "My friend in the human world told me I had to hold on to my heart during the war so I could keep being *me* afterwards, but it's broken now. I failed at that too." Misery crept up on her like a wolf, consuming her. Wouldn't it ever leave her be? Her grief alone could not bring back the Dollmaker or Jozef.

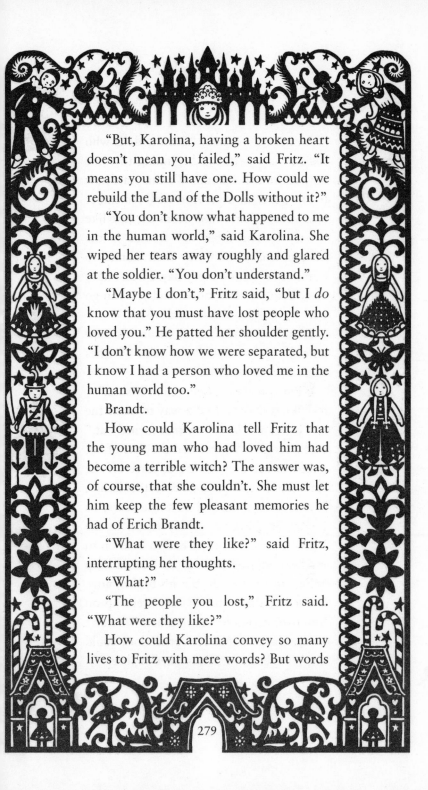

"But, Karolina, having a broken heart doesn't mean you failed," said Fritz. "It means you still have one. How could we rebuild the Land of the Dolls without it?"

"You don't know what happened to me in the human world," said Karolina. She wiped her tears away roughly and glared at the soldier. "You don't understand."

"Maybe I don't," Fritz said, "but I *do* know that you must have lost people who loved you." He patted her shoulder gently. "I don't know how we were separated, but I know I had a person who loved me in the human world too."

Brandt.

How could Karolina tell Fritz that the young man who had loved him had become a terrible witch? The answer was, of course, that she couldn't. She must let him keep the few pleasant memories he had of Erich Brandt.

"What were they like?" said Fritz, interrupting her thoughts.

"What?"

"The people you lost," Fritz said. "What were they like?"

How could Karolina convey so many lives to Fritz with mere words? But words

279

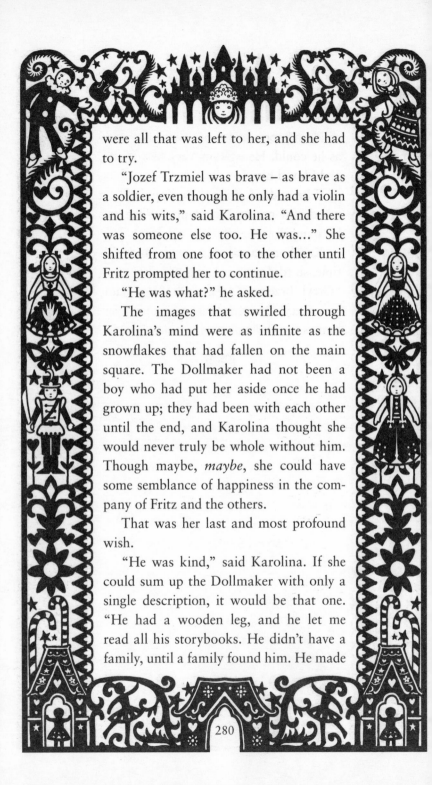

were all that was left to her, and she had to try.

"Jozef Trzmiel was brave – as brave as a soldier, even though he only had a violin and his wits," said Karolina. "And there was someone else too. He was..." She shifted from one foot to the other until Fritz prompted her to continue.

"He was what?" he asked.

The images that swirled through Karolina's mind were as infinite as the snowflakes that had fallen on the main square. The Dollmaker had not been a boy who had put her aside once he had grown up; they had been with each other until the end, and Karolina thought she would never truly be whole without him. Though maybe, *maybe*, she could have some semblance of happiness in the company of Fritz and the others.

That was her last and most profound wish.

"He was kind," said Karolina. If she could sum up the Dollmaker with only a single description, it would be that one. "He had a wooden leg, and he let me read all his storybooks. He didn't have a family, until a family found him. He made children happy, and then he saved as many as he could. He was my very best friend, and I loved him."

Fritz nodded along. "He sounds like a wonderful person," he said. "What was his name?"

Karolina raised her head, and this time, she did not attempt to stop her tears. "Cyryl Brzezick," she said. "His name was Cyryl Brzezick, but everyone knew him as the Dollmaker of Kraków."

CHRONOLOGY

28 June 1914: World War I (or the Great War) begins in Europe with the assassination of Archduke Franz Ferdinand of Austria. The German and Austro-Hungarian empires (including what is now Poland) fight against Britain, France and Russia.

6 April 1917: The United States of America enters the war on the side of the Allied Powers – Britain, France and Russia.

11 November 1918: World War I ends with the surrender of Germany and its allies.

28 June 1919: Germany signs the Treaty of Versailles with the Allied Powers. Many Germans feel the document is unfair because it places responsibility for the war solely on them. Poland is recognized as an independent country by the treaty.

July 1921: Adolf Hitler becomes the leader of the National Socialist German Workers' Party, or Nazi Party, in Germany. The Nazis are extremely anti-Semitic, meaning they are prejudiced against Jewish people, holding them responsible for Germany's problems.

October 1929: The US stock market crashes, leading to an economic depression all over the world.

30 January 1933: Hitler becomes the chancellor of Germany. He vows to make the country strong and prosperous again and has a plan to expand German borders.

March 1933: The first concentration camp is created in Germany at Dachau. People who speak out against Hitler and his Nazi regime are imprisoned in the camp and are eventually made to do forced labour.

23 August 1939: Nazi Germany and Russia (now called the Soviet Union) sign the Molotov–Ribbentrop Pact, becoming allies.

1 September 1939: Germany invades western Poland, thus beginning World War II.

3 September 1939: Britain and France declare war on Germany.

17 September 1939: The Soviet Union invades eastern Poland.

27 September 1939: The Polish government flees to Paris (they would later escape to London). Poland is now occupied by the Germans.

23 November 1939: All Jewish people in Poland are required by law to wear a patch or armband bearing the Star of David. Many of their freedoms are taken away.

May 1940: The Auschwitz concentration camp in southern Poland opens and starts receiving prisoners.

27 September 1940: Germany, Italy and Japan sign the Tripartite Pact, becoming allies.

3 March 1941: All Jewish residents of Kraków are forced to move with few possessions into the Kraków Ghetto. Food is scarce. Children are not permitted to go to school. Jewish adults are often forced to do manual labour for the Germans.

22 June 1941: Germany betrays the Soviet Union and invades the country.

October 1941: Auschwitz is expanded to include a death camp, Auschwitz-Birkenau. This is part of Hitler's

"Final Solution" – his plan to annihilate all Jewish people in Europe.

11 December 1941: The United States enters the war following the Japanese bombing of Pearl Harbor. They fight on the side of the Allied Powers against Germany and Japan.

Spring 1942: The Germans begin to deport Jews from the Kraków Ghetto to death camps such as Bełżec.

2 February 1943: The war turns against the Germans when they fail to capture the Soviet city of Stalingrad.

March 1943: The Kraków Ghetto is closed. All remaining residents are sent to Auschwitz-Birkenau to be murdered, or to the Płaszów slave-labour camp.

27 January 1945: Auschwitz prisoners are freed by Soviet Union soldiers. Over a million people were killed there between 1939 and 1945, and the number of Jewish people killed in all the Nazi death camps totalled six million.

7 May 1945: Germany surrenders and World War II ends in Europe. Hitler commits suicide the week before and many of the top-level Nazis escape to South America and Middle Eastern countries.

2 September 1945: Japan surrenders and World War II is finally over. The number of Allied soldiers who died in the war totals more than fourteen million.

AUTHOR'S NOTE

In the summer of 2005, when I was a teenager, I visited Poland and stood in a place called Brzezinka, the "meadow of the birch trees". More than a million people were murdered there by the Nazis during World War II. Most of these victims – men, women and children – were killed simply because they were Jewish.

I left Brzezinka – better known as Auschwitz-Birkenau, the most infamous of the Nazi concentration camps – after three days. But what I saw there haunted me for many years. Few Americans had ever visited Poland at that time because it was part of the Eastern Bloc and I struggled again and again to articulate my experience when I returned home. Perhaps it is not surprising that I eventually wrote a story about it.

At first, I didn't think my tale had anything to do with the Holocaust. It began with a simple scene in which a soldier-turned-toymaker brought a feisty doll to life. I had no idea what the outcome of the story might be, but I was intrigued enough by the characters to want to find out. When I realized that their journey together would end at Auschwitz-Birkenau, as too many journeys did between 1941 and 1945, I wondered if I could keep writing. How would I even begin to describe what had happened there? Yet the more I thought about it, the more I knew that I needed to tell the story about what I had seen in Brzezinka, to warn where blind hatred can ultimately lead.

 285

In 2016, I returned to Poland for the first time in more than a decade as part of a volunteer project to help maintain the Jewish cemetery in Oświęcim, better known as Auschwitz. While visiting an exhibit about pre-war Jewish life, I was struck by the vibrancy of the Jewish community that had once existed in the town ... and by how brutally it had been erased during the German occupation. Most of Oświęcim's Jewish residents were killed during the Holocaust, and that void, a space where life should have been, could still be felt very keenly all those years later.

It seems vital to me to remember the Jewish victims of Nazi terror, especially at a time when racism, fear and xenophobia govern so much of the world. The existence of that hatred reminds me that there are still people like Erich Brandt, who choose cruelty and bigotry, or those like Dombrowski the baker, who turn away from the terrible things happening around them.

But I know that there are people like the Dollmaker too.

The sad fact is that the magic he wielded in this book did not exist during the Holocaust. Yet there was another kind of magic at work in Europe during World War II: the courage and compassion of very real individuals who, like the Dollmaker, chose to help their Jewish neighbours. The Dollmaker comes from my imagination, but I believe that there are always good people like him in the world. These were ordinary men and women who, for the most part, went on to live perfectly ordinary lives after 1945. During the dark years of the war, however, they acted in extraordinary ways. Today they are honoured as the Righteous Among the Nations by the state of Israel. You can read more about them on Yad Vashem, the World Holocaust Remembrance Center's website (yadvashem.org/righteous).

If there is one thing I hope you take away from this book, it's what Karolina told Brandt: "You always have a choice." We can choose to participate in hateful acts, to look away from them … or to ease the pain we see in the world through bravery and kindness.

Please, be kind.

Please, be brave.

Please, don't let it happen again.

ACKNOWLEDGEMENTS

Thank you to my magical agent, Jenny Bent, who saw a spark of potential in this story and helped support and guide me through this journey from beginning to end.

I am grateful for my incredible editors at Random House and Walker Books, Beverly Horowitz, Denise Johnstone-Burt and Daisy Jellicoe, for all their insight and tireless effort to bring this book to the world in its best form.

I would not be where I am today without the wisdom of Dr Theodora Goss, James Patrick Kelly and Nancy Holder. You are the best mentors a writer could hope to have!

My heartfelt thanks to Jen, Elizabeth, Sarah, Lew, Dallas, Steve, Elaine, Doc, Suri, Pam, Kelsey, Nora, Paul and Andrea, who read various drafts of this book and many others. We will always have our Hogwarts in Maine!

My gratitude to Li and River for their friendship, support and encouragement over the last three years.

To Dr Caroline Sturdy Colls, Kevin Colls, Mick Britton, Steven Reese, Joann Siegienski, Bruce Mussey and the

forensic archaeology students of Staffordshire University
– thank you for the work you do and for allowing me to
share my own with all of you.

All my love to my mother, who read every single version
of this book; my sister, who always inspires me; and my
father, who told me that the pen weighs nothing.

ABOUT THE AUTHOR

R. M. Romero lives with her family and a menagerie of
pets in Colorado. *The Dollmaker of Kraków* is her debut
novel. Visit her online at rmromero.com